*It Wa...*

when her son walked in on her while she was
kissing Morgan.

When he had left the room, Kate and Morgan
exchanged glances. "Let's go downstairs
where we can talk," she suggested. "And
have some breakfast," she added. "I don't
know about you, but I missed dinner last
night."

Morgan grinned. "Strange as it may seem, I'd
forgotten all about food. But you're right. I'm
starving."

In the kitchen, she turned to him. "I don't
know how you felt when Tony walked in, but
I wanted to sink through the floor."

Morgan nodded. "Me, too. That's why I think
we ought to get married."

---

**AMANDA LEE**
lives in Howard County, Maryland, with her
husband, two children and two cats. A woman
of many talents, she particularly enjoys writing
about two of life's greatest pleasures—romance
and food. Her lively sense of humor sparkles in
the dialogue of her characters.

Dear Reader,

Silhouette Special Editions are an exciting new line of contemporary romances from Silhouette Books. Special Editions are written specifically for our readers who want a story with heightened romantic tension.

Special Editions have all the elements you've enjoyed in Silhouette Romances and *more*. These stories concentrate on romance in a longer, more realistic and sophisticated way, and they feature greater sensual detail.

I hope you enjoy this book and all the wonderful romances from Silhouette.

Karen Solem
Editor-in-Chief
Silhouette Books

# AMANDA LEE
# End of Illusion

*Silhouette Special Edition*

Published by Silhouette Books New York

**America's Publisher of Contemporary Romance**

SILHOUETTE BOOKS, a Division of Simon & Schuster, Inc.
1230 Avenue of the Americas, New York, N.Y. 10020

ISBN: 0-671-53665-6

First Silhouette Books printing May, 1984

10 9 8 7 6 5 4 3 2 1

Map by Ray Lundgren

To Linda
who helps make things work out for the best
and to Norman and Howie
who make it all possible

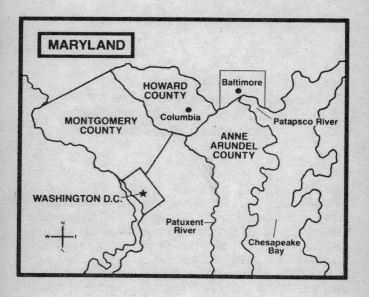

# Chapter One

*I*t was still a good fifteen minutes before the Saturday morning seminar was scheduled to begin, but already the small auditorium was almost full. From her vantage point in the back row, Kate Davenport surveyed the audience with intelligent hazel eyes.

Not the run-of-the-mill college crowd by a long shot, she noted with interest. These students were better dressed and more serious in their demeanor. And a good number had begun to gray around the temples— probably as a result of run-ins with their teenagers, she observed wryly.

But then, this was exactly the group the workshop on "Single Parent–Teen Relations" was supposed to attract, Kate reminded herself. In fact, as her boss, Dean Porter, had emphasized, it was one of the special programs designed to demonstrate that McCoy University could be responsive to the community's needs.

Kate settled back in the not-too-comfortable seat, smoothing the soft plaid wool skirt down over her knees. As the newly appointed assistant dean of continuing education, she was anxious that this first workshop come off well. Although the community outreach program had been set up by her predecessor, it was to be one of her main responsibilities.

Conscious of her visibility, she had been careful with her appearance, wearing her best navy blazer and taking time to tame her mane of chestnut hair, which she had always considered her best feature. With a new undercover makeup foundation, she'd even managed to hide the spray of freckles across her high cheekbones and tilted nose. And that was no mean accomplishment.

But still she couldn't keep from nervously reaching into her pocketbook for the fourth or fifth time to make sure she had brought along several pens and pencils.

Relax, she told herself sternly. There's no need to be jittery. Look at all the progress you've made this last year and a half. Bart did his best to make a dent in your self-confidence, but you're light-years away from the dependent little wife you used to be. Yet the pep talk was only partially successful. Up until a month ago Kate had been a senior administrator in the admissions office. She hadn't believed her luck when she'd won this new job over a dozen other applicants with more experience. And now she wanted to justify Dean Porter's confidence.

A ripple of anticipation running through the audience made Kate look up. The university had engaged Luke Taggart and Mary Froman, authors of *The Single Parent Dilemma,* to run the workshop. And the very professional-looking pair had just stepped up onto the dais at the front of the auditorium.

They were beginning their opening remarks, when a late arrival blocked her view. Kate glanced up in annoyance as he squeezed in front of her and the others in her row, heading for one of the few vacant seats left. "Excuse me," he whispered as he passed, not quite missing her suede pumps. Stifling her automatic "ouch," Kate had a quick impression of dark hair, a strikingly masculine face and a tall muscular form clad in a fisherman's knit sweater and brown cord pants. Another attractive man not caring whose toes he stepped on, Kate observed with a flash of resentment.

But she was too polite to take out her own prejudices on a stranger. Nodding her acceptance of the apology, she tried to turn her attention back to the team at the podium. It wasn't easy, for there was something about the man that kept distracting her. Even though he was five seats away, she found herself noticing when he shifted in his seat, trying to settle his six-foot frame in the tight space.

This is ridiculous, she told herself sternly. You're here to listen to the lecture. And besides, Dean Porter is expecting a report. With resolution, Kate picked up her notebook and pen and refocused her complete attention on the speaker.

"We've recently discovered that insanity is hereditary," Mary Froman was saying. "You get it from your teenagers."

The audience laughed. And Kate felt herself responding to the light tone set by the visiting psychologists.

For the first thirty minutes, Taggart and Froman talked about some of the more typical problems parents of teenagers encounter.

"We want you to know you're not alone," Luke Taggart explained.

"We've found," Mary Froman added, "that sharing problems can be very helpful. So, for our first workshop exercise, we'd like you to break up into small groups and talk a little about your relationship with your teenager. Give a bit of background about yourself first. Each of you should take about five or ten minutes. To make it easy, why don't we go by rows. Each row get together and assemble in one of the small classrooms down the hall. We'll meet back here in an hour."

Kate glanced quickly down toward the compelling stranger who was standing up and waiting for the rest of the row to file out. She hadn't expected this sort of exercise, and certainly not with someone like him. As others got up and started moving out, Kate briefly considered joining another group. But as she took a step toward the front of the auditorium, she felt a restraining hand on her shoulder.

"I think you're going the wrong way," a deep voice observed.

She didn't have to look around to know who it was. And she didn't want to look around and betray the flush on her face.

"Maybe you're right," she mumbled.

But the latecomer in the fisherman's knit sweater wasn't intent on taking charge of just her. "Let's grab the first empty classroom," he suggested to the rest of the milling group, a note of authority in his baritone voice.

It took a few minutes to accomplish that objective, since the closest rooms were quickly filled by other discussion groups. And when they finally pulled chairs into a circle, an uneasy silence hung in the air.

"Really, this is more than I'd bargained for," the petite blond woman next to Kate mumbled loudly enough for everyone to hear.

Kate nodded her agreement as she studied the rest of the participants. There were two other women besides herself, and three men. But the one who really held her interest was the man who had taken charge. However, there was nothing about his air of authority or his ruggedly attractive face with its strong nose and chiseled chin that changed her first impression. What was he doing here, anyway? she wondered. He looked like the type who would be too much in control to let a wayward teenager run roughshod over him.

Stop investing so much energy in idle speculation, she scolded herself. But, unfortunately, there was something elemental about the man that made it impossible to ignore him as she would have liked.

At that moment, the object of her troubled thoughts glanced up and caught her staring. Kate felt his own speculative gaze, which held hers captive for several heartbeats. His arresting brown eyes reminded her of a Bengal tiger's. And, she added to herself, he could be just as lethal. Quickly she began looking for another pen in her pocketbook.

When he spoke she half expected some sort of wisecrack. That would have been her late husband's style. But this man wasn't Bart. Instead of trying to win points by embarrassing a member of the group, he responded honestly to the blond's stage whisper.

"Nobody was ready for this. But let's give it our best shot. Why don't we start by introducing ourselves. I'm Morgan Chandler," he stated, and then looked toward the older man on his right.

"Ted Patterson," his neighbor replied.

It took only a moment for the six people in the circle to introduce themselves. And then their new leader looked expectantly at Kate. "Want to begin?" he questioned.

Kate gulped. "I, uh, I'm not actually taking this seminar. I'm on the university staff."

"You mean you're not a single parent with a problem teenager?" Morgan questioned with a raised eyebrow. "Do we have a spy in our midst?"

The rest of the group laughed nervously and Ted

Patterson broke in. "Whatever our positions, I hope we're going to keep what goes on here confidential."

Kate felt herself redden at the implication. "Of course your confidences will be respected," she assured. "And I'm actually in the same boat as everyone else," she added quickly. "I am a single parent with a problem ten-year-old. And I'm hoping to get some pointers today."

"In that case, why don't you tell us about it," Morgan prompted, his golden-brown eyes intent on her face again. There was something in his expression that made her feel his interest was more than polite curiosity.

"Really, I'd rather not go first," she tried to back out. Despite her new position as assistant dean, she had never been comfortable speaking before a group, especially strangers. Now she felt her palms going cold at the prospect. Why was this man forcing the issue, anyway? She should have followed her first impulse and joined another group.

But she was here now, and Mr. Chandler was not going to let her off the hook. "If you're on the staff, you should be setting the example for the rest of us."

He had her there. "I don't know where to begin," she floundered. But there seemed no way to back out gracefully now. Kate took a deep breath and tried to gather her thoughts.

"I've been a widow for a year and a half," Kate explained, willing the tremor out of her voice.

"Sorry," someone commented.

"That's all right," Kate replied. "I've learned to cope with just about everything—except my son." But the tense way she gripped the pen in her hand belied her statement. "Tony and his father had such a good relationship. They used to play ball in the back yard and go to soccer games and spend hours in Bart's workshop. Bart's death was a real shock to Tony. At first I expected his grief. But he doesn't seem to have gotten over it." As Kate talked, she found it easier to relate the details she had been holding inside for so long. "Tony's grades have slipped from straight A to barely passing. He's dropped all his friends. And he's indifferent to anything I suggest we do together. He acts as if the TV is the most important thing in his life."

The faces in the group were all sympathetic to her outpouring.

"How did you handle your own grief?" someone asked.

To her surprise, Kate began to voice the candid conclusion that she'd never revealed before. "I didn't grieve at all," she stated flatly. "From my point of view, the marriage was over a long time ago. The only reason I didn't leave Bart was that he was a good father and thought the world of Tony."

Wondering what they must be thinking, Kate looked around the room again. But it was Morgan Chandler's gaze that held hers. She couldn't read the reaction hidden in the tawny depths of his eyes, but for a moment it seemed as though there were only the two of them in the room, sharing some silent communication on a very basic level.

Kate forced herself to break the unspoken exchange and return her attention to the group. What was the man after? she puzzled, her mouth unconsciously curving into a frown.

"I wonder if Tony needs a man he can relate to," a woman across from Kate observed. "Isn't there an uncle or a grandfather who could fill the gap?"

Kate shook her head in denial. "Some people think that a man is the answer to every problem," she began, and then paused for effect, stealing a look at Morgan from under lowered lashes. "But I know that's not true." Then, realizing how her little speech must have sounded to the woman, she softened her statement. "You could be right in this case," she conceded. "However, my father and brothers are out west in New Mexico, and it's hard to establish a warm relationship across two thousand miles."

That was all she was willing to say out loud. But inwardly she thought again that if she'd had any sense, she never would have let Bart talk her into moving to Maryland.

There were a few more comments and suggestions. And Kate marveled at how everyone in the group had responded so positively not only to her problem, but to herself as a person. Bart had undermined so much of her self-confidence, that she was always wary of the impression she made on strangers. But her worries seemed groundless today. And what's more, her palms were no longer cold. This experience had brought her some much-needed positive reinforcement.

Kate's story had broken the ice, and others began to talk about their own problems. She listened with interest and sympathy and tried to add her own constructive suggestions. When Ted Patterson began to speak, Kate understood quickly why he did not want his story bandied about. His son had been caught vandalizing the neighborhood elementary school. The blond next to Kate, whose name was Sandra Downing, had a daughter with drug problems. And someone else had an ex-spouse who was trying to stir up trouble.

Morgan Chandler waited till last. And, despite herself, Kate found she was waiting to hear what kind of problem he couldn't cope with.

"My wife left the year after my daughter was born," he began.

*She was probably smart to get out from under the thumb of a dictatorial husband,* Kate thought smugly.

"She decided her career was a lot more important than making a home," he continued. "I wanted to help her do both, but she opted not to try."

Kate looked up in surprise. That was just the opposite of her own experience. Bart had been jealous of her even going back to college, and hadn't been willing to lift a finger to help.

"But that's ancient history," Morgan summed up quickly. "Obviously, it's my daughter I'm concerned about. Charlotte didn't want Julie and I did. Raising her was easy through preadolescence. But I wouldn't have been so confident of my parenting abilities if I'd known what was in store when she turned thirteen. We always had a close relationship. But when she hit her teens, she became downright possessive. If I brought a date home to the house, she'd sit there like a mother who thinks no one is good enough for her son. And if I didn't tell her I was out with someone, I began to feel as if I was cheating on my wife."

The group laughed sympathetically. And Morgan shook his head wryly. "It may sound funny, but I realize now that Julie's been the one who's managed to break up two or three promising relationships."

Since he was the focus of attention, Kate was free to study him now. His dark hair was a little less than stylish, with flecks of silver that highlighted its healthy sheen. As she inspected each of his features, Kate couldn't help but feel the pull of those expressive eyes framed by thick lashes. He looked like the kind of man who would have no trouble with the opposite sex. And without warning, she suddenly entertained a bit of sympathy for those women whose relationship with Morgan had been sabotaged by his daughter.

Luckily there was no way Morgan could know Kate's inward observations. "That was the initial problem," he was saying. "We had a very frank talk, and I thought everything was all straightened out. But things have gotten much worse now that she's fifteen. Julie told me she doesn't care what I do now, and that I don't have any right to interfere in her life, either," he continued, shifting uncomfortably in his hard-backed desk chair. Kate could tell that this candid disclosure was getting difficult for him.

Morgan cleared his throat before continuing. "To prove her point, she started retaliating by doing things she knows I wouldn't approve of with the boys she's dating—like lying about who she's with and staying out until two or three in the morning."

"Sounds like you're damned if you force the issue, and damned if you don't," someone commented.

"Exactly," Morgan agreed, uncurling his long legs and trying again to find a comfortable position in the cramped seat. "And to add another ingredient to the mess, Julie has a well-meaning grandmother who thinks the sun rises and sets on her only grandchild."

Kate suddenly realized that she was beginning to feel stiff too, and stretched out her own legs. She'd been so intent on the give and take in the little room—and especially the story Morgan Chandler had recounted—that she hadn't been thinking about her physical comfort at all. It was amazing, she reflected, that perfect strangers could be having this kind of discussion. But now that it had been forced upon them by the seminar, it didn't seem uncomfortable at all—in fact, it seemed very natural and cathartic.

At that moment, the public address system in the building sprang to life, interrupting her thought. "I hope you've found our initial exercise helpful," Luke Taggart's cheerful voice intruded. "Let's all come back to the auditorium for some general comments."

Kate watched the other people in her group get up and stretch. An hour ago they had been strangers, but now they were sympathetic comrades. As if by unspoken agreement, they all reclaimed their previous seats. And when Luke Taggart and Mary Froman had finished their morning session, Sandra suggested that they all have lunch together.

"That's a good idea," Morgan seconded, turning and giving Kate a very persuasive smile. "And I'll bet our university staffer can tell us the best place to eat."

The power of that devastating look threw Kate off-balance for a second. But fortunately, she had already been thinking about restaurants in the area with good food and fast service, and didn't let on that the man could render her speechless with just one smile. "The best place within walking distance is Giovanni's Pizza," she suggested. Her proposal was greeted with a unanimous "lead on."

As they strolled past trees decked in their vibrant autumn finery of orange, gold and red, Kate found herself appreciating the day for the first time and took a deep breath of the crisp air. The delightful change of seasons had been one thing she'd grown to love about the East Coast. And fall was her favorite time of all.

Morgan, who had fallen into step beside her, grinned. "You're another fall person, aren't you?" he questioned. "I can tell by the way you step on every leaf and listen to its crunch."

Kate couldn't help grinning back. "It's something I couldn't do back in New Mexico," she returned lightly. His low-keyed, humorous comments on the short walk had her almost relaxed. Morgan Chandler wasn't so intimidating after all, she told herself.

But when they all piled into a large booth, she noticed that he made a point of sliding in next to her. Tightly sandwiched between Morgan and the wall, Kate found it impossible not to be aware of every muscle in his leg. The intimate contact was more than she had bargained for. It was difficult to concentrate on what kind of pizza to order, much less make light conversation. But there was no way to lessen the pressure of his broad shoulder and hard thigh against her. Nor was there any way to be less aware of his masculinity. It had been a long time since she had sat this close to a man. With anyone else, she might have been able to ignore the contact that was at once so intimate and so impersonal. Why not with this particular man?

When his napkin slipped from his lap to hers and his hand brushed casually down her thigh to retrieve it, Kate sucked in her breath at the electric jolt his touch created. The intensity of her reaction was a surprise. It hadn't been since the early months of her marriage that she had responded this way. And what was Morgan's reaction? she wondered, taking a nervous sip of soda and observing him surreptitiously from under veiled lashes.

His face gave no clue. If she was disturbing his equilibrium as much as he was disturbing hers, he hid it well.

No one else in the group seemed aware of the effect Morgan was having on her either. As they ate their pepperoni-and-mushroom pizzas, they continued the discussion that had drawn them together that morning. Kate was too tense to participate intelligently. So she made a show of listening intently to the conversation around her. Morgan, she noticed, was content just to listen as well.

Kate let out a sigh of relief when the lunch was finally over and they could return to the relative safety of the auditorium. The afternoon session was primarily a lecture. Luke Taggart had some pointers that Kate found particularly useful—especially his advice on dealing with conflict. "Conflict, especially with those you love, is painful," he pointed out. "And we'd all like to sweep it under the rug. But it's really better to bring it out in the open and try to resolve it."

His words made Kate realize that, with her son, she had indeed been taking the easy way out. And she resolved to try to start a useful discussion the next time Tony withdrew into his shell.

The seminar ended on a very positive note. As the group stood discussing their experience for a few minutes, the consensus was that it had been a success. Kate was glad—both on a personal level and for the university. They really had managed to do something important for members of the community, she thought with pride.

As the group broke up, Morgan Chandler stopped in front of her. "How about joining me for a cup of coffee," he queried casually, his tone sounding confident of her agreement.

For a moment, Kate considered the offer. She had gained new respect for him during the day's session. And she was physically attracted to him, she admitted to herself. Look at the way she had reacted to his nearness at Giovanni's. But her physical response to the man was exactly the reason she shouldn't go out with him. Getting her life together had been difficult enough. But now that everything was finally starting to fall into place, she didn't want to risk the complication of a man in her life, especially not a "take charge" one like Morgan.

"I'm sorry, but I have other commitments," she explained softly; yet the closed expression in her hazel eyes didn't encourage him to find out if she were free some other time.

"I see," he said in a clipped voice, as if her refusal had hurt. "Well, it was nice meeting you." With that he turned and strode down the corridor.

All at once, Kate wanted to call after him. Maybe she was being ridiculous, she told herself. She was thirty-two years old, after all. She could certainly handle a casual cup of coffee without getting emotionally involved. But he had already gone. And there was nothing she could do about it now anyway.

The room had cleared except for the seminar leaders, who were packing up their materials. Kate went up to thank them on behalf of the university and then went upstairs to her office to write up a few impressions of the day.

Fifteen minutes later, when she returned to the parking lot, there was a definite chill in the air. Buttoning her blazer, Kate wished she had brought along a coat. Dusk was falling, and she noticed that the dimly lighted lot was deserted, except for her car and one other. The hood of the other car was up, and the owner's head had disappeared underneath. All that was visible was a pair of brown cord pants and a tan leather jacket. As she approached she could hear a string of epithets issuing from under the hood.

"Need some help?" she inquired.

The owner of the car straightened and turned. "What I need is a mechanic. I don't know a damn thing about cars except that they always break down when you least expect it." The speaker was an irritated Morgan Chandler.

Kate tried to bite back the smile at the corners of her lips. "Well, I do know a little about cars," she offered, coming around to peer under the hood. "What are the symptoms?"

Morgan looked doubtful. "It won't start," he stated flatly, and then challenged, "What do you think you can do about it?"

She was seeing another unexpected side of the man.

It evidently irritated him when he lost control of a situation; and even though he needed help, he seemed almost to resent her assistance. The revelation had quite a different effect than Kate might have expected. There was something about his present vulnerability that appealed to her, whereas his supreme confidence had put her off.

"When you say it won't start, what exactly do you mean?" she prompted. "Does the engine turn over? Does the ignition make a whining sound? Or is there no response at all?"

"It whines," Morgan conceded. "But it won't turn over."

"It could be the starter, then. Or the electrical system," Kate told him. "Why don't you try it for me."

A minute later Kate had confirmed her first diagnosis. It sounded as though he did need a new starter.

"And just how do you know?" Morgan challenged when she delivered her verdict.

"After my husband died, I didn't want to be at the mercy of the auto repair shops. So I took the course the university offers on do-it-yourself auto repair. I found out I didn't like getting engine grease on my hands. But at least I know how to do minor repairs, and I can spot a repair man who's trying to rip me off."

Morgan shook his head ruefully. "Maybe I should have enrolled too. Do you have any suggestions about what I should do?"

Kate glanced around at the deserted lot. It was already dark and she was cold. "You're probably going to have to have it towed. Why don't I drop you off at a service station?"

"Could you stretch that to my townhouse?" he inquired. "It's not too far, and I can get a ride back tomorrow to meet the tow truck."

Kate found herself making a quick decision. It would be rather "ungentlemanly" to leave a man in distress. And besides, she couldn't help feeling a tinge of remorse for her earlier brush-off.

"OK," she agreed, wondering if she would regret her generosity later.

# Chapter Two

As soon as Morgan had settled his large frame into her compact red Mustang, Kate began to wonder if giving him a ride had been a good idea. Once again, she felt crowded by his physical presence. And, as in the pizza parlor, there was no way to give herself more space. Every time she shifted gears, she had to consciously keep her hand from brushing against his leg. And even though he didn't say anything, she had the impression that he was evaluating the way she handled the car—ready to give backseat directions just in case she didn't meet his driving standards.

Yet he said nothing beyond a terse, "Turn right at the next cross street," or, "You'll be turning left at the next light."

Was he still upset over her earlier refusal to stop off for a cup of coffee? Kate wondered, shooting him a quick side glance. But his impassive face told her nothing.

From her point of view, the silence between them

was becoming more and more uncomfortable. And she found herself searching for some light subject that would fill the gap in conversation until she could drop him off. But all the questions that came to mind were continuations of the frank discussion they'd had in the seminar. She couldn't help wanting to know if he was dating anyone now or if he was as aware of her as she was of him. However, these were questions she would never ask. And furthermore, she reminded herself, she wasn't interested in getting involved with Morgan Chandler. So why was she so concerned about the intimate details of his life? She didn't want to pursue that line of thought too thoroughly. Instead, she turned her mind toward thinking of something less personal to talk about.

Finally she settled on a topic that seemed a safe compromise. "Um," she began, clearing her dry throat. "What do you do for a living?"

Shifting in his seat, he turned so he could face her slightly. "I'm an architect."

"Oh." Now what? she wondered. Apparently he was going to make her work to keep this conversation going. "What do you design?" she tried again.

"My firm specializes in shopping malls."

She thought he was going to drop the conversation again, but then, after a moment's thought, he surprised her by confiding, "But my real interest is in restoring old homes."

By that time his directions had led them to a narrow street of three-story red brick row homes in various stages of renovation. "Stop about halfway up the block," he instructed, pointing at one of the wider houses, obviously in need of a great deal of repair.

"You live here?" Kate questioned, unable to hide the surprise in her voice.

"Not yet," he returned. "But I will in the not-too-distant future. This is my pet project. I bought one of those city homesteads, and I'm in the middle of restoring it." There was a definite note of pride in Morgan's voice, which told Kate that the project must be a very special one for him.

"You're not doing all the work yourself, are you?" she wondered out loud.

Morgan shook his head. "All the design work is mine, and I've done some very unusual things with the interior spaces. But I've had to contract out the plumbing, the electrical work and the major structural changes."

His tone conveyed his enthusiasm for the project, and suddenly Kate's interest was piqued. Just what kind of home was this man designing for himself? she wondered.

"Want to come in and see it?" Morgan questioned.

Despite her curiosity, Kate hesitated. In the car coming over, she had told herself she wanted to terminate this encounter as soon as possible.

Morgan seemed to sense her reluctance. "Actually, you're the first person I've invited in—besides Julie and my contractor, that is."

The admission made Morgan more approachable again. In a way, it seemed as though he were trying to put the relationship back where it had been before she'd turned down his invitation after the seminar. And his next statement seemed to confirm her analysis. "Conditions inside are pretty primitive, but I can offer you a cup of instant coffee and some chocolate chip cookies."

Kate couldn't help smiling. "All right," she agreed. "But I can only stay for a few minutes."

Morgan reached for the door handle on his side, but when he pulled, it wouldn't open.

Kate found herself blushing. "Tony's too old for a

kiddie lock, but I keep forgetting to get it changed," she explained. "I'll have to open the door from the outside."

Morgan waited while she walked around to the passenger side and let him out. Then she stood aside to follow him up the broad marble steps that were a trademark of Baltimore row homes.

Suddenly she was conscious of how quiet the neighborhood was. None of the houses seemed occupied. And besides the two of them, the street was deserted.

"No neighbors?" she questioned.

Morgan shook his head. "The houses on this street only went up for sale this summer. So most of the homesteaders are just getting started. Nobody lives here yet. If we'd come a few hours earlier, you would have seen trucks full of lumber and building supplies. But most people knock off early on Saturday night."

The explanation was a bit unsettling. She hadn't bargained for being this alone with Morgan. But she would look like a fool if she protested now.

Pushing her doubts to the back of her mind, she waited while he turned the key in the lock and then shoved his shoulder squarely against the heavy door.

"Every time I come in here, I tell myself I should move 'replace warped door' to the top of the priority list. And then I forget about it again," Morgan chuckled as he flipped the light switch in the hall and then stood aside for Kate to enter.

She hadn't known exactly what she'd expected, but it wasn't this. Illumination was provided by a single two-hundred-watt bulb dangling from a wire suspended two floors up. Morgan had removed the ceiling of the living room so that second-floor bedrooms opened off a balcony. But the renovations were still in progress. The floor was littered with lumber and chunks of plaster, and her host had to grab her arm to guide her progress across the parquet oak floor.

"Steady," he cautioned. "If I'd made my usual Saturday morning stop over here, I would have known the contractors hadn't cleaned up. Sorry!"

As he spoke he led her across the debris and down a short hall toward the back of the house. "It'll be more livable back here," he promised, flipping on another light.

The kitchen was in better shape. Even though none of the appliances was in place, she could see what Morgan was trying to accomplish. A side wall had been stripped to its original brick, complete with an outsized fireplace. And a greenhouse breakfast nook had been added to the back of the room, making the area into an inviting enclave.

Rich wood cabinets had not yet been hung, but they were unpacked and stacked next to a long butcher-block island. And the old oak flooring had been stripped and refinished with loving care.

Morgan stood waiting for her reaction. "I know it's hard to get the feel of it all yet, but can you tell what I'm trying to do?"

"Oh, yes," Kate assured him. "This is going to be quite a place."

Morgan sighed with satisfaction. "Actually, this room kind of grew on me," he admitted. "I hadn't really planned to spend so much time and effort on the kitchen, but the possibilities became more and more appealing, and finally I just went with my instincts."

"Well, your instincts seem to be on the right track," Kate approved. "But since the stove is hardly functional yet, how are you going to get me that cup of coffee?"

"Oh, I have a hot plate set up in the library," Morgan told her. "This is about all I can show you, since the new stairs aren't in place yet. But we can look at the blueprints.

Kate didn't have the heart to tell him that the blueprints wouldn't mean much to her. Instead she let her host extract the bulky rolls from a shelf in the pantry. Following him into the library, she looked around with interest at the newly built-in shelving framed with pieces of antique molding.

"There's a salvage depot in the city where you can pick up materials from houses that have been torn down," he explained. "They've got everything from marble mantelpieces to handmade cherry banisters and the kind of oak parquet nobody makes anymore. And the price is right. There's even a discount for home-steaders," he added.

Kate turned from her inspection of the bookcases to find him busy plugging in the hot plate and pouring water from a large picnic jug.

"Make yourself at home," he threw over his shoulder. Kate would have obliged, except that the only place to sit was a twin mattress and box spring set sitting directly on the floor. It was covered by blue sheets and an old quilted comforter.

When Morgan turned and saw her hesitating, he laughed. "I told you it was primitive here. I've been known to get so involved with the renovation that I lose all concept of time. On weekends like this, when Julie is at her grandmother's, I sometimes end up spending the night here. That's why I moved a bed into the library. But it does just as well for a couch."

By this time the water was boiling, and Morgan handed her a steaming cup along with a bag of bakery cookies. "Hope you don't mind powdered cream, but I wasn't planning on company. Sit down and I'll go over the blueprints with you."

Kate stood watching as he settled down on the

makeshift couch and patted the space next to him. She didn't want to sit down on what had been his bed. But there really wasn't anything to do but join him. When she reluctantly sat down, she couldn't help the shiver of awareness that flowed through her body as her shoulder brushed against his.

But Morgan seemed to take no notice. "Hold this end of the roll," he instructed, as he began to unwind several large sheets.

Kate had to set the cookies and her coffee mug on the floor to comply.

"This is the back elevation," he pointed out. "You can see where the greenhouse has been added to the original structure." Then, turning to a sectional view, he continued, "I've put a loft into Julie's room and added a skylight in the bathrooms. And look at the balcony off the master bedroom. Notice how the side walls have been expanded to give more privacy."

Kate tried to focus her attention on the large blue-tinted architectural drawings, but she was finding it extremely difficult to ignore Morgan's closeness again. The musky scent of his after-shave heightened her senses to tingling awareness. And the slight huskiness in his deep voice made her shiver. Giving him a sideways glance, Kate took in the curl of his thick, dark hair as it framed his ear and brushed his collar. She had to stifle the crazy impulse to push it back. As Morgan leaned over to point out where the solar storage units would be located under the greenhouse, his arm brushed against the front of her blouse, and she jumped as though she'd been touched by a hot poker. Get a hold of yourself, Kate admonished, reaching down for her coffee cup and taking a long sip.

"Sorry," Morgan murmured, rolling up the sheets and reaching for his own mug.

For a moment they both sipped in silence. When

Kate finally set her cup back on the floor, Morgan followed suit and then began to unroll the next set of sheets. Kate wished she could tell him that she wasn't really interested. Yet the words just wouldn't seem to come to her lips. She had wanted to avoid any further physical contact with Morgan. So how had she gotten into this situation? she wondered. And, more to the point, just how was she going to get out of it?

As though unaware of her discomfiture, Morgan had launched into a detailed explanation of the energy conservation measures he had designed for the house. "There's no central furnace," he enthused. "I'm adding a double shell on the outside walls for extra insulation. The house will be solar heated. But every room will have its own baseboard unit as a backup. That way you don't have to waste energy heating spaces that aren't occupied."

"Um," Kate responded, shifting slightly to widen the gap between herself and this all-too-attractive man beside her.

"I guess this is pretty boring," he admitted, misinterpreting her response.

"Oh, no," Kate protested. "But I am going to have to be leaving soon," she added, seizing the opportunity he had offered. She made as if to stand up, but to her surprise, Morgan laid a restraining hand on her shoulder. "I know we've just met," he began, "but if you leave now, I think both of us will have missed an important opportunity."

"Opportunity?" she questioned, wishing she could wriggle out from under his grasp without falling into his lap. The hand on her shoulder was gentle, yet it held her with the force of an iron band.

"Yes. There are a thousand questions I want to ask you, but I'll settle for just one right now if you'll answer it honestly."

Kate nodded uncertainly.

"Is sitting here making you as aware of me as I am of you?"

Kate's hazel eyes widened in amazement. He had just voiced the same thought she had been wondering in the car. But it was the last question Kate had expected from Morgan Chandler. "What—what do you mean?" she stammered.

"I think you know what I mean. But if I have to answer the question myself, I'll tell you that sitting here makes me want to take you in my arms and kiss you. What would you do if I did?"

His directness made her breath quicken. And yet she tried desperately to hide her reaction. "I only said I'd answer one question," she reminded him lightly.

"But you haven't given me even one honest answer so far. So I guess I'll just have to find out for myself."

Leaning forward, he pulled her swiftly into his arms, and before she could protest, his lips had covered hers. The gentle attack took her so completely by surprise that she didn't have time to muster any defense. Her lips parted and Morgan instantly took advantage of the opportunity. With warm sensuality he deepened the kiss, his tongue teasing the corners of her lips before darting forward into the sweet moistness of her mouth. The way he had suddenly pulled her into his arms wasn't her only surprise. Unaccountably, she was responding to this man in a way that she'd not responded in years—even with Bart.

Although she wanted to remain passive, she found her own tongue moving forward to meet his. And, at the same time, her hands went to the back of his neck to tangle in the thick hair she'd wanted to touch earlier.

Nevertheless, his sigh of satisfaction at her response brought the old doubts flickering through her consciousness. Things had started this way with Bart. But the promises that he had seemed to offer had never been fulfilled. Her hands came up to push against the hard wall of Morgan's chest. When he felt her protest, his lips left hers. He loosened his embrace just enough for her to pull back a few inches.

"What's the matter?" he whispered, his breath feathering her ear.

"I can't do this." Kate looked down at the intricate pattern of his sweater, unable to meet his eyes.

But he wouldn't allow her to sidestep him so easily. With his index finger, he lifted her chin so that she was forced to meet the tawny brown of his eyes. "Tell me why not," he demanded.

Kate took her lower lip between her teeth. It wasn't fair. He was making this as hard as possible. She was physically attracted to him. She'd admit that to herself. But she'd been physically attracted to Bart, too. And where had that gotten her? Yet, there was no way she could tell this virtual stranger about *that*.

"I'm . . . I'm just not ready to get involved with someone," she offered lamely. And I probably never will be, she added to herself.

Morgan's searching gaze seemed to penetrate the deception. "I won't make a secret of the fact that I'd like to get to know you a lot better," he told her, his finger gently stroking the side of her face as he spoke. "But I won't ruin my chances by pressing you now if you'll agree to see me again."

Kate was torn in two. Experience told her she should say good-bye once and for all to Morgan Chandler. But her emotions were singing a different song.

Morgan seized on her uncertainty. "Tell you what," he began with a boyish grin. "Let me prove how trustworthy I am."

Intrigued, Kate raised an eyebrow. "And just how do you propose to do that?" she challenged.

"I'll set the alarm on my watch for ten minutes. And when it beeps, we'll call a halt to whatever we're doing."

Kate cocked her head to one side. Was he really saying what she thought he was saying? "You can't be serious," she exclaimed.

"Oh, I'm perfectly serious."

Before she could think of a reply, Morgan had checked the time on his digital watch and begun to set the alarm. This was the most outrageous line anybody had ever tried on her, and Kate didn't know whether to laugh or run.

"And how do I know I can trust you to come to a screeching halt when your time is up?" she questioned.

"Oh, I was a boy scout. My word is my bond." The little speech was delivered lightly, yet it seemed to come from a basic honesty.

As Kate looked thoughtfully into his twinkling eyes, he grinned. "Stop wasting time; we're already thirty-four seconds into our experiment," he pointed out.

Why should she trust him? Kate wondered. When had Bart ever made himself stop when his own pleasure was involved? But Morgan wasn't Bart, another part of her mind argued. She'd known him only a few hours, and the differences were already quite apparent. Just maybe, Kate thought, she could trust him—at least for ten minutes. Besides, he was giving her an opportunity to find out more about her own reactions without the risk of starting something she couldn't finish. When he pulled her back into his arms, she did not protest.

Wondering just what to expect, she felt his lips brush the top of her head and then trail feather kisses to her ear. His fingers stroked her cheek again, and then he turned her head up once more so that their lips could meet.

Somehow, because he had set the bounds on how far

this would go, Kate was able to respond to his gentle caresses with more openness than she would have believed possible. She felt her lips opening once more to the persuasive pressure of his. And when his tongue began new explorations, she couldn't hold back a sigh of pleasure. She felt weightless, as though she were floating on her back in a warm, inviting pool. And her arms went around his shoulders, so that she could stroke the strong muscles under his nubby sweater. But her own caress only served to whet her curiosity about Morgan Chandler. She felt a part of herself that she had long kept buried welling up like an untapped spring. She wanted to know more about this man. And she knew he felt the same about her.

When his hands reached under her blazer to brush against her back through the soft fabric of her blouse, his lips meanwhile nuzzling the side of her neck, she didn't pull away. Instead, she concentrated on the exquisite sensations his explorations were creating.

Encouraged, his hands moved lower to boldly free the blouse from the back of her waistband. Before she knew it, he had slipped his hands under the silky material so that he could caress the skin of her back. The feel of his hands on her bare flesh sent little unfamiliar shivers coursing through her body.

She couldn't analyze her reactions. She only knew how good his strong fingers felt on her silken skin. Part of her wanted very much for his hands to move around to the front of her body. And, as if in anticipation, her nipples hardened.

Morgan, too, seemed to sense her arousal. Slowly his hands inched to the sides of her body, stroking her ribs in an unhurried pattern that came closer and closer to her lacy bra.

Kate's breath quickened. She was lost in a sea of sensation that seemed to be spreading through her

body like a raging fire in a drought-parched forest—
"Beep. Beep. Beep. Beep." A high-pitched sound that
seemed to be coming from under her blouse intruded
into her consciousness.

Morgan raised his head, and she heard him swear
under his breath.

Obviously he did not want to return to reality. And
one part of Kate, lulled by the sensuality of his
lovemaking, wanted to retreat back into the soft cocoon that his embrace had woven about them.

Shakily he withdrew his hands from her blouse so
that he could shut the alarm off. With obvious effort,
he was trying to pull himself together. But his breathing
was as ragged as her own. "You don't know what this
'trustworthy' business is costing me," he confided in a
voice that was noticeably huskier than before. "I don't
suppose you're going to beg me to throw my watch out
the window?" he added hopefully.

Kate felt herself flush as she pulled hastily away from
his embrace and struggled to put her clothing to rights
as soon as possible. Morgan's little demonstration had
gone quite a bit further than she had intended. She had
learned enough of her own uncontrolled response to
this dangerous man to make her wary of any more
"experiments." Quickly, she tucked her blouse back in
and ran a nervous hand through her hair.

"I take it that means no?" he persisted, his eyes
searching her face.

Kate lowered her gaze as a bubble of apprehension
began to rise in her chest. He had meant what he said,
hadn't he? The last thing she wanted was to end up
fighting him off.

But Morgan instantly responded to the change in her
demeanor. "I always keep my word," he assured her,
"no matter what the personal cost. But in this case, I do
expect some kind of reward. You will see me again,

won't you—now that you know you can turn me on and off like clockwork?"

"Morgan, I . . ." Kate began.

But he shook his head. "Don't give me an answer now unless it's yes."

When she didn't respond, he continued. "Then I'll call you in a day or two. Okay?"

This was all going too fast. And she needed time to think about whether she could handle Morgan Chandler, or whether she even wanted to try. But it was easier to agree now than start an argument.

"Okay," she conceded.

"Then you'd better give me your phone number, or I won't be able to reach you," he pointed out.

"You can get me through the Office of Continuing Education at the university," Kate reminded him. "And I do have to be leaving," she added, looking around for her pocketbook. Before he could stop her again, Kate had gotten up off the mattress and was on her way to the door. But once there, she turned and looked back at Morgan, who was just getting to his own feet. The expression on his face made her want to soften the abruptness of the departure. "I do like what you're doing with the townhouse," she offered. And with that, Kate headed down the hall toward the front door.

# Chapter Three

Despite the warped front door, Kate had done her best to exit Morgan's townhouse with a show of calm nonchalance. But once she had slid behind the wheel of her car and locked the door, her hands were shaking so badly that it took three tries to fasten her seat belt.

Nothing much happened in there, she told herself firmly. *So why are you reacting like this?* But she knew the answer very well. It wasn't what had actually happened. It was the potential for what might happen. In a very real way, Morgan Chandler was a threat to everything she'd been trying to accomplish these last two years. Although it had been far from easy, she knew that being independent and working out her own problems had helped her grow as an individual. The last thing she needed now was an involvement with a take-charge man, no matter how sexy or charming he might be.

Yet her logical arguments did little to quell the unsettled feelings in her lower abdomen. "It's just hunger," Kate mumbled out loud, wishing her words were really true.

Tony and Mrs. Kelly, her sitter, had already eaten by the time she arrived at her townhouse in suburban Columbia. And so she fixed herself a quick supper of soup and salad. Even though the light meal satisfied her hunger, Kate had to admit that it would take more than food to make her forget her encounter with Morgan.

Sighing, she pushed back her chair and began to clear the table. As she rinsed her dishes and stacked them neatly in the dishwasher, she tried to focus on the positive aspects of the day. After hearing the other members of her group tell their stories, she knew her problems could be a lot worse. Tony wasn't into drugs or anything else illegal. The two of them just had a communication problem. Morgan seemed to have one with his daughter too, she mused. If she saw him again, maybe she'd get to meet Julie. And then Kate caught herself up short. Why was she letting her thoughts be pulled back to Morgan? Hadn't she told herself she didn't want to become involved with him?

Deliberately she began to think about the pointers she'd gotten from the seminar. Mary Froman had suggested, for example, that games were an excellent meeting ground for parents and children. And Luke Taggart had cautioned that direct questions often put a youngster off. Maybe she could put some of their theories into practice.

Her clean-up chores completed, Kate peered into the semidarkened living room. Tony was in his usual place —in front of the TV set. But now his thatch of straight red hair was bent over the controls of a video game. Crossing the room, Kate sat down on the couch and cleared her throat. But Tony's hazel eyes lifted only to the screen, where a cosmic invasion force was threatening to envelop his ship.

"I had a really interesting day," Kate ventured. "You wouldn't believe how well the university's outreach program is doing."

Tony grunted.

"Did you and Mrs. Kelly have fun?" she continued the one-sided conversation, not knowing how else to proceed. This time Tony spared her a pained look before firing another missile.

Despite all her good intentions, Kate suddenly wanted to march across the room and snap off the set. But she knew that was no way to open communication, and so she made herself count to ten before she did something she'd regret. What would Morgan do to get through to her son? she wondered. Probably sit down and challenge Tony to a game.

"How about if we play against each other?" she suggested.

Tony shook his head. "You know you're no good at this, Mom. It's more fun playing the computer." But his voice wasn't edged with the sarcasm she might have expected.

Should she try again? she wondered. Or perhaps the end of the day, when everybody was tired, simply wasn't the best time to try and open lines of communication. Kate stood up to leave. "I'm going to take a shower."

Tony swung his head in her direction. "Say, Mom, I'm on a winning streak now, but if you really want to learn, maybe I could show you sometime."

Kate grinned. "I may just hold you to that offer." With that she turned and headed for the stairs. It might be a small victory, but this was more progress than she'd made in months.

There was an even bigger victory Sunday afternoon when she offered to help Tony with his spelling and he didn't stalk off to his room. Although most subjects

came easily to her son, spelling was a real effort. Before
Bart's death, she and Tony had established a weekly
routine of going over his new words together and trying
to come up with memory joggers that would help him
pass his test. But they hadn't had a session in months.

"*Cemetery* is really hard to spell," he complained
now, screwing his face into a scowl.

"Didn't your teacher tell you that only *e*'s are buried
in the cemetery?" Kate questioned.

"Hey neat." Tony grinned. "But I bet you can't think
of a way to remember *principal* that easy."

Kate thought for a minute. "You're right," she
agreed. "*Principal* is a lot tougher."

Tony, too, furrowed his brow in concentration.
"Hey, I know: the principal is always your pal!" he
finally exclaimed.

Kate gave him a congratulatory pat on the back and
he beamed. They spent the next half hour companiona-
bly going through the rest of his word list. Her only
regret was that the lighthearted mood didn't carry over
into the evening—when she and Tony had a minor
battle over bedtime.

Nevertheless, she couldn't help feeling optimistic. If
Tony had opened up with her this much, certainly
they'd be able to go even farther.

She was still mulling over the possibilities as she
pulled into the McCoy staff parking lot on Monday
morning. And her thoughts were so absorbing that she
didn't see several secretaries trying to stifle giggles as
she opened the door to her office.

But the sight that greeted her stopped her short. Tied
to the back of her chair was a huge cluster of red, blue
and yellow helium balloons. Openmouthed, she ad-
vanced into the room. Who in the world was responsible for this zany surprise?

"Don't just stand there like a dummy. Look at the

card," a voice behind her urged. Kate whirled to find
the department's administrative assistant, Mary Ellen
Collins, grinning broadly.

"Is this some kind of joke? Are these really for me?"
Kate questioned. "It's not my birthday," she added in
befuddlement.

"Well, it may not be your birthday, but they're for
you, all right. The delivery boy asked for Kate Davenport. And he wanted to make sure you'd be in today."

Still almost unable to believe this whimsical display
was for her, Kate crossed to her chair and untied the
small white envelope attached to one of the strings.

"I enjoyed the outreach activities on Saturday more
than you'll ever know. And I'm looking forward to an
even more stimulating session very soon. Scout's
honor. Morgan."

Kate couldn't stop herself from blushing. Although
the gesture itself was charming, the accompanying note
was pushing his luck. She understood the double
meaning of Morgan's note quite well. Anyone else
reading it might have thought he was talking about the
seminar. But she knew that he was really referring to
their extracurricular activities at his townhouse. Playing
around with Morgan had certainly been stimulating, all
right. And just the thought of things getting any more
heated made her stomach knot.

"Well, aren't you going to share it with me?" Mary
Ellen prodded, referring to the note Kate gripped. The
younger woman whirled. She'd forgotten all about the
fact that she had an audience.

"Oh, uh, this ridiculous 'bouquet' is just from some
guy who got a lot out of Saturday's seminar."

"Sure, I'll bet. No one goes to this much trouble
unless he's interested in more than a seminar."

Kate felt her flush deepen. There weren't many
people who would have dared to tease her about her

social life. But even in the short time they had been working together in Dean Porter's office, the two women had become good friends. A divorcée who had remarried several years ago, Mary Ellen had recognized the symptoms of Kate's troubled background, and over shared lunches she'd drawn out the younger woman and offered encouragement.

"Well, out with it." Evidently Mary Ellen was not going to let her off the hook.

Kate's eyes began to sparkle with mischief as she met her friend's level gaze. "Actually, he's trying to make amends for stepping on my foot Saturday," she volunteered.

"And after this alleged incident?" the other woman questioned.

"Well, it's a long story. But somehow I ended up letting him talk me into coming back to his townhouse to see his blueprints."

"Don't you mean etchings?" Mary Ellen's eyes had taken on a sparkle of their own.

"No, blueprints. He's an architect."

This information only whetted her assistant's appetite for more. But luckily Kate was saved from further explanations by the buzz of the office intercom. It was Dean Porter, anxious for a report of his own—on how the seminar had gone, not what had happened afterward.

"You're not going to get off so easily," Mary Ellen called after Kate as she hurriedly exited her office. "We'll continue this discussion at lunch."

Kate paused for a moment to compose her features before knocking politely on her boss's door.

"Come on in," he called in his pleasant tenor. The youthful voice was at variance with the dean's elderly appearance. Now close to retirement, he had earned his head of white hair and deeply lined face from years as the university provost. And as a reward for surviving thousands of encounters with obstreperous students, he'd been given the plum job of dean of continuing education for his remaining years at McCoy.

She was lucky to have the opportunity to work with someone so dedicated to and knowledgeable about the university, Kate reflected, as she slipped into one of the padded seats opposite his desk. The only drawback was that he had become set in his ways. Once he got a bee in his bonnet, he couldn't be dissuaded.

"Well, I trust everything went well," he began cheerfully, pulling out a pen and note pad.

Kate nodded. "Froman and Taggart were everything their advance publicity promised and more." For the next few minutes she found herself describing their presentation as the dean made careful notes.

"And what about the group participation?" Dean Porter persisted. "What kind of response did we get from the members of the community?"

"Well, I can't speak for all the groups, but the one I joined was quite effective. I think the participants learned as much from sharing their own experiences as from the lecture itself."

The dean's pale blue eyes lit up, and he leaned forward across his wide mahogany desk. "I'd like to hear some of the details."

Kate hesitated. She knew how reluctant members of the group had been to speak until they'd been assured that she'd keep the information confidential. And although she had no question of Dean Porter's integrity, his line of inquiry was making her uncomfortable. But perhaps she could get away with talking in generalities instead of specifics. But Dean Porter's probing questions brought out a good deal more than she would have chosen to reveal on her own. About the only thing she held back was the names of the participants. And even though she had stressed several times in the conversation the confidentiality of the revelations, she couldn't help feeling a bit uneasy when she returned to her desk a half hour later.

Maybe she should document her concerns, she decided. But before she could write the memo, a phone call from the print shop distracted her. They couldn't read her hastily scribbled corrections to the galley for the next community outreach program announcement, and it was impossible to get things straight over the phone. She had to dash across campus and look at the sheets herself to decipher the instructions.

By the time she got back, most of the staff had left for lunch. But Mary Ellen had loyally waited for her return.

"I passed up a trip to that new Szechuan restaurant down on Charles Street," she informed Kate with a mischievous twinkle in her eye. "I hope you'll make it worth my while."

Kate knew how much Mary Ellen loved Chinese food. If her assistant had made this sacrifice, she must mean business.

"Come on, let's grab something from the carryout across the street," her friend suggested. "The weather's still warm enough to eat outside."

There was no graceful way to turn down the invitation. And so, twenty minutes later Kate found herself on a sunny park bench unwrapping a thick corned beef sandwich.

"All right, I want all the juicy details," Mary Ellen insisted after taking a bite of her own hot pastrami.

Kate deliberately pulled a small carton of orange juice from her brown paper bag before answering. Then she took a deep breath and plunged in without giving herself time to think. "Well, his name is Morgan

Chandler. He's tall, dark and handsome. He's restoring one of those urban homestead townhouses. He's really sure of himself in almost everything, and comes across as knowing what he wants and how to get it. Just being alone in the same room with him makes me nervous. I'm afraid I'm really attracted to him. And I'm scared to death about where things might lead."

Mary Ellen gave her friend a careful look. "Well, that was some speech for you," she finally ventured. "This Morgan Chandler must be *quite* a guy. So what are you afraid of?"

Kate gestured helplessly with her hands. "You know it's been such a struggle to get this far after the way Bart undermined my self-confidence. I've worked hard for my independence. And if I get involved with Morgan, I'm putting all the progress I've made on the line."

"Oh, come on. You just met him on Saturday. Surely he's not that potent."

Kate couldn't help grinning. "Well, I don't know about that. It only took him ten minutes to have me melting in his hands like chocolate on a hot day."

Her friend chuckled. And then her expression grew thoughtful. "You just gave me a little speech about independence and progress, but deep down, that's not what's really bothering you, is it?"

Kate looked away. "That's certainly part of it . . ." she began.

"And the rest of it is that you're afraid you're going to make the same mistake you made with Bart, isn't it?"

Kate looked down at her half-eaten sandwich. Suddenly her appetite was gone. "I thought I was in love with Bart, you know," she confessed in a small voice. "And it wasn't until after the wedding that I found out how bad living with him was going to be. If I could be that blind to the way he really was, how do I know I won't do it again?"

"In the first place," Mary Ellen began, "you were only nineteen when you married Bart. You didn't have the maturity or the judgment you have now. If you're honest, you'll admit you're not the same person, Kate."

The younger woman opened her mouth to speak, but Mary Ellen shook her head. "The lecture's not over," she stated. "In the second place, nobody's forcing you into a lifetime relationship with this guy. So he wants to date you. So let him. If he turns out to be like Bart, all you have to do is give him his marching papers."

Kate chewed on her knuckle for a moment. Mary Ellen had a point. She wasn't the naive little girl who had fallen for Bart Davenport's superficial line. Yet even with that assurance, she still had doubts about whether she could handle someone who came on as strong as Morgan Chandler. On the other hand, she had discovered something in his arms that beckoned her to find out more. Maybe she should give the relationship a chance.

The luncheon conversation did a lot to bolster her self-confidence, and when she picked up the phone later that afternoon to hear Morgan's husky baritone, she was able to sound reasonably calm and collected.

"Well, did you get my little surprise?" he asked.

"Oh, I got them all right," Kate agreed. "Lucky for me no one else opened the note. Really, Mr. Chandler, don't you think you went a bit too far? Saturday you promised not to rush things, and today you've already got your track shoes on."

Morgan chuckled. "You may be right," he agreed. "Let me make amends by taking you out to dinner tonight."

"Taking me out to dinner tonight is making amends for rushing things?" Kate couldn't help questioning. "I don't even know if I can get a sitter on such short notice," she added.

"That doesn't matter," Morgan assured her. "If you can't, I'll go out for hamburgers or something."

Kate was silent for a moment, and Morgan used the opportunity to try another tack. "Listen, if you just can't accept my gracious invitation any other way, think of it as a *quid pro quo* for giving me a ride. And, by the way, you were right about the car; it did need a new starter."

A few hours earlier, the aggressive technique might have scared her off again. But fortified with Mary Ellen's words of wisdom, she found herself agreeing to see him that evening.

How should she dress? Kate wondered, as she stood in front of her closet at five-thirty, inspecting her wardrobe. Mrs. Kelly hadn't been available until eight, and so she wasn't sure whether they'd be eating in or out. Finally she settled on a pair of deep-brown culottes and her favorite bittersweet overblouse, which emphasized the slimness of her waist. The severity of the blouse's cut was softened by the puffy Victorian sleeves and pleated front.

Her efforts were rewarded by the warm look of approval in Morgan's eyes when he arrived. And he didn't look bad himself, she noted silently, taking in his burgundy pullover and gray cords.

"Are you ready to go?" Morgan questioned.

Kate shook her head. "The sitter can't come till eight, so maybe we'll have to take you up on those hamburgers after all."

"Why don't we check with Tony?" Morgan suggested.

"Be my guest," Kate invited, wondering just how the two of them would get along.

But when she drew her date into the living room, Tony barely looked up from his video game. After mumbling something that might have been "hello," he turned quickly back to the screen. Undaunted, Morgan plopped down on the floor beside him and began to compliment his strategy at Crystal City Adventure. Within fifteen minutes Tony had turned the controls over to Morgan and was enthusiastically coaching from the side.

Kate watched his technique with admiration and not a little envy, noting how careful he was not to better Tony's score. Inside half an hour, the man and boy sitting on the carpet sharing the game controls looked like best buddies. And Tony was clamoring to accompany Morgan and his mother to dinner.

How would he really respond to the proposition of being saddled with a ten-year-old on their first date? Kate wondered, watching Morgan from under lowered lids. But she needn't have worried.

"We'd love to have you come along to dinner," Morgan assured her son. "And I'll bet you even know the best place around here to eat."

"Yeah," the boy agreed. "The mall. They have all these neat food stands down there, and you can get anything you want."

Morgan favored the two of them with a grin. "I'm game if your mother is," he said, ruffling Tony's tousled red locks.

They piled into Morgan's now-functioning Datsun and headed for Columbia's large, enclosed shopping mall.

Tony practically pulled Morgan through the large glass doors to the lower level where more than a dozen individual food vendors vied for customers' attention.

"I always start with French fries," Tony confided. "And then I either have a pizza or a hamburger."

Morgan surveyed the line of red-and-white-tile eateries bordering a large but crowded common table area. He looked almost as enthusiastic as Tony, Kate thought, trying not to show her amusement.

"Listen," Tony explained. "The first thing you have to do is stake out a table. Mom can do that."

Morgan turned and looked questioningly at Kate. "Do you think you can handle that assignment?"

She nodded. "I'll get myself a salad when you two come back."

By the time she'd located a table in the crowded dining area, Tony and Morgan were threading their way back in her direction, each carrying a paper plate of French fries covered with beef barbecue.

"What in the world is that?" Kate wanted to know, pointing to the unlikely combination.

"I'm not too sure myself," Morgan admitted, "but Tony and I talked each other into it. And I might regret it later," he added almost under his breath.

"Well, I'm playing it safe with my usual broccoli-cauliflower salad," Kate said, getting to her feet.

"Do you always play it safe?" Morgan teased.

Kate shook her head. "No, only ninety-five percent of the time."

When she returned with her light meal, the two at the table were deep into a discussion of the relative merits of the Baltimore Colts versus the Washington Redskins. And after that they went on to soccer and baseball.

The lively conversation gave Kate the opportunity to study Morgan unobtrusively. He honestly seemed to be having a good time. And the laugh lines around his light brown eyes crinkled good-naturedly.

And yet she didn't feel excluded as she often had

when Bart and Tony had gotten together. There was a warmth in Morgan's personality that seemed to reach out toward her. Was she reading too much into this? she wondered. Only time would tell.

After their meal, the threesome strolled down the mall to the ice cream parlor.

"Why don't you ever try anything new, Mom?" Tony complained. "You had that same dumb salad you always eat. And now I know what kind of ice cream you're going to pick: rocky road."

"Am I that predictable?" Kate asked, surprised in spite of herself. Maybe she had fallen into more ruts than one without knowing it.

Sensing her indecisiveness, Tony drew himself up importantly to his full four feet, ten inches. "You've got to try something new tonight," he insisted. "Let Morgan pick for you."

Things seemed to be going so well with Tony this evening that Kate decided to indulge him a bit more. But no way was she going to let a virtual stranger control something as important as her ice cream choice.

Morgan had already begun inspecting the long list of exotic flavors. Then he turned to give her a speculative look. "Yes, why don't you try something new tonight?" he echoed her son. "You might find you like it."

Before she could wonder whether he was talking about ice cream cones or something else, he added, "Let's see, are you the peppermint-cheesecake type?"

Above Tony's head, she shot him an exaggerated grimace.

"Peaches 'n' cream?"

She shrugged noncommittally.

"Bubble gum ice?"

Kate heard Tony giggle as she rolled her eyes.

"Oregon blackberry," Morgan tried again.

That didn't sound too bad, Kate decided, giving Morgan a quick nod. After all, there were at least twenty-five other flavors that sounded worse. Morgan ordered her cone along with a peanut butter crunch for Tony and a mocha almond swirl for himself. And Kate had to admit, as she licked her creamy purple ice cream, that trying something new had its advantages. She might even order Oregon blackberry again, she decided.

"Can we play some more Crystal City Adventure?" Tony asked Morgan eagerly when they arrived back at her townhouse.

Morgan shook his head. "Not tonight, Tony. Your mom and I have plans this evening."

When the boy began to protest, he held up his hand. "But if you do your homework tonight and go to bed on time without squawking, I promise to come back real soon. Is it a deal?"

Tony hesitated for a moment. "Deal," he agreed.

Kate had to admire Morgan's style. Not only did he have Tony under control, but he had casually arranged another visit as well.

After giving some last-minute instructions to Mrs. Kelly, who had let herself in while they were at the mall, Kate let Morgan escort her back to his car. This evening had done a lot to change some of her notions about the man beside her. His interest in Tony had seemed genuine. And her son had responded like a morning glory to the sun. She had read somewhere that kids could sense character instinctively. Maybe she should trust her son's judgment.

On the other hand, now that she was alone with Morgan again, part of her couldn't help wishing for a little help from Tony. She had to admit that his presence had changed the context of things with Morgan and made her feel safer. As if to emphasize the point, the all-too-attractive man beside her turned on the engine and shifted into first, giving Kate the distinct impression that he was shifting gears in more ways than one.

# Chapter Four

There's a terrific little tavern down at Fells Point called Kermit's. I thought we could have an after-dinner drink down there," Morgan suggested, giving her an expectant glance.

Kate nodded. "That sounds fine," she agreed, wondering what they were going to talk about for the rest of the evening. An hour ago, with Tony along, there had been no awkward silences. In fact, she was surprised at how much she had enjoyed their visit to the mall. But suddenly things weren't so easy anymore. She was very conscious of the intimate environment of Morgan's expensive sports car, as she studied his profile from under lowered lashes.

As she'd discovered on Saturday, there was something very sexy about this man. And just the thought of their little "experiment" in his unfinished townhouse sent a shiver down her spine. Don't get carried away, she scolded herself. But she couldn't keep her eyes

from returning to his rugged profile which snapped into
sharp focus every time they passed under another
streetlight.

Just then, Morgan turned toward her and caught her
staring. And suddenly it became even more important
to fill the silence between them.

"I, uh, I really think you did a wonderful job of
handling Tony," she blurted.

He chuckled, his voice warm and rich in the semi-
darkness. "I'm glad the technique worked with him.
Actually, I must confess I've tried the same thing with
Julie—and I never got to first base."

The tension between them was broken and Kate
joined in his laughter.

"Well, there goes my 'super parent' image," he
admitted.

"Oh, you blew that when you came to the seminar,"
Kate reminded him. "If you'd been perfect, you
wouldn't have been interested in what Taggart and
Froman had to say."

"Ouch," Morgan responded.

"You never told me what you thought about the rest
of the day," Kate prompted. "Did you get some
pointers that will help you with Julie?"

"Well, the best part for me was the group discussion," Morgan revealed, looking at her meaningfully.
"What about you?"

Deliberately not asking what he'd liked about that
particular session, Kate began to relate the small but
nevertheless significant progress she'd made with Tony.

"I've tried some of the suggestions, too," Morgan
revealed. "But with mixed results."

For the next twenty minutes they discussed the
Saturday seminar. And Kate wondered if Morgan were
as glad as she for the ready-made topic of conversation.

However, ready-made or not, Kate found the

exchange—or perhaps it was the company—absorbing. And so she was somewhat surprised when she looked away from Morgan's face, to discover how quickly they had arrived in the Fells Point area. Moments later Morgan stopped the car and backed into a tight space on the street.

While he parked, Kate glanced around the historic waterfront community with its red brick row houses and inviting night spots.

"I've got something to confess, too," she offered playfully as he helped her out of the car. Although she'd been dreading the ride downtown, she had to admit that she'd actually enjoyed herself almost as much as at the mall.

Morgan arched a questioning eyebrow.

"I've lived near here for five years, but I really don't know my way around Baltimore very well. Would you believe this is my first trip to Fells Point?"

"Then you're in for a treat. And I'm glad I'm the one who's going to introduce you to one of Baltimore's favorite pleasures."

Moments later he was ushering her into the cozy nautical atmosphere of Kermit's Pub. Right inside the entrance were two large saltwater aquariums filled with a variety of colorful and exotic sea creatures and fish. Kate stopped for a moment to watch the antics of a sea horse that seemed to be playing hide-and-seek with the gracefully swaying sea grasses. Morgan stood behind her watching over her shoulder for a moment. And then he leaned over to whisper in her ear.

"Don't you want to see the dancing girls on the bar?" Morgan inquired.

Kate's head snapped around. *Dancing girls on the bar? What kind of place was this anyway?* And then she caught the mischievous twinkle in her companion's eyes.

"You are kidding me—aren't you?" she questioned.

"You'll just have to come back and find out."

Kate allowed Morgan to escort her farther into the darkly lit room. She peered cautiously at the long polished wood bar, but there were no dancing girls— only one of the most extensive collections of liquor bottles she'd ever seen. And that gave her an idea.

As they slid into one of the high-backed leather booths, she gave Morgan a speculative look. "Do you believe turnabout is fair play?" she asked innocently.

"I sense a trap in that question," he informed her. "But suppose I answer yes for the moment."

"Okay," she agreed. "Then allow me to choose a drink for you—since you picked an ice cream flavor for me."

"Oh, so you're trying to find out whether I play it safe or not," Morgan returned lightly. "I like a woman with initiative."

Kate grinned, pulling open the large drink menu and giving it careful consideration. "Let's see. Are you the Hurricane Joe type?"

Morgan rolled his eyes toward the ceiling.

"Sloe gin fizz?"

He started coughing.

"Amaretto and Seven-Up?"

Morgan wrinkled his nose. "Surely you jest."

Kate shook her head. "You're probably the Scotch-on-the-rocks type. But you ought to try something different for a change. How about . . ." She closed her eyes, moved her finger in a wide circle and plopped it down in the middle of the menu. It landed on something called a seafarer's delight.

"Listen, that's not fair," Morgan protested. "I gave your ice cream cone some real thought. You're treating that drink menu like a Ouija board."

Kate looked down at the description. "It doesn't

survive," Morgan pointed out. There was a look of admiration in his eyes, and something else too.

This might have been an opportunity to confide that her disastrous marriage was a big part of her reluctance to get involved with another man. But Morgan could probably read that between the lines whether she said it or not, Kate decided.

However, her story had obviously triggered some thoughts of his own. "It's funny how a bad marriage can leave a scar that takes years to heal," he observed.

He must be speaking from personal experience, Kate deduced, remembering back to some of his remarks during the group discussion. And his next words confirmed her supposition.

"My wife deserted me when Julie was just a baby. Charlotte was a dancer and she decided that her career was more important than marriage and its responsibilities." He paused, looking out toward the bar. But Kate knew his gaze wasn't really focused on anything in the room. He looked like a man confronting some long-buried pain.

"Charlotte had me convinced that everything was wonderful. And you can imagine my surprise when I came home from work one evening to find Julie with a baby-sitter, and a note on the dining room table saying that my wife had been accepted with the Kophry Repertory Company and had left with them on a three-month Canadian tour."

She could see the hurt and anger in his eyes that the memory still evoked. And Kate found herself reaching across the table to place her hand over his.

"The worst part, you know, is that she was using me," he went on, unable to keep the bitterness out of his voice now. "If she'd just said she'd wanted to end the marriage, that would have been different. It would have hurt, but at least it would have been honest."

Kate nodded, understanding just why this episode was so painful for Morgan to recall.

"But she stayed around," he continued, "letting me support her until she could set herself up with something she thought was better. And all the time . . ." He stopped abruptly and gave her a curious look. "I didn't really mean to get going like that," he apologized.

"No, sometimes it's good to talk, instead of keeping things bottled up inside," Kate reassured him. "And you're right; I'm not the only one who's been scarred by a marriage partner," she added.

"Did I say that?"

Kate shook her head. "Not in so many words."

Morgan squeezed her hand, and all at once she felt much closer to him than she had at the beginning of the evening.

"It *was* a bad experience. But, like you, I think I've learned from it and come out stronger."

"What did you learn?" Kate questioned softly.

"That trust and honesty are the only basis for a lasting relationship. If you don't have them, you don't have anything worth keeping." But then he forced a smile. "I think that's enough of the heavy stuff for a while, don't you?"

Kate smiled. "We've probably had enough heavy stuff to last a week," she agreed. But just as they began to take up a lighter topic, the noise level in the bar suddenly escalated.

"It always gets like this on Monday nights when the bowling leagues come in," the waitress explained when she came back to see if they wanted a refill.

Morgan shook his head. "No, we can't even hear ourselves think anymore," he told her.

Kate was suddenly disappointed. She sensed that Morgan had let his guard down with her—that he had shown her a side of himself that few other people were permitted to glimpse. And now, having gotten to know Morgan better, she didn't want the evening to end quite so quickly.

Morgan apparently was as reluctant as she to call it a night. "Tell you what," he began as they paused by the fish tanks once again on the way out. "Why don't we go back to my place for a while?"

Kate wanted to agree. But all at once she couldn't help remembering the last time she'd been alone with Morgan, and she didn't trust her attraction to him.

Morgan seemed to read her thoughts. "Julie should be home from the library by now, so you'll be able to meet her."

That made his offer seem a lot safer. And, besides, she did want to meet his daughter. "All right," she agreed. "But we can't stay out too late. I have to be in the office by nine tomorrow."

"Oh, I promise you'll be home tomorrow before nine," Morgan quipped.

Kate gave him an elbow to the ribs accompanied by what she hoped was a disparaging look. But he only grinned. "Just joking, of course," he qualified.

Morgan's house turned out to be a tidy split-level in Catonsville, one of the nearby suburbs. "I don't know how you commute all the way from Columbia into town," he told her as they pulled up into the driveway.

Kate looked with surprise at the brick-and-frame exterior, which was exactly the same as three other models on the street. Somehow, after the exciting things he was doing with the house downtown, she hadn't expected that he would be living in such an ordinary development.

Morgan seemed to be waiting for her reaction, and she racked her brain for something complimentary to say. But the exterior seemed so conservative that she found herself blurting, "I'll bet you didn't design this house."

Morgan's rich, appreciative laughter filled the car. "Actually, you're wrong. This development was my first effort when I came to work for Stone and Krammer Associates. And since the development is all sold out, they're letting me live in the model until my townhouse is finished."

Kate felt embarrassed—as though she'd just told someone their child was ugly. But Morgan put her at ease instantly.

"It's not really my taste either. But Stone and Krammer wanted something distinctly middle class."

"Well, I think you achieved that quite well," Kate returned lightly.

"There are some surprises inside, though," Morgan promised, opening the door. Kate found herself standing in a spacious, two-story foyer leading to a cozy family room. The house was dark and quiet.

"Julie," Morgan called, flipping on the light. "I've brought someone home to meet you." But there was no answer.

Briefly, Kate wondered if Morgan had really expected his daughter to be at home. The look of puzzlement and then annoyance that crossed his chiseled features quickly convinced her otherwise.

"She went to the library with her friend Amy Lockwood. I'm going to call and see if they're both over there. Why don't you make yourself comfortable." He pointed toward the family room before tramping up the steps toward the kitchen.

Kate wandered back, noting the warm feel of the room with its Navajo throw rugs and comfortable leather couches. She'd barely settled down on a couch behind the freestanding fireplace, when Morgan came back in. His eyes were blazing and the annoyance on his face was replaced by anger. "Amy says my daughter left the library with her boyfriend of the moment, Jeff Hudson, over an hour ago. She knows she's not supposed to go out on a date on school nights."

Kate opened her mouth to comment, but Morgan was too wound up now to stop. "Last week she promised she wouldn't be home any later than nine o'clock. When I get my hands on that kid, she'll be grounded for a month!"

"Do you think Taggart and Froman would endorse your method of dealing with this incident?" Kate asked quietly, trying to make him see the situation more objectively.

Morgan shot her an exasperated look. "I bet Taggart and Froman don't have a fifteen-year-old daughter who turns every household rule into a test of wills."

"Surely it can't be that bad," Kate began.

Morgan sighed and sat down heavily beside her on the couch. "Maybe I am overreacting," he admitted. "But sometimes I get so upset with that girl. Things will go along all right for weeks, and then something like this happens."

"But you don't really know why she went with Jeff," Kate soothed. "Maybe they're on their way home right now."

Morgan took a deep breath, obviously trying to regain his equilibrium. For a moment he said nothing, and then he turned and put his hand on her shoulder. "I'm lucky you're here tonight. Otherwise I probably would have gotten angrier and angrier and I might just have thrown away what little progress I've made recently with Julie."

He looked so lost then, that Kate felt herself melting. She could tell that he cared deeply about his daughter and that this breach of the rules really concerned him. After all, he'd raised Julie by himself since she was a baby, and that made him feel doubly responsible for her.

Just as she had in the bar when he'd shared the story of his broken marriage, she felt a strong urge to comfort him, to make him feel better. And so, instinctively, she reached out with gentle fingers to brush back the lock of hair that had fallen across his forehead.

It was like a moment in slow motion. And then suddenly, his captivating eyes were locked with hers. A current seemed to be flowing between them now, and it didn't have anything to do with comfort.

Morgan's strong hands moved gently down her arms, sending little shivers of sensation along their path. And then he was folding her into his arms, and pulling her close against the warmth of his body.

Kate was caught off balance, as though she were the needle of a compass, drawn off course by a strong magnet. And yet the pull was so intense that she was powerless to fight it.

"Kate," he murmured, his voice at once rough and velvety in her ear. For a time, he simply held her there, as though the contact with her body were all he craved. Kate, too, savored the moment, acknowledging silently how good it felt to be just where she was. As a child, she had always liked being cuddled. But Bart had never been the cuddling kind, and she had forgotten how safe and secure it felt being this close to someone special.

The thought made her realize how quickly she'd come to think of Morgan in that way. He *was* special, she told herself. He was that rare kind of man who could show a woman his vulnerability as well as his strength.

She found her arms stealing around his waist, enjoying the solid feel of his well-muscled form. "When I was little, I always wished for a teddy bear that could hug back," she confessed, not sure why that particular revelation had leaped into her mind.

Kate could feel the laughter vibrate through Morgan's chest. "I don't know whether to be flattered or insulted. Don't tell me you think of me as a teddy bear?"

Realizing how her words must have sounded, Kate was momentarily embarrassed. "I didn't mean, that is, I wasn't—"

But Morgan gently grasped her chin with his thumb and forefinger and tipped her face up so that he could look into her hazel eyes. "Maybe it's not so bad, after all. Did you sleep with your teddy bear?"

Kate's eyes widened, but Morgan quickly defused the loaded question. "Well, if you did take Teddy to bed, it would have to have been at your instigation," he pronounced very seriously.

Kate heaved a small sigh of relief.

"But I envy Teddy's special place in your heart, nevertheless," Morgan added, his lips brushing the barest caress across her forehead.

The contact made Kate shiver with a mixture of anticipation and apprehension over where all this might be leading. "Aren't you going to set your alarm again tonight?" she whispered, searching the face only inches from her own.

Morgan shook his head. "No, tonight I think we'll just rely on the honor system."

Kate didn't know whether to be amused or relieved. But before she could ponder his answer further, his lips were descending slowly to hers.

In keeping with the mood he had created, his kiss was gentle and unhurried. Kate found her own lips parting in response. She knew that getting involved with him could be dangerous, but she was feeling so mellow that it was hard to see the harm in something that felt so right. And besides, she thought she knew how to keep things from becoming too heavy between them.

But despite her conscious strategy, Morgan was quick to sense the encouragement she unconsciously offered. Tantalizingly, his tongue swept along the sensitive inner surface of her lips and then teased the barrier of her teeth, creating a heady mixture of sensations for Kate.

He tasted deliciously of orange, coconut and rum— bringing a wayward, humorous thought to Kate's mind, and she couldn't suppress a tiny chuckle.

Morgan drew back, a frown crossing his features. "I've had strong reactions before to my kisses, but never that."

"Seafarer's delight," Kate whispered. "I'm finally getting a taste of it."

"Oh, is that what's tickling your fancy? Then let me offer you another taste," he suggested, bending to claim her mouth again.

Though his words were playful, his approach this time was not. It was as though he were determined that she would concentrate on him and not the little diversions she had set up as barriers to the type of communication he had in mind.

A moment ago his kiss had been unhurried, as though he were waiting to test her response. Now he was out to take away her freedom of choice. His lips took masterful possession of hers, and at the same time, his hands roamed purposefully down her back, kneading and massaging as they went.

Although all of the arguments against letting Morgan sweep her off her feet still stood, Kate could still not help but respond like a water-starved plant soaking up moisture from a sudden summer downpour. She was overwhelmed by so many sensations all at once. She felt the tantalizing pressure of his lips against hers, the warmth of his body, the electrifying touch of his hands. It was as though she were being enveloped by the total maleness of this man—the musky scent of his aftershave, the tickling roughness of his chin, and the hard wall of his chest.

And even with all of this, she found herself wanting more. She snuggled closer to the warmth radiating from his body, and at the same time her arms crept around his shoulders, her fingers reaching upward to caress the thick hair at the nape of his neck.

At her response, Morgan's touch grew bolder. Lifting her a few inches off the sofa, he drew her into his lap. And then his lips were trailing teasing little kisses along the line of her jaw and down the ivory column of her neck. He was momentarily stopped by the tight collar of her blouse, but not for long.

With deft fingers he began to unfasten the row of tiny buttons down the front, pausing to bestow a kiss at each inch of flesh revealed. When he was finished, the front of her blouse was completely open.

Realizing how far his explorations had progressed, Kate stiffened, trying to draw back from his embrace. But like a gold prospector on the scent of a big strike, Morgan had staked his claim and was unwilling to stop. He trailed his fingers along the full curve of her breast, pushing aside the lacy fabric of her bra. The all-but-transparent material was slight protection from his searing gaze. And yet he wanted more. His fingers went to the front clasp, releasing her passion-swollen breasts. When his fingers grazed their hardened tips, Kate's breath caught in her throat. But instead of continuing with the caress, he drew back, desire smoldering in his tigerlike eyes.

For her own part, Kate could not help but respond.

Her nerve endings were tingling with anticipation now. And her body arched forward, begging for his touch. Yet, strangely, the man who had brought her to this fevered pitch made no move to go further.

Looking up, she met his gaze with an odd mixture of longing and inquiry. "Morgan . . ." she began.

But he stilled her lips with a touch of his finger. "God, Kate, you're beautiful," he whispered huskily. "I just want to memorize the way you look."

From anyone else, the words would have brought a flush of embarrassment to Kate's cheeks. But from Morgan, they were as erotically stimulating as his touch. And she knew what he meant, because she felt the same way. The look of passion in his eyes was something she never wanted to forget either. Tenderly she reached up to run her finger down the strong line of his cheek before tracing the outline of his lips.

The gesture was a spur to his own action. With a groan, he lowered his head to her breasts, seeking first one hardened nipple and then the other with his lips and tongue.

For Kate, it was as though he had tapped a wellspring of long-suppressed sensations, creating a piercingly sweet ache that traveled downward through her body.

She felt her own hand steal under his sweater to stroke the warm skin of his back. And when they worked their way around to his chest so that her fingers could tangle in the springy mat of hair they encountered, she heard him sigh with satisfaction. "Oh, yes, Kate, touch me too," he urged her on, his voice a husky plea.

It was as though nothing else in the world existed except her and Morgan Chandler and the all-consuming feelings they were sharing.

That was why she wasn't aware of the key turning in

the front lock or the first indications that they were no longer alone in the house.

But Morgan was apparently not so insensible. "Oh, my God," he muttered, unceremoniously dumping Kate on the couch. "Julie's home," he added, answering the wild question in Kate's eyes.

Before she could begin to gather her wits, he had sprung off the couch and was hurriedly pulling the edge of his sweater down over his pants. "I'll keep her out of here for a minute," he whispered, already striding purposefully from the room.

For a moment Kate was paralyzed. She felt like a teenager caught petting on the couch. Only it was Morgan's daughter, not an angry mother, who was going to walk in and find her half-undressed.

Activated by that mortifying thought, her fingers began to pull the lacy cups of her bra together. But the catch, which had come undone so easily under Morgan's nimble attentions, refused to cooperate.

As she fumbled to put her clothing back in order and smooth her tangled hair, she could hear strident voices in the hall. "You didn't have permission to go anywhere but the library," Morgan accused. "And you're supposed to be home by nine on school nights, no matter what."

"Why are you blocking the door to the family room? Who's in there," his daughter countered, obviously intent on directing attention away from her transgression by putting her father on the defensive.

"Don't change the subject, young lady. I want to know where you were and who you were with."

But Julie was not about to obey his instructions. Having given up on the bra, Kate had almost fastened the row of buttons on her blouse when a teenager with long dark hair and uniquely colored eyes just like

Morgan's ducked under his arm and poked her head into the family room.

"Hi," she chirped with false brightness. "From the looks of things in here, I can understand why my dad's so uptight. But you'd think he'd be glad that I got home late. In fact, if you'd like, I'll go back out for another half hour and the two of you can finish whatever it is you started."

Kate couldn't suppress an astonished gasp. Had she really heard this girl correctly?

Apparently Morgan had caught the same baiting remarks. "All right, that's quite enough," he warned, the anger in his face clearly visible to Kate. But Julie, who could not see her father's expression, plowed blithely on, addressing herself to the disconcerted woman on the sofa.

"But I do have a question to ask, since my elders are supposed to be setting a good example. I've never seen you around here before, so I assume you've just met my father. Don't you have any more respect for your body than to engage in casual sex with someone you barely know?"

Kate could feel the color draining from her face. She wanted to try to defend herself against the cutting remark, but all she could do was sit there numbly and stare at the girl in disbelief. Seconds later, when her mind started functioning again, Kate realized that there *wasn't* a way to answer that outrageous question. But Julie hadn't really been after an answer, anyway. Having delivered her salvo, she turned and marched triumphantly from the room.

If Kate had been watching a play instead of being an intimate participant in this little drama, she would have enjoyed the series of conflicting expressions that chased one another across Morgan's face. It was obvious that he didn't know whether to follow Julie and chastise her for her outrageous behavior or to try to soothe Kate. Finally he settled for calling, "I'll deal with you later," up the stairs before coming back to rejoin Kate on the couch.

"God, Kate, I'm sorry," he began. "You know that if I'd known this was going to happen, I'd never have let things go so far . . ."

Kate shook her head. She felt shaken. What in the world had Morgan been thinking? He should have realized that Julie would be coming home. But then, she should have, too. Hadn't Morgan said as much?

"It wasn't any more your fault than mine," she told him in a voice that she couldn't quite hold steady. "But I think you'd better take me home now." The end of the sentence ended in a gulp. If she said anything else now, she might burst into tears.

Morgan seemed to understand. Without trying to prolong the discussion, he escorted her out of the house and into the car. And, as they drove back to Columbia, she was grateful that he didn't try to rehash what had just happened. Rather than start a conversation, he simply flipped on the radio to a classical station, and Kate let the strains of a Brahms symphony absorb her attention and relax her body.

When they pulled up in her parking lot, Morgan turned and looked at her questioningly. "Are you feeling any better?"

Kate nodded. She would have told him that anyway, but she realized it was true. The ride home had given her a chance to put the incident in perspective.

"I'm sorry you had to meet Julie under these circumstances. Believe it or not, her manners are usually a lot better. In a way, it's my fault she was on the attack. She's the type of child who strikes out blindly when she's cornered."

Kate considered the new information. Naturally,

Morgan would try to put the best possible face on this, she realized. What parent wouldn't?

Morgan waited for her response. But what could she say?

"Listen, Kate, even though I can see my daughter's side of this, I'm not blind to her faults. Subconsciously she's probably trying to mess up our relationship before it has a chance to get off the ground. You're not going to let that happen, are you?"

His words gave Kate something to think about. And the look on his face told her that this incident had taken as much of a toll on him as it had on her. Suddenly she didn't want to leave him feeling guilty about tonight.

"Don't tell me you've used that corny line about respect for your body and casual sex?" she asked, making her voice deliberately light.

His expression grew sheepish. "You know, you get to the end of your rope, and all those old things your parents told you come tumbling off your lips."

Kate found that she could even grin now. Actually, if the truth be told, the scene with Julie brought back some of her own rebellious teenage behavior and the anguish she later realized it had caused her own mother and father. "I think every girl wants to declare her independence from her parents. Some just use more drastic tactics than others."

"Intellectually I know you're right, but I can't help wishing I didn't have a crisis to deal with every other day."

"I know what you mean," Kate sympathized. "But don't be too hard on Julie. Part of her is still a little girl. And even though she wants to be independent, you're really all she's got. I guess she can't help seeing someone like me as a threat."

Morgan leaned down and gave her a quick kiss. "Don't call yourself 'someone like me,'" he commanded. "You're not just someone; you're someone very special."

"You are too," she found herself acknowledging. And then, turning quickly, she scrambled out of the car. But she couldn't stop from looking back at him one more time.

"Good night, Kate," he whispered huskily.

"Good night," she echoed, knowing that she was going to remember the warm look in his eyes long after she'd gone to bed.

# Chapter Five

$\mathcal{T}$he evening had given Kate a lot to mull over, and it was hard to get to sleep. As she shifted restlessly in her double bed, she found her mind sifting through problems she hadn't even known existed. Before she'd agreed to go out with Morgan this evening, she'd thought that independence was her primary concern. Well, that was still important. But now that she'd met Julie, she knew there was a lot more to the picture. Getting involved with Morgan meant having to deal with his daughter as well. And, although Kate had been feeling close to Morgan as she'd said good night, she wasn't sure if she could handle what Julie was dishing out.

But then her thoughts drifted back over the rest of the evening—from their outing with Tony, to their candid talk at Kermit's, to the passionate scene on the couch that Julie had so rudely interrupted. Before Morgan had come to pick her up, she had been wary of their next encounter. But during the evening he'd won her over—in fact, so much so that she had been lured gently into his embrace. And in all honesty, she had to admit that up until Julie's arrival she had been eager to sample all that Morgan was offering—and to give to him in return. If he had simply made a pass, it wouldn't have happened that way. But there had been a lot more to it than that. She had been bowled over by the way he'd related so easily to Tony. And she'd been drawn to him by the way he'd opened up and revealed some of his painful background.

By the time he'd proffered that taste of seafarer's delight, she'd been all too ready to accept. And now she wasn't sure she would have had the strength to pull back from his lovemaking on her own. Just the thought of the way he'd looked at her after he undid the buttons on her blouse made her tremble all over again. And the way he'd caressed her heated skin had made her eager for more.

Maybe Julie had really done her a favor, she tried to convince herself. Had Morgan's daughter been a few minutes later, the situation might have been even more embarrassing. How far would she really have gone with the persuasive Mr. Chandler? And, for that matter, how far did she plan to go?

The question made her sit up in bed and cup her chin thoughtfully in her palms. It was amazing how quickly things had gotten out of control. She couldn't deny her strong attraction to Morgan—or her strong sexual response either. Yet, at the same time, she knew that they gave him a hold over her that she wasn't quite ready to accept. She'd worked to make it on her own. And she had told herself that she wasn't willing to give it up. But what about her sexual needs? Up until now, her abstinence hadn't seemed like such a sacrifice. But a few moments in Morgan's arms had changed that. The first time in his townhouse had awakened feelings she didn't even know she possessed. Bart had never made her feel so primitive, so sexually alive. Tonight, it was as though Morgan had taken up where he'd left off at his townhouse. The moment he'd stroked her, she had started to purr like a contented cat. Did she want to give that up? she wondered. Might it be possible to have a sexual relationship without making a commitment to that person? She didn't know. But she was pretty sure a superficial relationship would be impossible for her. And where did that leave things? Back to allowing her relationship with Morgan to intensify on every level—and back to having to deal with his daughter.

But maybe that wasn't so bad. In just one evening Morgan had done a lot for Tony. Perhaps she could return the favor and help ease the strain between Julie and her father. After all, she could offer something that Morgan lacked: a woman's perspective. And besides, maybe it was just easier to deal with a teenager who wasn't your own—especially when you weren't handicapped by months or years of acrimonious encounters.

That thought made her suddenly optimistic. She did want to see Morgan again. And she would simply take each day as it came.

The next morning at work, Mary Ellen was eager for details of the night before. "Did you see him?" not "Good morning," were the first words out of her mouth.

"See who?" Kate asked innocently.

"I see by your evasive answer that you must have," her assistant countered with a satisfied smirk. "So how did it go?"

Kate shook her head. "I don't think I can give you a minute-by-minute account of every evening we spend together. Would you settle for a weekly update if it lasts that long?"

"Oh, ho," Mary Ellen retorted. "So it's too hot and heavy to even talk about in the office. But remember, I'll be sitting here panting at my desk until I hear the next installment."

At that moment Dean Porter poked his head into the reception area. "I need your input on plans for the May Day Career Fair. We only have seven months to get everything coordinated, so you'd better bring your folder in."

"I'll be right there," Kate assured him, glad of the chance to escape. She loved Mary Ellen like a sister, but she didn't feel comfortable talking about her relationship with Morgan—especially when she didn't know exactly where things were leading.

Nevertheless, as the day wore on, she found that she couldn't help expecting him to call. In fact, every time she answered the phone, her voice took on an extra warmth. Her enthusiastic "hello" drew comments from a computer supply salesman, the chairman of the history department and a philanthropic alumnus. And she was just about to reconsider her telephone voice when Morgan finally called.

"You certainly sound in good spirits," he remarked, his own voice reminding her of smoke and velvet. "Is that special lilt just for me?"

When she failed to reply at once, she heard him chuckle. "I'll take your silence for a positive response."

"You can take it any way you like," Kate replied lightly.

"Well, since you're so agreeable, how about seeing me again tonight?"

Kate hesitated. She knew she really wanted to see Morgan again, but the scene with Julie was still so fresh in her mind. Maybe it would be better to give herself a little distance. And yet she wanted to make it clear that a second invitation would be welcome. Quickly she considered several excuses. All of them sounded lame, but she finally settled on food shopping. "I'd love to see you," she told him, "but tonight I've really got to buy groceries. My pantry's practically bare, and poor Tony won't have anything for breakfast unless I replenish the shelves."

"I hate to think about you lugging all those heavy bags up from the parking lot," Morgan returned. "Why don't you let me take you?"

"Really, that's not necessary—" Kate began.

But Morgan didn't let her finish the sentence. "I insist. I'll pick you up around seven."

The kind of intimacy Kate had been worrying about wasn't really possible in the grocery store. And carrying the bags in from the car was the thing she hated most about shopping. "Okay," she agreed. "I'll see you later."

Morgan appeared just as Kate was stacking the last of the pots in the dishwasher. "Ready to go?" he asked.

Kate shook her head. "I can't shop without a list, and I need to sort through the week's coupons, too."

"Then I'll challenge Tony to a game of Space Invaders while you get ready," Morgan replied, heading in the direction of the living room.

As Kate sat at the kitchen table mentally planning the meals for the week, she could hear the two of them bantering in the other room. Again she thought about how well they got along and what Tony had been missing since his father's death.

Kate hadn't realized she was missing anything—until Morgan Chandler had charmed his way into her life. Forcing her mind back to the coupons on the table, she finished writing down the last few items on her list and peeked into the living room. Tony and Morgan were just finishing up a game.

"Want to go with us?" she asked her son.

"Aw, Mom, you know I hate grocery shopping."

"Okay, you can stay here. But don't cook anything, don't invite anyone over and don't open the door to anyone. If someone phones me, tell them I'm taking a nap and will call them back later."

"Sounds like you have a regular drill," Morgan observed.

"Yeah, we go through this every time she leaves me here alone—even if it's just for five minutes," Tony informed him.

"Well, it's a good idea," Morgan approved, leaning over to ruffle the boy's hair affectionately. "You're a special guy and I wouldn't want anything to happen to you."

Tony nodded gravely. His expression seemed to say that if Morgan thought the drill was a good idea, then maybe his mother wasn't crazy after all.

"Thanks," Kate whispered as she closed the front door. "I always worry about leaving him alone. If I'm going to be gone for any length of time, I get a sitter. But that's such a hassle for a forty-five-minute trip to the store. And he really is old enough to stay by himself for a while."

Morgan held up his hand. "Don't be so defensive, Kate. You don't have to convince me. Julie began baby-sitting for the neighbors before she was twelve. You have to start giving kids some responsibility somewhere along the line."

Ten minutes later, they pulled into the parking lot at a local supermarket. "This place is giving double coupons this week, and I want to take advantage of the savings," Kate explained.

"Are those coupons really worth all the effort of clipping them and keeping them straight?" Morgan questioned.

"Wait and see the difference at the checkout counter."

Inside, Morgan grabbed a cart. "I have the feeling I'm going to get a lesson from a pro," he quipped.

"Well, don't just stand there. Let's get started," Kate responded.

Her first stop was the produce department where she selected an assortment of fresh vegetables and salad fixings along with some tart, juicy apples. Then she began systematically working her way up and down the aisles. Morgan was assigned the task of pulling out coupons that corresponded with her purchases.

"They're arranged by categories," she told him, "so you shouldn't have any trouble finding the right ones."

"I don't believe how organized you are," Morgan accused. "Don't you ever have to go back an aisle for something you forgot? I spend half my time running back to get the stuff I missed. And then when I get home, I find that I didn't even buy the one thing that I went to the store to get in the first place."

"Then why don't you make a list?" Kate asked, tossing several boxes of breakfast cereal into the cart.

"Because I can't remember everything I need until I see it on the shelves."

They had worked their way down to the grains, and Morgan stopped the cart before a center display featuring jars of gourmet popcorn. He reached for a jar and set it casually in Kate's half-full cart.

"Hey," Kate objected, "that isn't on my list."

"I'll treat," Morgan offered. "Anyway, what could be better than snuggling down together in front of the fire on a crisp autumn evening with a bowl of hot buttered popcorn? Can't you just see yourself reaching into the bowl for another piece and brushing my hand? And if you were extra good, I'd let you feed me a kernel as I lean back indolently against the sofa.''

Kate shot him a wary look. Despite herself, she could easily picture the scene he had just described. And the intimacy of his voice brought a shiver of awareness down her spine. Even though he hadn't elaborated further, she knew what was in his mind for the rest of the evening. With Morgan Chandler, there was no telling where something as innocent as popcorn could lead.

Kate glanced up and down the snack food aisle. Three shoppers within hearing distance hadn't moved an inch since Morgan had started his provocative popcorn campaign. In fact, one elderly lady nearby had been concentrating so intently on their conversation that she'd loaded a dozen jars of macadamia nuts into her already packed cart. Although, in a way, the incident was funny, Kate still felt uncomfortable at being the center of attention. She looked accusingly back at Morgan, who had started the conversation in the first place.

The warning in her eyes brought only a quick amendment to his lips. "Of course, if you insist, the bowl will be between us. Now what could be more proper than that?"

"You can keep your popcorn," Kate told him quickly. "But if you don't behave yourself, those gourmet kernels won't be the only thing in hot butter," she added over her shoulder as she resumed her shopping. She'd better get the rest of the things she needed quickly. Who knew what Morgan was going to try and pull next?

As she'd feared, minutes later he halted her progress again in the cheese department. "I can't believe the selection they've got. In our neighborhood, you're lucky to get Cheddar and Swiss. But you've got everything from Camembert to Port Salut." He was already reaching for a wedge of Brie when Kate laid a restraining hand on his arm.

"Are you sure you had dinner before you picked me up?" she questioned. This time she was going to have control of the interchange. No way was she going to let him go off on the kind of sensual tangent inspired by the popcorn.

"Grocery shopping always makes me hungry, whether I've had dinner or not," he replied good-humoredly. "Let me treat you to some cheese, and you can provide the crackers."

"But we already passed that department," Kate complained.

Morgan lowered his voice to a conspiratorial whisper. "If you promise to give me a snack when we get back, I won't tell anyone that you had to go back a few aisles. And I won't insist on making the popcorn either. We can save that for another evening."

Kate grinned with a mixture of amusement and relief. "I'm not sure I could handle the popcorn tonight. And as for my efficient shopping habits—I don't consider it a violation of my sacred honor when someone *else* forces me to backtrack."

"In that case, I have a special request. I didn't want to mention it, but did you happen to see the woman making up fresh pizzas near the deli counter? They *really* looked good."

Morgan had put so much enthusiasm into the comment that Kate was left in no doubt that the pizza had really taken his fancy. Cocking her head to one side, she studied him with mock intensity. "Are you sure you didn't have any ulterior motives when you volunteered your services this evening?"

Morgan chuckled. "I may have ulterior motives, but

you're going to have to find out for yourself which ones they are."

Turning the cart around, he headed purposefully back toward the deli. "How 'bout mushroom, olives, green pepper and anchovies?" he threw back over his shoulder.

Kate grimaced and hurried to catch up with him before he gave the order. No way was she going to let him order anchovies—not if he planned to share it with her.

While Morgan waited for the order, Kate added the last few items to her already full basket. Then, with the pizza perched on top, they made their way to the checkout counter.

"Where are all those coupons I asked you to pull out?" Kate inquired.

Morgan reached in his pockets and pulled out two crumpled wads.

Kate rolled her eyes in exasperation. "In this store they make you put each one on top of the item it matches," she informed him. "So smooth them out and start matching."

"Yes, ma'am."

It took an extra ten minutes to make it through the checkout line. But even Morgan was amazed that she had saved fifteen dollars on her shopping bill with her use of the cents-off certificates.

"How did you ever learn to do that?" he questioned, after they had crammed her eight bags of groceries into the back seat of his car.

The innocent question brought back unpleasant memories, but they seemed like such a long time ago that to her amazement, Kate found that they had lost their ability to hurt her.

"Bart was really tight with the household money," she began. "To put food on the table and have enough money to run the house, I had to learn to scrimp and save every place I could. I used to get Tony's school clothes at garage sales. You'd be surprised at the bargains you can pick up that way."

Morgan shot her a disbelieving look. "You're kidding? Didn't he make a decent living?"

"Of course. But there were so many high-priority things he wanted—like the best stereo equipment and a fast car."

"That's terrible," Morgan commiserated.

"It wasn't quite as bad as it sounds. Actually, it got to be a challenge. And now, even though I don't have to cut corners so much, I still enjoy beating the system at the grocery store. The money I save goes into a special account for Tony's college education."

"You really do have something to be proud of," Morgan marveled. "And I don't just mean your ability to organize coupons. Few people have it all together the way you have."

Unwittingly, Morgan had given her an opportunity to tell him something that had been on her mind for the last few days. "You're only seeing the image that I've worked hard to cultivate," she began.

"Don't tell me you're really an undercover agent?" he quipped.

"Morgan, this is serious," Kate insisted. "It's true that my life is organized. But that was the only way I could function after Bart died. There were so many things I had to learn how to do. You know, Bart didn't let me handle any money except my household funds. I didn't even have a checking account in my name. It took over a month to get that mess straightened out with the bank."

Morgan turned to her as he stopped at a traffic light. He looked as though he were about to say something, but Kate hurried on. "I may have everything in order, but it's all fit together like the pieces of a jigsaw puzzle. Sometimes I'm afraid that if I rearrange even one little piece, the whole picture wouldn't make any sense any more."

As he shifted into first gear, Morgan's expression grew thoughtful and then tense. "So that's why you've been afraid to open up to me," he finally observed. "You've been worried that I'd rearrange your neat and tidy picture. Is that what you're trying to tell me?"

As Kate watched the strained lines of his face, she wanted to deny his interpretation of her words. But basically, he had cut right to the heart of all her doubts.

"Well, what are you trying to say? That you want to stop seeing me?" he demanded, his knuckles white on the steering wheel now.

The terse question brought an instant denial. "No!" she protested. "That's just the problem. I do want to keep seeing you."

Her words made some of the tension ease out of his body, and he reached over to lay his large square hand on top of one of her small ones.

"Well, I sure as hell want to keep seeing you, too," he assured her gruffly, giving her hand a squeeze. "So let's just take things as they come. Okay?"

Kate looked over at him and nodded. "Okay," she agreed.

"I hope that means you'll invite me in to share the pizza we just ordered," he prompted.

Kate shot him an exasperated look. "Listen, Morgan," she informed him. "Every time I think you're going to give me some control over this situation, you jump in and take over."

At her accusation, the expression on his face grew thoughtful. "You know, I'd never thought about it in those terms, but maybe you're right. I do try to take charge."

"Well, I think things between us will go more smoothly if you at least give me the illusion of some power."

"Yes, ma'am," Morgan retorted. "In that case, would it be all right if I come in and fix that pizza for us?"

Kate studied the handsome man beside her. Was he capable of taking this whole thing seriously, she wondered, or was he secretly laughing at her little plea for independence? There was only one way to find out. "All right. But you have to bring in the groceries while I put everything away."

"Sounds as though I don't have any choice," he grumbled good-naturedly, pulling into her parking lot. "Let's get the fun part over first."

Fifteen minutes later they stood in her kitchen surrounded by half-unpacked brown grocery bags.

"Could you put the tomato sauce in the pantry?" Kate asked, indicating a heavy bag in the middle of the floor. Morgan started to comply, but when he opened the pantry door, he couldn't help laughing.

"What's so funny about my pantry?" Kate demanded, turning from the refrigerator where she had just stowed a carton of milk.

"Maybe you're not as organized as I thought," Morgan retorted. "You already have half a dozen cans of tomato sauce. So why did you need ten more?"

"You have a lot to learn about economical shopping," Kate informed him. "First of all, the tomato sauce was on sale. And in the second place, I have a two-dollar rebate with fifteen labels. That means I really got them for a nickel apiece."

Morgan held up his hand. "Okay. I give up. There probably is a method to your madness after all."

Working together, they were quickly able to put everything in its place. "Tony is really good about staying out of the way when there are groceries to unpack. But I'll bet the smell of pizza will bring him out of hiding in a jiffy."

But Kate's prediction proved to be incorrect. Though the aroma of spicy tomato sauce and bubbling cheese filled the townhouse, Tony failed to appear.

"I'll go get him," Morgan offered, heading for the living room. In a moment she heard him tromping up the stairs, but he returned alone.

"Better tell Tony not to study in bed. He's fallen asleep with his math book on his chest."

Kate shook her head. "Math always put me to sleep, too. Did you turn off his light?"

Morgan nodded. "And I pulled off his shoes and tucked him under the covers."

"Sounds like you have the whole routine down pat. All you missed was a good-night kiss."

Morgan's eyes suddenly lit up with mischief. "I can still take care of that," he pointed out, closing the distance between them. Before Kate realized what he was about, he had backed her up against the counter and planted a none-too-brotherly kiss on her lips. In keeping with his playful mood, the demonstration of affection was more teasing than passionate. And, before Kate had time to feel threatened, it was over. She looked up at Morgan questioningly.

"It's not that I wouldn't like to go a little farther," he explained, "but I've taken your lecture about independence to heart. And besides, what I really want to do is build up the kind of relationship where we can trust each other. Something like that is worth the investment. So I'm willing to wait to claim my reward."

His words made Kate feel good. Apparently he was willing to give things a chance to develop between them without trying to force the sexual issue. Yet, at the same time, she couldn't help being a bit disappointed

that that one teasing kiss was all she was going to get.
Dealing with Morgan's honesty was almost as hard as
dealing with her own response to his sexual advances.

"Oh, you're probably more interested in the pizza
than in me, anyway," she joked, half hoping that he
would deny the accusation.

"That's a leading question that I refuse to answer
until after we've eaten," Morgan returned, reaching for
a slice.

As it turned out, that one teasing kiss was the only
intimate contact Kate had with Morgan all evening.
And over the next week, although he came by to see
her and Tony frequently, he made no move to take
things any farther.

Although she had made her little bid for independence, Kate found herself wishing that he would be
more aggressive. But how could she let him know she
wanted more without seeming forward? she wondered.

But before that problem could be settled, it was
temporarily pushed out of her mind by an announcement from Dean Porter.

"Kate, I was scheduled to attend the College Outreach Conference in New York tomorrow, but my
wife's uncle in Chicago died unexpectedly and we have
to rush out there. The registration is paid and the room
at the St. Regis has already been booked. Is there any
way that you could take my place?"

Could she? Kate wondered, mentally ticking off all
the things she'd have to do first. The key thing would be
getting a sitter for Tony. "I can let you know by
lunchtime," she told him.

Luck was with her. Mrs. Kelly was available for the
three days of the conference and was delighted to get
the job. Kate gave Dean Porter the good news well
before lunch and he immediately began briefing her on

sessions he particularly wanted her to attend. After that he gave Kate the afternoon off to get ready.

As she sorted through her closet, selecting and rejecting outfits, Kate found her spirits soaring. This was her first out-of-town conference and a real professional milestone. Who would have thought just a few months ago that she'd be representing the university at a national meeting?

And then her thoughts turned to Tony. How would he take her absence? But she needn't have worried. He was so anxious to attend Mike Hastings' overnight party on Friday that he swore up and down that he wouldn't give Mrs. Kelly any problem. It was the first invitation of that kind he'd received since moving to Columbia, and Kate shared his excitement. He seemed to be coming out of his shell. Maybe there was going to be less to worry about with him from now on, she told herself.

There were so many arrangements to make, that it was almost nine-thirty before Kate remembered one more thing. She had a date with Morgan Wednesday night. Was it too late to call? she wondered, glancing at her watch.

But she really didn't have any choice, since she was leaving on the seven A.M. Metroliner from Baltimore. The phone was picked up on the first ring, but it was Julie who answered, not Morgan.

"It's for you, Dad," she heard his daughter yell as though he were on the other side of the world. "But don't be long; I'm expecting an important call."

"I pay the phone bills around here, remember," he informed his daughter curtly before speaking into the receiver. But his tone changed abruptly when he discovered Kate on the other end of the line. "To what do I owe this honor?" he questioned. "You know this is the first time you've called me, don't you?"

"Unfortunately, I have to break our Wednesday date."

"Oh?"

"Dean Porter asked me to replace him at the College Outreach Conference in New York. I'm leaving tomorrow morning and won't be back till Friday afternoon." It was impossible for Kate to keep the excitement out of her voice.

"Well, you don't have to sound so happy about breaking a date," Morgan teased.

"Sorry. Couldn't we make it Friday instead?"

"I don't know if I can wait that long." Morgan paused. "In fact, I'll only agree to the postponement if you let me come over and say goodbye this evening."

"But it's late already," Kate objected halfheartedly. She was touched by the gesture. Under the circumstances, most men would be content to say good night over the phone. But Morgan wasn't *most men*. She knew that already, and what's more, she had to admit that she wanted to see him too.

"I'll be there in half an hour," he was saying. "But I won't stay long," he promised. "I know you need a good night's sleep."

True to his word, he knocked lightly on the door as her mantel clock was chiming ten. Although she'd eagerly awaited his arrival, once he'd stepped into her small foyer and closed the door purposefully behind him, Kate felt suddenly shy looking up at the man who had become an important part of her life all too quickly.

Morgan shook his head wryly. "You know, I've been so good all week, I figured I'd get my just rewards tomorrow night."

Kate didn't know whether to shake her head in exasperation or smile. She'd never met a man who could be both so honorable and dishonorable about his intentions all at the same time.

"And now I won't get to see you till Friday."

"Were you really being good in the expectation of a reward?" she couldn't help whispering.

"Damn right!"

Before she could respond, he had swept her into his arms. "My plan may have backfired, but you certainly can't deny me a fond memory to take to bed while you're away," he coaxed, his warm breath persuasive against her ear. The strategy was all too effective.

"Umm . . ." Kate found herself agreeing, as she snuggled closer against the length of his lean body. Although she hadn't told him, she'd been wanting something like this all week too.

When his mouth descended to claim hers, her lips opened in eager invitation. She could feel that old familiar warmth beginning to spread through her body as Morgan's hand moved up the length of her spine.

It would have been impossible for him not to sense her quick response. His hands slid down to press her tightly against the cradle of his hips. And at the same time, his lips left hers to nibble seductively at her earlobe.

"Are you going to keep me standing here in the hall, or are you going to invite me in?" he whispered huskily.

For a moment Kate wavered. Then she shook her head regretfully. "Let's not start something we can't finish."

Morgan sighed. "You're right; I did promise to let you get your beauty sleep," he was forced to agree, and yet she could tell just how much he wished the situation were otherwise. For a moment he pulled her even closer against his hard frame as if trying to memorize the feel of her pliant body. His hands stroked down her back from shoulder to hip, kneading and caressing as they went. Kate closed her eyes and leaned into him, her own hands unable to remain still on his neck and shoulders and then in the thick dark hair at the back of his head. She heard his muffled groan of pleasure.

And then, to her surprise, he released her and took a deliberate step backward.

"What did you say about starting something we couldn't finish?" he questioned, his voice husky.

Kate bit her lip. "I'm sorry . . ." she began.

"Don't be sorry. You don't know how much I'll be looking forward to Friday now," he promised.

"Yes," she admitted.

For just a moment he reached out and touched his finger to her lips. And then, quickly, he turned and opened the door. As he closed it behind him, Kate knew just how much she'd be looking forward to Friday too.

# Chapter Six

The scene with Morgan in the hall had hardly been conducive to sleep, and so it was almost midnight before Kate finally drifted off. Five A.M. came all too soon. Unable to get up as she had planned, she turned off the alarm and rolled over for another ten minutes of sleep. Half an hour later, when she woke up for real, there was barely time to complete her preparations and make it to the train station.

She was a little disappointed when her cab pulled up at the St. Regis. There was nothing remarkable about the gray stone facade. In fact, the only touch of glamour was the red carpet at the door. But once she'd entered the elegant lobby with its marble floors and sparkling chandeliers, her opinion changed rapidly. It was like stepping into the opulence of another era.

A uniformed bellman took her bags while she made her way to the ornately carved check-in desk. And then she was being whisked into a small art deco elevator.

"Are you here with the conference?" the bellman inquired, holding the elevator door for Kate before leading her down a carpeted hall.

"Yes," she confirmed. "Do you know where I'm supposed to register?"

"On the top floor. But most of the sessions will be on the second and third," he explained helpfully.

Kate's room surprised her. Although it wasn't really large, it was beautifully decorated with antique reproductions. The walls were papered in a delicate Laura Ashley print, and the Persian blue drapes and quilted bedspread carried out the romantic motif. It was a setting that made Kate feel deliciously feminine. And all at once, she couldn't help wishing that Morgan were there to share it with her. The wayward thought brought her up short. *Back to work,* she told herself sternly, checking in her briefcase for the confirmation letter Dean Porter had received several weeks ago. Since he had preregistered, she was going to have to have the records changed to her name.

After touching up her lipstick and brushing her chestnut hair, Kate was ready to make her presence known. But she hadn't bargained for the stubborn clerk at the registration desk. He had Dean Porter's name on his computer listing, and there was no way he was going to change the entry to Kate Davenport without authorization from the conference coordinator.

A few months ago, Kate might have sighed and resigned herself to a long wait. Now she insisted that everything be straightened out as quickly as possible. Still, by the time she was officially registered, she had missed the welcoming coffee and the opening ceremonies. But the first session, "Publicizing Outreach Events," more than made up for the disappointment. Kate took careful notes, knowing the dean would quiz her on the information. But she would have taken them anyway, she realized, since the material would prove invaluable for the university's next program.

By the time lunch came around, her hand was cramped from writing so much. Even so, she wanted to be certain not to miss the one o'clock seminar. To save time, she simply grabbed a tuna sandwich and a cup of coffee from the fast-service counter the hotel had set up for the convenience of those attending the conference.

For Kate, the afternoon sessions were just as hectic. Although she knew that Dean Porter considered these conferences as much a social as a business affair, she felt compelled to remain all business. She had so much to learn about university-community relations, and this was like a crash course. But more than that, her sense of thriftiness dictated that she get full value for the not insignificant sum McCoy was paying for her registration and expenses.

Many of the conference-goers skipped the late afternoon sessions, but Kate hung in for that last hour and a half. Since the crowd was now only half its former size, she had a chance to ask an important question at the session on counseling workshops. Dean Porter's insistence that she reveal the actual problems people had talked about in the small group discussion on single parenting had been troubling her.

What did the speaker think about the ethics involved? she queried.

"That's a good question," he replied. "But as long as you don't match names of participants to problems, you're abiding by the ground rules."

Kate smiled her thanks, and listened with interest as he related some of his own experiences in similar situations. His reassurance helped end the first day on a very positive note for Kate. She had thought she would be exhausted, but suddenly she didn't feel like simply going back and spending the rest of the evening in her room. Instead, after dropping off her briefcase and changing into some low-heeled walking shoes, she grabbed her midlength leather coat and headed for the strip of nearby shops she'd seen that morning.

If this conference gets any more frantic, I won't have the time or the energy to pick up anything for Tony, she reasoned. So I might as well get it over with now.

The shop windows beckoned with an array of New York souvenirs. Kate saw everything from huge lollipops shaped like a "Big Apple" to Statue of Liberty paperweights. But her practical mind gravitated toward the clothing—which Tony could always use. She was delighted to find a hooded sweat shirt proclaiming "I Love New York." And it was even on sale.

With her purchase tucked under her arm, Kate went in search of supper. But before she encountered any restaurants, she passed a boutique offering women's designer lingerie at discount prices. Unable to resist, she decided to take a peek inside, and within five minutes she'd fallen in love with a champagne beige gown-and-peignoir set. Bart had never provided the resources to indulge herself in expensive nightwear, and once she'd had to manage by herself, it was much easier to rationalize splurging on an outfit she could wear to work than on a sexy nightgown that no one besides herself would see.

However, she was unaccountably in the mood to give herself a treat. Here she was in this exciting city for the first time, and she wanted something in addition to carefully inscribed notes to bring back.

I'll just go see how it looks, Kate told herself, heading for the tiny dressing room in the back of the shop. I don't have to buy it. However, even in the very unromantic surroundings, the rich satin and lace of the gown did wonderful things for her figure and brought out the peach beige of her skin.

Before the practical side of her nature could come up with any objections, she was fishing in her wallet for a credit card.

On the way back to the hotel, she thought of another way to rationalize the purchase. The university was paying her per diem for the conference. She was getting a flat sum for meals—whether she ate at the Ritz or McDonald's. She hadn't spent much for lunch, and a sandwich and salad would satisfy her for dinner.

As it turned out, a sandwich wasn't so much of a sacrifice. Not far from the hotel was the most fantastic deli she'd ever seen. It seemed possible to gain ten pounds just on the enticing aromas that enveloped her when she stepped inside the door. And selecting from the voluminous menu was an exercise in self-control. She finally settled on a bowl of homemade chicken noodle soup and a corned beef sandwich on rye that turned out to be stacked three inches high.

From her table in the back of the crowded room, Kate watched the other diners as she munched her mouth-watering sandwich, enjoying the hint of garlic in the seasoning. The noise level was incredible, and she could hear conversations in a variety of languages. She felt the vitality of the city as her mind cataloged the day's new experiences. Her only regret was that there was no one to share her impressions.

The overstuffed sandwich and soup proved as filling as a full-course meal. Kate was feeling pleased with her resourcefulness in finding this inexpensive eating place so close to her hotel. With this menu, she could eat here all week and not get bored.

But as she stepped out of the restaurant, she knew the fast pace of the day was finally catching up with her. Though the evening was still relatively young, she had the beginnings of a slight headache. All she wanted now was a hot bath and a good night's sleep.

The first was easy to take care of. After she emerged from the steaming water and dried herself, she decided to try on the champagne beige gown once again. Somehow it fitted the romantic mood of the room, she mused as she turned back the covers and slipped between the crisp white sheets. But the headache she'd tried to bathe away was not going to let go so easily.

Why hadn't she thought to bring aspirin with her? she asked herself, wondering if it was worth getting dressed and going down to the hotel drugstore. Or maybe some soothing music would do the trick. Consulting the guide on the dresser, she found a classical station on the bedside console.

She had just adjusted the volume to a soft background level when the phone rang. Who had her number besides Mrs. Kelly? she wondered. Could something be wrong with Tony? But when she picked up the receiver, it was not the thin soprano of her baby-sitter which greeted her but the rich baritone of Morgan Chandler.

"I tried you earlier, but you weren't in," he explained, and Kate couldn't help catching the slight note of reproach in his voice.

"Well, the wild party doesn't start for another hour," Kate retorted, "so I was out grabbing a bite of dinner first."

"I'm not calling to check up on you," he added quickly. "If you can't be here for our date tonight, long distance is the next best thing."

Kate couldn't help smiling. Despite her hectic day, she had missed Morgan. It was nice to know he had missed her, too, she thought, realizing all at once that the sound of his voice had been what she'd needed to banish her headache.

"So how is the conference going?" he asked.

"Informative. Hectic. Exhilarating. A little intimidating," Kate summarized. She was struck with the sudden insight that when she had been wishing for someone to share her day with, it was Morgan she'd had in mind.

"That's certainly an intriguing opening. How about some details," he encouraged.

For the next ten minutes she did her best to comply. And then she realized that it was all on his nickel. "It was wonderful of you to call, but this must be costing you a fortune," Kate felt forced to remind him even though she was reluctant to end their conversation.

"Actually, it's my pleasure. And it's got to be cheaper than taking you out to dinner," Morgan quipped.

"Not if you'd taken me to the deli where I ate," she countered playfully. "By New York standards it was a real bargain, and the corned beef was the best I've ever had." And then a funny thought crossed her mind and she giggled into the receiver.

"What's so funny about a corned beef sandwich?" Morgan demanded.

"The garlic," Kate answered. "If you'd been at dinner with me, you probably wouldn't want to kiss me good night."

"Oh yes I would," Morgan corrected. "When you ordered corned beef, I would have had it too."

"Is that the way you men make your menu selections?"

"Drastic situations call for drastic measures."

Without her realizing quite how it had happened, the conversation was suddenly on a more intimate note. Trying to get things back to more neutral ground, Kate changed the subject. "I got a chance to do some shopping after dinner," she told Morgan.

"Sounds exciting. Did they honor your coupons in New York?"

"No." Kate decided not to take offense at his little dig. "But I did find a great bargain on a hooded sweat shirt for Tony. It'll be perfect for when he plays soccer."

"And what did you get for yourself?" Morgan inquired.

Kate looked down at the satin and lace gown she was wearing. Somehow it seemed just too intimate a piece of apparel to mention to Morgan. And yet, she couldn't bring herself to lie.

"Just a nightgown," she finally admitted.

"The tone of your voice makes me think otherwise," Morgan prompted silkily. "If you're too shy to describe it, then I'll just have to guess. You can tell me if I'm getting warm." Before she could demur, he added quickly, "Let's see, you'd look delicious in peach. Is that its color?"

"No, champagne beige," Kate found herself blurting.

"You'd look wonderful in that too. It would bring out the warm glow of your skin." His words were like a caress, and Kate couldn't stop from responding. She felt what was, indeed, a warm glow start in her face and spread downward to the gentle curve of her breasts, visible at the deep vee of the gown's neckline.

"And the material," Morgan continued. "Is it sheer and lacy?"

"You're half-right," Kate conceded, hearing the intake of his breath on the other end of the phone line.

"My God, do you mean I'd be able to see right through that gown?" he groaned.

"No," Kate was quick to correct him. "It's satin, with a touch of lace." Somehow she couldn't believe that she was relating such intimate details. And yet, what was the harm? The man was two hundred miles away, after all. What could he do via long distance?

But she had ample opportunity to find out. "This bit of lace," he probed; "I can just see it on the bodice. Am I right?"

"You *are* warm," Kate congratulated. And I'm getting there too, she admitted to herself.

"Ah," Morgan breathed. "Let me try my luck a little further. Either you have a great memory for detail, or you're wearing that sexy gown right now. Which is it?" he questioned huskily.

Dare she admit that she was lying here in bed, dressed in the seductive creation they were describing together? Kate wondered.

But she didn't have to answer.

"You'd tell me right away if it were in your suitcase, so I know you've got to be wearing it," Morgan deduced. Before she could confirm or deny his hunch, he went on, "Look down and tell me about the neckline. How much of your tempting décolletage would I be able to see?"

"Morgan!" Kate reproved him.

But his answer was a deep chuckle. "Going to make me guess again?" he asked.

Which would be worse, Kate wondered, describing the plunging neckline or having him conjure up something even more revealing? "It's just this side of modesty," she finally hedged, and then, unable to deny an impish impulse, she added, "But it plunges all the way down to my waist."

"Do you mean I'd be able to see the full curve of your breasts?" Morgan whispered huskily. His silky words brought back the memory of the last time he'd stroked that full curve to aching awareness. She didn't have to look down to know that her body was remembering as well. The sensitive peaks of her breasts had tautened and were straining against the delicate material of the gown.

"I hope you know that this conversation is driving me up the wall," she heard him growl softly over the phone line.

"Me, too," Kate admitted, surprised at the words that had tumbled from her own lips. She had assured herself that it was all right to play this erotic game with Morgan, that she was perfectly safe. But she had underestimated his ability to reach her—even though he was miles away.

"You don't know how much I'd like to grab the first plane to New York," he confessed. "But that's impossible, of course. Maybe we'd better just say good night— so I can go take a cold shower. But you have to promise me one thing first."

"What?" Kate questioned.

"That you'll be waiting for me in bed when I call tomorrow at ten—and that you'll be wearing that sexy gown again."

"Morgan!" Kate exclaimed.

But his only answer was a wicked chuckle. "Remember, tomorrow at ten," he repeated.

She could still hear that chuckle echoing in her mind as she turned off the light and tried to settle down under the smooth sheet and warm wool blanket. Even though she was tired, it was almost impossible to relax now. She couldn't help replaying their all too sexy exchange over in her head again. Even in memory it had the power to heighten all her senses.

And then a sudden thought struck her as she went over the details of the conversation yet again, pondering just exactly what questions Morgan had asked and in what order. It hadn't been until near the end of the conversation that he'd suggested she was actually wearing the nightgown in question. But he must have been making that assumption all along. "The dirty dog," she groaned, and then couldn't repress a grin.

However, her next thought was more unsettling. Somehow, the fact that he'd been picturing her in this gown all along was very provocative.

It was almost two before Kate finally got to sleep, and her seven A.M. wake-up call came all too early. But somehow in the cool morning light, she realized it was going to have to be business as usual today. Quickly she showered and then dressed in the russet suit she'd brought along. Over breakfast of a coffee and Danish, she studied the conference schedule. There were several concurrent sessions that appealed to her, but she finally settled for a panel discussion of "Conference Pitfalls and How to Avoid Them."

During the busy day, she hadn't allowed her mind to wander back to Morgan Chandler. But as she opened her suitcase to change shoes before going to dinner, she saw the champagne beige gown that had provoked their suggestive interchange of the evening before. He said he was going to call her again tonight, Kate thought with a little pang of anticipation. And he would be expecting her to wear the gown again. She hadn't exactly promised that she would comply, but somehow she knew she would.

Ten-thirty that evening found her sitting in bed dressed as requested, wondering why Morgan hadn't called. For the past forty minutes, she had been trying to read the *New Yorker* magazine she'd picked up at the lobby newstand.

*Was this Morgan's idea of a joke? Was she being stood up over the phone?* Ten minutes ago, after she'd read the same sentence a dozen times, she'd even called downstairs to check whether there had been any messages for her. But no one had called.

She had just tossed the magazine on the nightstand and was about to snap off the light when the phone rang. Eagerly she reached out her hand, but stopped in midair. He had made her wonder where he was. Let him suffer the same anxiety for a few seconds. But then a horrible thought crossed her mind. What if he gave up too easily? With that, she grabbed the phone, her breathy "hello" sounding overanxious, even to her own ears.

"Well, that was worth waiting for," Morgan drawled.

"What do you mean? You're the one who kept me waiting," Kate couldn't help complaining.

"But it wasn't my fault! I kept getting, 'We're sorry; all circuits are busy. Please try your call again later,'" Morgan whined, imitating the nasal recording that Kate had heard herself all too many times.

She was instantly contrite. Trying to get through unsuccessfully must have been just as frustrating as her waiting anxiously for his call. "I'm sorry. I didn't know," Kate apologized. "What do you suppose tied up all those lines?"

"Didn't you see the evening news?" Morgan teased.

"No, I've been so busy with this conference that I feel as though I've lost track of the world. Has something important happened outside the St. Regis Hotel?"

The suppressed laughter in Morgan's voice should have warned her that his answer would be facetious. But she had let him set her up. "You mean you didn't hear that a trunk cable between Baltimore and New York melted down from the heat of a certain conversation last night? They had to rush fifteen eavesdropping operators to intensive care."

"Morgan!" Kate squeaked. "How could you lead me on like that! You're making me wonder if you really couldn't get through this evening."

"Oh, that part's true all right. I was getting ready to send you a telegram but I was afraid they'd come and arrest me if I sent the message I had in mind."

As she had the night before, she felt herself flushing. If phone lines really *could* overheat from conversation, they'd both be in trouble with the FCC.

As if tuned to the same frequency as she, Morgan picked up their conversation where he'd left off the night before. "You are wearing that sexy gown again, aren't you?" he asked, his voice as silky as the shimmering material itself.

"Um, yes," Kate admitted. And then she had an idea. If he could play this game, so could she. "And what are you wearing?" she asked boldly.

"Nothing . . . much," he chuckled.

Kate sucked in her breath.

"Not to worry," Morgan qualified. "I do have on a pair of cutoffs."

"You're trifling with me again," Kate accused. But the image of his broad chest and narrow waist refused to be dismissed from her mind. She hadn't actually seen him in that unattired state, but she had run her fingers under his shirt and she could picture that naked expanse of chest very well.

"You bet I am," he shot back. "That's the whole purpose of this telephone call. But I'm not going to let you change the subject on me. Let's get back to that gown that drove me crazy all night. I think we got as far as the vee neck. I spent from two to three A.M. wondering whether you were wearing anything underneath it." There was an expectant pause on the other end of the line. "Are you?" he finally asked.

Kate could feel her heartbeat accelerating. No, she didn't have anything on underneath. And she was suddenly aware of how sensual the silky material felt against her bare skin.

"Well?" Morgan prompted.

When she still didn't answer, he went on. "Are you going to make me play Twenty Questions again? Okay.

I'm guessing that I'd be able to see a lot more of you than I ever have before through that translucent material."

Kate looked across the room at her reflection in the large dresser mirror. Even in the dim light she could see the outlines of her slender legs topped by a shadowy triangle. The thought of Morgan having the same view made her nipples harden with arousal. "I'm not sure I can handle this conversation," she whispered hoarsely into the receiver.

"I'm not sure I can either," he answered, his voice equally husky. "But I'm not sure I can stop, either, until my wicked curiosity has been satisfied. Let's press on now," he ordered, clearing his throat. "Can I assume confirmation of my last assumption?"

"Please—" Kate began.

But he stopped her. "I'd be willing to quit this line of interrogation if you would model the gown in question for me tomorrow night. But with Tony around, we both know that would be impossible."

He ended on such a regretful note that Kate found herself confiding, "Tony's going to be at a sleepover party tomorrow." And then her hand flew to her mouth as she realized what she'd revealed.

"Hot damn!" Morgan exclaimed exuberantly.

The two syllables were like a power surge on her end of the line.

"Kate," he added quickly. "You don't know how much I want to be alone with you tomorrow night."

But she did know. Because suddenly she realized that she wanted to be alone with him too. She had convinced herself that there was no harm in playing Morgan's little game over the phone and that she was perfectly safe two hundred miles away, but now she knew better. Morgan's seductive words had stoked her warm response to him into a blazing need. "I want to be alone with you too," she admitted in a trembling voice, knowing full well what she was committing herself to.

"Do you want to go out to dinner—first?" he asked, the last word of his sentence hanging in the air between them like the promise of spring on the first warm day of early March.

"No," she whispered. "I'll be home in time to fix us something. Why don't you come over around seven?"

"At least let me bring some wine, then," Morgan offered. "And I'll be counting the hours," he added.

"Me too," Kate admitted softly before they said good night. It was going to be another restless night. But tomorrow was another proposition.

*Chapter Seven*

The conference would be ending at noon so that participants could check out and get home for the weekend. Though two morning sessions were scheduled, there was only one more seminar Kate wanted to attend. It was on budgeting, a subject that should have captivated her interest. Yet, it was impossible for her to translate the speaker's well-thought-out guidelines into coherent notes. Though she scribbled furiously during the first half hour, when she looked down at her paper, she found unconnected words and phrases interspersed with flowing doodles. She was shocked. She had never doodled in her life. What was the matter with her? But the question was really unnecessary. She knew what the matter was. Her mind was no longer on the conference. It had leaped hours ahead to this evening— when she had agreed to see Morgan Chandler alone. And that was making it impossible to concentrate on the here and now.

With a sigh she closed up her notebook and stuffed it

in her briefcase. She might as well leave the session and go back to her room and pack. There was no use staying in New York now. When she checked the train schedule, she found there was an earlier Metroliner she could take back to Baltimore if she could get to the station within the next hour and a half. She could get ready in time. But, remembering the stop-and-go ride from the station to the hotel, she knew that whether she could make it or not really depended on the New York traffic. As it turned out, luck was with her. She arrived at Penn Station with fifteen minutes to spare. And the train wasn't even crowded. There were only half a dozen people in the nonsmoking car, so she was able to slip into one of the four facing "conversation" seats near the door. Since she had no companion, she spread her coat on the seat opposite, put her feet up, and stretched her legs out.

Although the extra space made it easy to get comfortable, Kate found it difficult to really relax. Now that she was alone for three hours with her thoughts, the uneasy path they insisted on taking was anything but relaxing. She had practically assured Morgan that she was going to let him make love to her tonight. How in the world had that happened? But she knew.

She had been foolish enough to assume that a phone call would be safe—it would be all right to relax and enjoy the sexual byplay that somehow always simmered beneath the surface of their conversations. But she had been wrong. Morgan's silky, seductive teasing had had as much power over her as if he'd been right there in bed with her.

Kate let out the breath she'd been unconsciously holding. What was she going to do? The sensible thing would be to call him as soon as she got to Baltimore and break their date. But she knew instantly that that would be impossible. He had pushed her frustration level beyond the point where it was bearable. And he was the only one who could ease the aching need he had created and nurtured.

And that was just the point, Kate told herself. It was Morgan Chandler she wanted, and not just any man. Over the last few weeks she'd come to care about him deeply. If it weren't true, she would never be considering keeping the "date" they had tonight.

Kate leaned back against the cushioned seat and closed her eyes. She had finally admitted something to herself that she had tried for a long time to hide. It was inevitable that she was going to bed with Morgan. And tonight was almost surely going to be the night.

The realization suddenly freed her mind from all the questioning and turmoil that fed on her indecision. Her eyes opened again. If what was going to happen was a *fait accompli*, then she might as well make the most of it. And besides, planning this evening with Morgan would be a lot more fun than worrying about the consequence.

The delicious thought brought a little smile to her face. What was she going to wear, for instance? Morgan had suggested the nightgown that had started all the trouble. But she certainly wasn't going to greet him at the door in *that*. And what was she going to have for dinner? She'd better think about the meal now so she could stop at the grocery on the way home. It would have to be something elegant—and at the same time something that could be prepared in advance. After all, she wanted to spend more time getting herself ready than the food.

By the time the Metroliner pulled into the Baltimore station, she had made a list organizing everything. Dinner would be marinated flank steak, salad, baked potato and the apple pie she'd made several weeks ago and frozen for a special occasion. If this wasn't special, she didn't know what was.

Kate arrived home in time to hug Tony, hear how things had gone without her, and then see him off to his party. If he hadn't seemed so happy to be leaving, she might have felt guilty about her own anticipation for the evening without him. But he seemed so excited and proud to be included in this sleepover that she found herself feeling as happy for him as for herself.

Humming along with the radio, she set about getting dinner started. After marinating the flank steak, she made the salad and wrapped it in a damp tea towel to crisp in the refrigerator. Then she scrubbed the potatoes and took the pie out of the freezer. Although Kate had to admit that she really wasn't much of a baker, pies were the big exception. Her mother had taught her to make them juicy and delicious, with a flaky crust that practically melted in the mouth. And it would be the perfect ending to the deliberately man-pleasing meal she'd planned.

Once dinner was under control, she was free to begin her own preparations. She started by washing her heavy chestnut hair and then wrapping it in a towel so she could enjoy a long, luxurious soak in the tub.

Should she pin her hair up or leave it loose? she wondered, as she blew the tresses dry. But as she brushed it into natural curls around her shoulders, she decided on the latter course. The excitement that shone in her hazel eyes was matched by the free and easy style. It was perfect for her mood for the evening—seductive and reckless.

And once she'd made that admission, it was easier to pick an outfit. In the back of her closet was a creamy white angora sweater that she'd gotten for a New Year's Eve party and never worn since. When she'd bought it, she hadn't realized how much the low neck and open weave revealed of her figure. But the comments that evening had left her in no doubt that it had raised male temperatures a few degrees all over the room.

A few minutes later, as she stood looking at herself in the full-length mirror, she hardly recognized the seductive woman who stared back at her. Kate had always thought of herself as somewhat conservative. But this woman was daring and exciting. The sexy sweater hugged her every curve. But the long chocolate brown hostess skirt she'd selected to go with it was another matter. Its velvet folds hinted at more than they revealed, except where she'd purposely left the bottom of the side split unbuttoned. As she twisted and turned she could catch glimpses of her gold-braided sandals and an inviting expanse of leg that went well above her knee.

Her face, too, had enjoyed special treatment. Honey peach blusher brought out the color of her cheeks, and soft turquoise shadow did wonderful things for her eyes. The whole effect made her feel deliciously seductive. What would Morgan think? she wondered, her excitement and anticipation building. She wanted to be sexy for him. But that wasn't all. Over the weeks she had come to know that he cared for her and Tony. She felt the same way about him, but she had been more afraid than he to let it show. When he saw her tonight, she wanted him to realize how deep her feelings really were.

She was just adding a touch of perfume when the doorbell rang. She looked at her watch. Morgan was fifteen minutes early. He must be as anxious as she to get the evening started.

Hurrying down the stairs as fast as the skirt and her evening sandals would allow, she caught a delicious whiff of the cinnamon and apple flavor of the pie she'd popped in the oven between her bath and makeup session. That would make a lovely greeting as well. With an expectant smile on her lips, Kate opened the front door. Morgan Chandler stood rigidly on her front step. One look at his tense expression froze the welcome on her lips.

"Morgan, what is it? What's the matter?"

"This is the matter," he growled, holding up a crumpled tabloid newspaper section and waving it under her nose.

"You're not making any sense . . ." Kate began, but before she could finish, Morgan pushed past her into the townhouse.

"I guess you've been too busy to read the paper, then," he jeered. "But since you're responsible for this article, you must have known it was going to be in Friday's special education supplement."

"Article," Kate repeated stupidly. "What article?"

"Don't play dumb with me," Morgan grated. "There's no one else who could have provided the press with the details of that small group discussion we both attended. You know—the one where you promised that everything said would be kept confidential."

"But I never . . . But I didn't . . ." she started to defend herself. And then she blanched, a measure of understanding dawning. Against her better judgment she had told Dean Porter some of those confidential details. He must be responsible for the article.

Morgan noticed the change in her expression and took it for an admission of guilt. "To think I trusted you," he spat out. "But it's obvious that you had a long talk with the guy who wrote this article. Where else could he have gotten all these details?" She saw his knuckles whiten on the crumpled newspaper.

Suddenly it was almost impossible for Kate to stand up. Weakly, she slumped back against the wall of the small foyer, fighting to control the hot tears that stung the backs of her eyes.

"Morgan, you've got to let me explain," she choked out.

"I don't have to let you do anything," he cut her off. "You've already done it."

"No," Kate managed. "You're wrong. I didn't talk to that reporter. It must have been Dean Porter. He must have disclosed information from my conference report."

"So you can't even admit your own mistakes," Morgan accused, shaking his head. "This is hopeless."

An iron fist already seemed to have a stranglehold inside Kate's chest. And Morgan's words made it tighten so that she could hardly breathe. It was almost as though he'd delivered a physical blow, and she stared at him in pain.

At that moment the buzzer on the oven went off. It took a long moment for Kate's confused brain to understand what the sound meant. And then comprehension dawned. The pie. It was going to burn if she didn't take it out.

Suddenly, getting dessert out of the oven seemed like the most important thing in the world. Turning without a word, she left Morgan standing rigidly in the vestibule and hurried down the hall to the kitchen. It took only a moment to place the steaming pie on the rack to cool. But when she returned to the foyer, it was empty. Morgan was gone.

Any strength that remained in Kate's legs ebbed away and it was only the banister that kept her from falling. Holding it as though it were the only stable thing in the middle of an earthquake, she let her body slide down to the floor until she was sitting in a dejected heap, her back against the wall. She felt weary; a dull ache radiated throughout her body. Twenty minutes ago she had been so full of happy anticipation for the evening. But those joyful feelings seemed as far away as a distant galaxy. What was she going to do? What could she do? In a way Morgan had some justification for his anger. She hadn't wanted to give so many details to Dean Porter. Yet she hadn't been able to hold back under his questioning. She'd felt guilty at the time, but just this week in New York, she'd been reassured by experts who had to deal with the issue that she hadn't done anything unethical.

The realization helped restore her equilibrium. Looking up, she noticed for the first time that she was actually sitting on the cold floor of the front hall. This was ridiculous. Hauling herself up, she turned back to the family room where she'd tossed the afternoon paper carelessly on the coffee table. The article Morgan had waved so angrily in her face must be inside. What exactly had it said, anyway?

Heart pounding, she thumbed through the supplement. Near the back was a half-page article on McCoy's outreach program. As she scanned the columns, she realized it was based almost entirely on an interview with Dean Porter, and even attributed a number of quotes to him. There were only two paragraphs that dealt with the small group discussion she and Morgan had attended. Although some of the parents' problems were sketched in general terms, no names were mentioned.

Kate threw down the paper, her own defensive reaction bubbling up in anger. The nerve of that man to come over here accusing me of breaking his trust! she fumed. If he'd taken the time to read the words in print thoroughly, he would have known that nothing personal had actually been revealed. To think that she'd spent all afternoon getting ready for him.

Jumping to her feet, Kate marched into the kitchen.

She might as well pitch out the dinner she'd so lovingly prepared that afternoon. But as her hand reached for the flank steak in its pungent marinade, she paused. Just how was it going to hurt Morgan Chandler if she threw out eight dollars' worth of meat? She might as well save it for her and Tony's dinner tomorrow.

Yet that didn't satisfy her need to let off steam. She wanted to do something violent like smash eggs against the wall or hurl dishes onto the floor. But she could never permit herself that kind of destructive release. And besides, who else was there to clean up except herself?

But then again, she couldn't sit around here doing nothing. Tromping back upstairs, she looked around her bedroom and spied the overflowing hamper of dirty clothes she'd had to leave before dashing off to New York. She usually made Tony carry them down to the basement laundry room. But since he wasn't here, she had a better idea. Dragging the laundry hamper to the top of the stairs, she reached inside for a pair of jeans, rolled it into a ball and hurled it down the stairs, imagining that it was a cream pie hitting Morgan Chandler in the face. The little fantasy was immensely satisfying, she thought, picking up a heavy towel and slinging it after the jeans. By the time the contents of the hamper had landed in the front hall or on the bottom stairs, she was feeling somewhat calmer.

But suddenly she didn't feel much like washing laundry—or doing anything else. It had been a long day. She might as well just leave the hall the way it was and just go to bed.

Sighing, she turned and headed back to her bedroom. But as she crossed the room, she caught a glimpse of herself in the full-length mirror on the door and stopped. The outfit that she had so expectantly put together was now in disarray from her pitching practice in the hall. The skirt was twisted so that the side slit was down the back. The sweater had ridden up around her waist. And her carefully arranged hair was a riot of chestnut waves framing her troubled face. Grimacing, she pulled the sweater over her head and tossed it on the chair in the corner. Next she unbuttoned the skirt and laid it across the chair back. She was just running her hands distractedly through her hair when the doorbell rang.

Who in the world could that be? she wondered, glancing at the clock. It felt like the middle of the night, but she was surprised to see that it wasn't quite eight. Maybe it was the paper boy. After slipping into a velour robe and quickly zipping the front closure, she grabbed her purse and headed for the front door. But when she opened it a few inches, she was surprised to see not the paper boy but a sheepish-looking Morgan Chandler standing in the illumination of the outdoor light.

"Go away," she ordered, trying to push the door quickly closed. But he was faster than she, wedging his foot in the small opening before she could shut him out.

"Kate, I've got to talk to you," he insisted.

"I've taken all the abuse I care to this evening," she informed him coldly. "Why don't you just leave me alone?"

His features contorted. "I don't blame you for being upset," he admitted. "I was way out of line. Let me come in and apologize."

Kate shook her head adamantly. "I don't think there's anything more I care to hear from you. If you'd just taken the trouble to read that article carefully, you would have realized that there were no real grounds for your accusations."

"That's just it," Morgan pleaded. "After I left, I did read it carefully. You're right. I'm a total ass. Please let me in."

Despite all the misery she had suffered that evening, Kate couldn't stifle a glimmer of amused satisfaction at this turn of events. Here was Morgan Chandler groveling on her doorstep, apparently ready to take any punishment she might see fit to deal out. "And why should I let a total ass into my house?" she questioned.

"Because he wants a chance to make amends for ruining your evening," Morgan prompted.

Kate opened the door a crack wider. "And just how do you think you can make amends for accusing me of being a grasping, dishonorable woman willing to do anything to drum up free publicity for the university?"

Morgan winced. "I guess that *is* what I implied," he confessed. "You've got to believe I'm sorry, Kate. I realize now how much I overreacted. This trust thing has gotten to be such a . . . a . . ."

"Neurosis," Kate supplied.

"That I'm like a wounded bull seeing red whenever I believe the principle has been violated," Morgan finished on a self-deprecating note, his tawny eyes anxiously fixed on Kate's face.

For a long moment she studied his drawn expression. There was no doubt that he regretted the hurt he had caused her. Was there any sense in being obstinate about his apology? she debated.

Stepping back, she opened the door wider. "All right, come in," she relented.

As Morgan stepped over the threshold, his foot landed on a pillowcase. He had to catch the doorjamb to keep from falling flat. "What in the world . . ." he exclaimed, looking around at the laundry all over the foyer.

Kate reddened. "Actually, it's the fallout from a little game I just invented."

For a moment he looked at her in disbelief. "Care to tell me what it was?" he asked curiously.

Kate shook her head. "It's nothing I'd like to share right now."

"I understand," Morgan conceded. "But I hope when you were in a destructive mood you didn't throw the dinner out too."

Kate shook her head. "No. I decided you weren't worth wasting all that expensive meat."

"Expensive meat?" he echoed. Suddenly, he looked as though he were hoping that despite what had happened, Kate might still invite him to dinner. But he didn't dare ask, of course.

And Kate wasn't yet ready to pick up where the evening should have started. "I'm afraid your little tirade has taken my appetite away," she informed him curtly.

Morgan's eyes met hers. "You have every right to be angry at me. But please hear me out."

Kate looked down. Despite the somewhat mollifying conversation of the last few minutes, she was still hurt and upset. And yet, she had told herself she cared about Morgan. Didn't she at least owe him a hearing? "Okay," she finally said. "Come on into the family room."

Morgan followed her down the hall. When he reached the family room, he glanced at the couch and then at Kate's unreadable expression. Resolutely, he sat down in the chair across from the TV while she took the couch.

"All right. I'm listening," she told him.

"Kate, when I picked up the evening paper and saw that article, in my mind it was Charlotte all over again."

"You've got to forgive me if I find that statement hard to follow," Kate clipped out.

Morgan sighed. "But it does make sense," he insisted, leaning imploringly toward her. "Once you've been played for a fool like that, you can't help waiting for it to happen again. Don't you remember that I told you Charlotte spent a lot of time convincing me that everything was all right between us, and I believed her? That's when she stuck it to me."

Kate knew this whole apology must be costing Morgan a lot. It was evident in his haunted eyes, and she found herself shifting nervously in her seat.

"Someone else in my position would have salved his ego by simply despising a woman like Charlotte," he continued. "But I couldn't. I loved her then, and that's why it hurt so much when she left." The pain in his eyes was so naked that Kate felt her heart contract. It seemed selfish to hold onto her anger when he was revealing so much of his inner feelings.

"Despite the way I opened up with you at Kermit's, there aren't many people I've talked to about my marriage," he continued.

Kate nodded.

"But I have to make you understand," Morgan went on. "It's been a long time since I've cared strongly about anyone except Julie. And I thought maybe I never would again—until I met you. That's why the article on the conference blew me away. I'd finally let myself . . ." He paused, searching for the right word. "Open up to somebody," he finally whispered. "And then when I saw that article, I thought I'd been set up again."

Kate studied Morgan's drawn features. The whole speech had been a hard one for him to make. But now Kate could understand better what had set off his tirade. It had been a defensive reaction which he hadn't been able to control. And if he hadn't really cared about her, he would never have come back. He would have simply slammed the door on their relationship and walked away.

Standing up, she crossed the room swiftly and knelt by his chair so that her eyes were on a level with his. "It's all right. I do understand," she began. The words brought a flood of relief to his troubled features. But she knew she had to make him understand that while she sympathized with his motivation, she couldn't leave herself open for this kind of episode again. "Morgan," she added, "I have to believe we both learned something tonight. And if it put our relationship on a more honest basis, then it was worth the misery it caused us both. But I don't think I could take something like this again."

She felt Morgan's hand on her shoulder, pulling her gently to him, but she held back. "What assurance do I have that this won't happen again?" she questioned, and then held her breath, waiting for him to speak.

"I can't swear that I'll never have any other doubts," he finally answered, his voice edged with regret. "I know myself too well for that. But I can promise that I won't shoot first and ask questions later. If there's ever something like this between us again, I'll not only give you a chance to explain, but I'll do my damnedest to believe what you say."

Was that enough? Kate wondered. Maybe not, but it was going to have to do for now. Morgan had been as honest with her as he could. He couldn't promise her a rose garden. But at least he'd promised to deal with the thorns before she got wounded again. And after all, what assurances were there in life, anyway?

"Kate?" Morgan prompted, raising her chin so he could look intently into the hazel depths of her eyes.

For her answer, she pressed her hand around his.

Neither spoke, but an intimate understanding flowed between them. Slowly Morgan's fingers began to caress her cheek. Light as a feather, his touch was gentle but at the same time sensual. Kate closed her eyes and savored the feeling. After the acrimony of their confrontation over the newspaper article, it was like a balm to her battered emotions. Unconsciously, she leaned closer, and her hand began its own tentative caress. Hooking her thumb under his hand, she began to stroke the pad of flesh at the base of his palm. It was such a small gesture, and yet Kate could feel a shudder go through his body. Or was it through hers? She didn't know.

He leaned over a few more inches and brushed a kiss across her forehead. And then, unaccountably, she heard him chuckle.

"What is it?" she whispered.

"If I have to keep leaning over like this, I'm going to throw my back out. Maybe I'd better join you down there on the carpet."

In the next second he had moved down beside her and pulled her over onto his lap. It felt so right to be there, Kate admitted to herself, snuggling close against the broad expanse of his chest. Her cheek rested on the fabric of his shirt where she could appreciate the fresh, inviting smell of newly laundered clothing. But beneath that she could sense the exciting male scent of Morgan himself. Over the phone in New York, it had just been his voice and its wicked insinuations that had sent her imagination romping. But now, here in his arms, all her other senses were responding as well.

"God, Kate, it's so good to hold you in my arms again," he murmured, his lips against her hair. And then he buried his face in the chestnut richness, savoring the closeness that they both had craved so much during the past few days.

"For me too," she confessed. "Last night on the phone you about drove me crazy with wanting this."

At her admission, Morgan lifted his head. And Kate tilted her own face up so that she could read his expression. To her surprise, the corners of his eyes were crinkled with mischievous amusement. "It was harder on me than it was on you," he informed her as gravely as possible.

The double meaning of his words was not lost on Kate, and she felt her face grow hot.

"I guess I've discovered the secret of making you blush," Morgan congratulated himself, leaning down to press his lips against the center of one reddened cheek.

The gesture had started off in fun, but with the contact of his lips against her soft skin, they both suddenly knew that the game had moved on to something more serious. The light banter had been a way of reestablishing the bond that had been stretched almost to the breaking point between them. But now it had snapped back, drawing them together in heated anticipation.

"Morgan," Kate whispered, "when I was waiting for you this afternoon, all I could think about was . . ."

He pulled her even tighter into his arms. "This," he supplied. And then his lips were seeking the warmth of her mouth. There was no need for him to urge her lips open. They parted for him like a flower yielding up its honeyed nectar.

Last night and the night before, when he had seduced her with his sensual words, she had imagined them sharing a welcoming kiss. But rich as it had been at the time, the fantasy just couldn't compare with the reality of Morgan's lips on hers. They were eager and demanding, yet soft and persuasive, all at the same time. And as his tongue slid into the warm cavern of her mouth, she beckoned him to discover more.

When he finally drew back the merest fraction, it was to speak her name. "Kate, oh, Kate, I missed you so much," he groaned, so close that she could almost taste the words as they flowed between her lips.

"I know," she mouthed, "me too," sending the admission back as a caress. She could feel her words literally vibrate between them.

"I've wanted to do this . . . and this . . . and this," he growled, his lips demonstrating the sensual thoughts his mind had conjured up. And then his hands trailed down the front of her velour robe, setting her nerve endings tingling as his fingers sought the fullness of her breasts. Even through the thickness of the fabric, the pleasure was so intense that she gasped. And yet she wanted more.

And Morgan evidently shared her desire. His fingers found the zipper tab of the robe, pulling it slowly down until it opened to reveal the creamy cleavage at the top of her bra. As his lips began to explore this newly discovered terrain, Kate felt a delicious little shiver, and her own head lowered so that she could press her cheek against the richness of his dark hair.

Encouraged by her reaction, he slid the zipper even lower and slipped two fingers under the edge of the lacy bra. Kate held her breath, waiting for him to find her hardened nipples.

But instead of going on, he stopped and raised his head. Although his words were light, his voice was heavy with suppressed emotion. "I only have about ten seconds of control left. If you want to stop me, you'd better do it now."

Kate searched the liquid depths of his eyes, seeing her own passion mirrored there. "I don't want you to stop," she answered, her own voice barely audible.

"Are you absolutely sure you know where this is

leading?" he asked, giving her one more opportunity to call a halt.

"To my bedroom," she answered, unable to keep the impish glint out of her hazel eyes.

"In that case, I'm going to insist that you model that gown I've heard so much about," he replied huskily. "That is, of course, if you let me up off the floor here."

Kate scrambled off his lap and then offered her hand to help him up.

"You'd better not do that with your robe hanging open like that," he advised, "or we may not make it upstairs, after all."

Kate hadn't thought of the revealing picture she must make. With shaking fingers she started to draw the zipper back up, but he stopped her quickly. "Don't spoil the view," he pleaded.

Arm in arm they headed for the stairs, but at the entrance to her bedroom Morgan paused. "I hate to let reality keep creeping in, but I have to ask if you're protected."

Kate swallowed, touched at his concern and yet reluctant to answer. She knew she couldn't get pregnant again, but she didn't want to discuss the details now. "You don't have to worry," she assured him, turning to open the door.

The first thing Morgan saw was the famous nightgown, freshly laundered and laid out across the bed. Looking from it to her, he grinned. "Well, I see we were both thinking about the same thing."

Snatching the satin and lace creation off the spread, Kate turned and disappeared into the bathroom. There was just a moment of hesitation when she caught sight of her passion-bright eyes and glowing complexion in the mirror. The woman looking back at her might have been a reckless stranger. Without giving herself time for further contemplation, she undressed quickly and slipped into the delicate negligee. But the sight of her body, revealed through the translucent material, brought a shiver of both excitement and apprehension. Was she sure she wanted to go through with this? she asked herself. But it was far too late to turn back now; and besides, she knew she wanted Morgan with all her mind and body.

When she emerged from the bathroom a few minutes later, the room was bathed in the soft amber glow of the lamp on her dressing table. Morgan was waiting for her in bed, propped up against the pillows so that the wide expanse of his hair-matted chest was visible above her printed sheets. Her heart missed a beat and her mind skipped down to ponder what lay hidden below the covers.

As he watched her hesitate in the doorway, he stretched out an arm in invitation. "Better get under the covers, because if you don't, I'm coming out to fetch you."

His little threat was all the incentive she needed. Quickly she crossed the distance between them and slipped into bed. The first thing she noticed was the way his body had warmed the sheets for her. But before she had time to fully appreciate the small service, Morgan had turned and pulled her into his arms. For a moment he simply held her close, savoring the intimate contact he had craved for so long.

Kate closed her eyes, luxuriating in the feeling of melting against his burning length.

"Much as I'd like to keep on holding you this way, I've got to satisfy my curiosity about you in that gown," he whispered huskily.

"Didn't you just see me come to bed?" Kate questioned.

But Morgan only chuckled. "That didn't count. It

wasn't up close—like this." Before she could demur further, he had swept aside the covers and laid her gently on her back. As his heated gaze roamed over her body, lusciously revealed by the creamy fabric, Kate knew what it was to be adored. His hand reached over to trace the line of lace where it edged the deep vee of her bodice. Although it was the lightest of touches, her breasts swelled in instant response.

She heard his indrawn breath. "So beautiful," he murmured, extending his explorations further under the lacy edge of the fabric. Kate waited expectantly, the sensitive peaks of her breasts begging for his attention. But his teasing touch never quite gave her the satisfaction for which she hungered. Frustration made her move restlessly beneath his hands, enjoying the exquisite torture and yet wanting more than that.

"Morgan, please . . ." she beseeched. But he stilled her words with his lips.

"Everything in good time," he promised, punctuating each word with a leisurely kiss. "This week has been an eternity for me. But now that the reward is within my grasp, I want to savor it."

His lips left hers then to trail tantalizing little kisses along the line of her jaw. And then his teeth gently claimed the lobe of her ear. "There's so much I want to know about you—every nuance, every detail," he whispered huskily, his breath warm and intimate against her cheek.

His slow seduction was setting each one of Kate's nerve endings on fire. And passion made her bold. Her own restless hands sought the firm muscles of his back and then slid lower to grasp and knead the flesh of his hips and buttocks. Her reward was his little growl of surprise and pleasure. Encouraged, her hands slipped around to the front of his body so that she could caress the hair-roughened skin of his thighs. But he was not about to submit to the same torture he was so skillfully administering. With a quick maneuver, Morgan changed positions so that he could capture both of her hands and bring them up above her head.

"What are you trying to do, drive me crazy?" he growled.

"No, I'm just helping you to understand what *your* teasing is doing to me."

Morgan couldn't suppress a wicked grin. "You mean, you'd like things to proceed a little faster?" he inquired solicitously, the smoldering desire in his eyes sending delicious tremors through her body.

As she watched, mesmerized by the play of emotions on his face, his gaze fastened on the tiny bows that held the straps of her gown together. Almost in slow motion, he shifted his grasp so he could hold her wrists captive with one hand. With the other, he gave a tug on each bow, parting the two halves of each delicate strap. The deliberate sexiness of the gesture made Kate's breath quicken. She knew beyond a doubt what he was going to do next. But still, when he began to lower the bodice of the gown, she was unprepared for the flood of longing that seemed to wash over her. As he bared her breasts, his hungry eyes seemed to revel in the sight of what they had uncovered. His searing look made her nipples harden as though he had touched her with his hand.

"So lovely," he murmured. "As lovely as you looked in that gown, you're even more beautiful without it."

He bent, then, to test the swollen texture of one straining peak with his lips and tongue. And then he turned to give the other the same attention. Kate arched against him, and as his hands freed her wrists, she pulled him closer.

It was as though a dam of passion had burst. Impatiently, Morgan slipped the gown past her hips and over her feet. And then he was working his way back up her body, kissing and caressing, stroking and exciting every inch of her. Kate felt the flood tide of her passion surging violently, threatening to drown her in its intensity.

"Morgan, I need . . ." She stopped unable to articulate what it was she was seeking so desperately.

"Kate, I know it's been a long time since you . . ." He, too, let the rest of the sentence trail off. "And I don't want to hurt you," he whispered, and yet he had gone too far to turn back now. His first possession of her was tentative and gentle, testing for resistance before going further. But the passionate response of her body told him what he needed to know. Her hips surged forward to meet his, begging for total possession. With one powerful thrust he completed the union of their bodies.

He paused for a moment to hold her close and kiss her, as though savoring the reality of what was finally happening between them. And then, with controlled urgency, he began to move inside her. The rhythm at first was slow. But it built in power and intensity, carrying Kate up and up to heights of rapture beyond her imagining.

It had never been like this for her before, never.

"Morgan," she gasped, something close to fear in her eyes.

But he seemed to understand. She felt him deliberately stop moving inside her, watching her face intently as he did.

"Don't be afraid. Don't fight it," he whispered. "Let it happen for you."

Leaning down, he brushed his lips against her eyebrows and then nuzzled his face reassuringly against her cheek. And then, slowly, he began to move within her again, until it was she who begged with her eyes and body for him to increase the pace.

"Kate," he breathed, obeying her unspoken plea. She was like a comet blazing out of control now, glowing brighter and brighter with the depth of her need for release. And even though traveling at the speed of light, her body was still finely tuned to his. It was he who triggered the final quantum leap that seemed to send her very being out of the galaxy. And it was Morgan to whom she clung, overwhelmed with the intensity of what was happening. For a long moment, she and Morgan were poised on the edge of infinity together. And then, slowly, leisurely, they were being drawn back to earth.

"God, Kate, that was incredible," Morgan sighed.

"For me, too."

She felt his arms tighten around her. "I know," he whispered.

As he held her close, she couldn't help marveling now at the sense of contentment she felt. Morgan's arms around her were like a cocoon that sheltered her from everything but the reality of this bed and this moment. If only the rest of life could feel as right as this, she thought, snuggling closer.

Waking up the next morning was like coming out of a beautiful dream. For a long moment Kate snuggled under the covers, reveling in the feeling of warmth and contentment that still enveloped her. But when she stretched out her arm luxuriously, she suddenly realized that something was missing. The man who had shown her just how satisfying physical love could be was no longer in her bed.

Throwing back the covers, she sat up and then shivered. She had forgotten that Morgan had shed her nightgown in the heat of passion last night. That thought alone should have been enough to warm her up on this crisp autumn morning. Yet she still padded across to the bathroom to retrieve the green robe she had left there before coming to bed. It and all the towels were missing.

Wrinkling her nose in puzzlement, she stuck her tousled head back out the door. But before she could pursue the mystery further, she'd have to find *something* to wear. In the back of her closet was a knit caftan that she'd used as a cover-up at the pool. Pulling it over her head and slipping into terry scuffs, she went in search of Morgan. He was not on the first floor. And neither was the laundry she had pitched down the stairs the night before. Comprehension began to dawn. It looked as if her guest had decided to make himself useful.

As she headed down the stairs to the basement, she could hear someone humming "Là ci darem" from *Don Giovanni*. At least, that's what she thought it was, since the delivery of the tender love song was so off-key that it was hard to be sure. Crossing the recreation room on tiptoes so as not to disturb the performance, she paused for a moment in the doorway. Morgan was dressed in a light blue jogging suit, and for a fleeting moment she wondered where it had come from. Where were the shirt and slacks he had worn last night? As if to answer her question, he opened the dryer and pulled out his shirt, flapping it vigorously to help the permanent press along. After carefully hanging it up, he began to extract newly laundered sheets and towels from the dryer and toss them into a wide basket. As he worked, he started another aria—this one the "Toreador Song" from *Carmen*. It was just as awful. Kate was touched that he was being so thoughtful, yet he looked so pleased with both his domestic and musical abilities that it was hard to keep from grinning. And the grin soon escalated to a full-fledged chuckle. Morgan didn't even bother to acknowledge the insult with a look. "So you think my singing is funny, do you?" he questioned. "Or maybe it's my laundry technique."

"You really don't want me to comment on the singing," Kate assured him. "But it's wonderful of you to help with the chores. There's only one thing . . ."

"Yes?"

"I *am* a little picky about the way things are folded." As she spoke, she couldn't keep her glance from flicking toward the casually loaded basket.

"Naturally," Morgan agreed. "I wouldn't expect less from you."

Somehow Kate didn't know whether he was delivering a compliment or a snide remark. However, in the next second, he was picking up the basket and heading for the stairs. "Then let's make this a group activity," he tossed over his shoulder.

Kate followed him up to the bedroom, where he smoothed back the spread and then dumped the whole pile of laundry on top. "I do like your fabric softener," he commented with a deceptively innocent smile as he selected a fluffy yellow towel. "You don't know the problems I have with static cling at home."

Kate was speechless—until she saw the way he was folding the towel. It wasn't right at all. "No, stop," she commanded. "I fold them the long way first."

He stopped in mid fold and gave her a strange look.

"It's easier," she defended. "That is, it's not easier to fold them that way, but it's easier to hang them up once you've done it."

Morgan lifted his eyes heavenward. "I think I'm going to need some special instruction in your technique." With that, he held out the towel. But when she stepped forward to get it, he seized her by the waist and tossed her into the pile of warm laundry on the bed. Her look of utter surprise had barely registered before he joined her.

"What in the world?" Kate began. But he stopped her with a kiss. It was impossible for Kate not to give in to the moment. If the bed had felt cozy when she awakened, it was now a deliciously warm nest. The toasty heat and fresh smell of the clean clothing tingled her senses invitingly.

Morgan seemed equally enchanted with this unique environment he had created especially for the two of them. "I've never tried this before," he admitted, nibbling softly on her ear. "But I think I could really get into laundry even if you don't like the way I fold your towels."

Kate silently agreed. There was something decidedly decadent and yet strangely exciting about making love to Morgan in this outrageous milieu. With beckoning hands, she reached up and pulled him closer, suddenly realizing just how much he was aroused.

"Well, I guess you don't need any starch, do you?" she couldn't help teasing.

He grinned back. "No indeed," he acknowledged, before recapturing her mouth in a kiss that made it clear that he intended to take up where they had left off the night before.

Her hands slipped under the edge of his warm-up jacket to discover that he was wearing nothing underneath. Curious, then, she slid her fingers down to the elastic band at his waist—to find that he was similarly unattired beneath his knit pants.

"If you're looking for my underwear, you're looking in the wrong place," Morgan chuckled. "They're somewhere on the bed with the rest of this stuff. Luckily I keep this outfit in my car so I can stop at the gym sometimes on the way home from work," he continued.

"Otherwise you might have discovered me in your laundry room wearing one of your towels."

"You wouldn't!" Kate squeaked.

"Don't be too sure," Morgan returned. But before she could continue the discussion, he was discovering her own little secret. She didn't have anything on under her caftan, either.

"How convenient," he whispered, one hand sliding up her leg while the other tugged industriously at her zipper. But the passion smoldering in his eyes told her his mood was no longer playful.

As his hand found her breast, Kate arched to his touch, suddenly eager to find again those dizzying heights that she had discovered last night.

However, at that moment a loud slam penetrated her consciousness. And then she heard her son's voice. "Mom, where are you? I'm home," Tony called.

Kate and Morgan instantly sprang apart. By the time Tony had pounded up the stairs and into the bedroom, they had managed to be standing at the side of the bed, holding a wrinkled sheet between them.

"Morgan's helping me fold clothes," Kate sputtered.

Fortunately, her son seemed to see nothing amiss. "Hi," he told her assistant sheet folder. "I'm glad Mom's got someone else roped into doing laundry."

Kate saw Morgan's complexion deepen. "Well, your mom was just about to show me the right way to do it."

Kate had to bite her lip and look away to keep Tony from realizing that there was more to this conversation than might be apparent on the surface. "How was the party?" she asked, trying to change the subject.

"It was really neat!" her son enthused. "Mike Hastings has videodisks of all the *Star Wars* movies, and we stayed up all night watching them.

"*All night?*" Kate echoed. "I'm surprised you're not asleep on your feet."

Her son yawned. "Actually, I may lie down for a little while. See you later."

When he had left the room, Morgan and Kate exchanged glances. "He's probably going right to sleep, but let's go downstairs where we can talk," she suggested. "And have some breakfast," she added. "I don't know about you, but I missed dinner last night."

Morgan grinned. "Strange as it may seem for me, I'd forgotten all about food. But you're right. I'm starving."

In the kitchen, after she had filled and plugged in the coffee pot, she turned to him. "I don't know how you felt when Tony walked in, but I wanted to sink through the floor."

Morgan nodded. "Me, too. That's why I think we ought to get married."

# Chapter Eight

$\mathcal{K}$ate almost dropped the saucer she had been about to set on the counter. "What did you say?"

"I said, I think we ought to get married."

"Why?" Kate blurted, before sinking down into the chair opposite the man who had just sprung this surprise proposal. Suddenly she didn't feel as though her knees would hold her up.

Morgan reached across the table and took her hand. "I'm serious, Kate," he insisted. "I feel just as uncomfortable about the realities of two single parents conducting an affair in front of their children as you do."

Kate sighed. "But marriage, Morgan, that's a big commitment. We've only known each other a few weeks. What makes you think it would work?"

Morgan squeezed her hand and forced her to meet his eyes. "After last night, how can you argue that we don't know each other, Kate?" he persisted.

She wanted to look away, but the power of his gaze

held her captive. Last night had been very special. She had responded to Morgan's exciting yet tender love-making as she never had to Bart. But was one memorable night enough on which to base a marriage? On the face of it, that sounded foolhardy. How much did she really know about Morgan? Certainly not enough to chance another disaster like her first marriage. And yet, when she thought about simply sending Morgan away, something inside her chest tightened painfully.

The man seated at the table could see the emotions and doubts chasing each other across her face. "Don't shut me out, Kate. Tell me what you're thinking," he urged.

She chose her words carefully. "Morgan, last night was wonderful for me, too. But . . ."

He arched his brows expectantly.

"But," she continued, "I just can't make such an important decision on the basis of sexual compatibility. And then there's something else you haven't mentioned—love. That's what most marriages are based on, you know."

Morgan brought his hands together, trapping hers in the warmth of his grasp. "Kate, we've both learned the hard way that love is just an illusion. We both thought we were marrying for love the first time around. And look where it got us."

She dropped her gaze, looking down at her small hand trapped between his two large ones. What he said was true. She couldn't deny that. But unlike Morgan's, her first experience hadn't destroyed her belief in the existence of love between a man and a woman. It had simply made her more cautious in giving her heart before she knew her love was returned.

"We have something more enduring than love," Morgan was saying. "Our relationship is based on honesty and trust. I think we can build together on that. Besides, you're good in the laundry," he added with a chuckle.

"Morgan," Kate began hesitantly, "I'd be lying if I didn't acknowledge that there was something special about our relationship from the beginning."

His face lit up at that admission. "I thought so, too," he whispered huskily.

"But I need more time. I've fought hard to be self-sufficient. And it's scary to think about giving up what I know works for me. And then there are the kids. How is this going to affect them? Can the four of us really function as a family?"

"I think our marriage would work for our kids as well as for us, Kate," Morgan argued. "Tony and I already get along together, and Julie needs a mother at this critical stage in her development. But if you're not sure it would work, let's hear your alternative."

"Couldn't we keep dating?" Kate asked.

"Yes, of course we could," Morgan agreed. "But I think that might prove awfully frustrating."

It was Kate's turn to lift a questioning eyebrow.

"I didn't like the way Tony walked in on us this morning any more than you did," Morgan pointed out. "It's more than that, though. I feel as though I'm setting up some sort of double standard with my daughter if I sleep with you and at the same time expect her to refrain from hopping into bed with her boyfriends."

Kate nodded. "I see what you mean," she acknowledged pensively. "So where does that leave us?"

Morgan thought for a while. "How does this sound? Let's try getting together as a foursome and see how that works out. If we pass that hurdle, then you and I can give our personal relationship a week's trial by taking a vacation together."

"How much time are you giving me altogether?" Kate wanted to know.

"I'd like to say three minutes," Morgan quipped, "but how does a month sound? Thanksgiving would be a good time for the two of us to get away."

Kate felt a little as though she were being railroaded into a course of action that could only lead to one decision. But to be truthful, she *was* willing to go along. "All right," she told him, her eyes meeting his.

She could see how relieved he was at her answer. And yet he strove to keep the moment light. "Well, now that's out of the way, how about that breakfast you promised me."

"Are you the bacon-and-eggs type?" Kate asked, more than willing to go along with the change of subject.

"This morning I think I might be the apple-pie type. I did smell one baking last night, didn't I?"

"You mean, in the middle of your fit you actually noticed?" Kate couldn't keep the note of incredulity out of her tone.

"Oh, yes, I'm very perceptive where food is concerned. That apple pie is one of the things—not the major thing, but *one* of the things—that brought me back here."

"Morgan!" Kate admonished. But she was already opening the refrigerator to get out the pie. "Do you want it with ice cream?"

"Of course. How could I turn something like that down?"

It was an unusual breakfast, but Kate enjoyed it too—as much for the company as for the food. It had been a long time since she'd sat across the breakfast table with anyone but Tony. And she had to admit that she liked it.

As he finished the last bite of his second piece of pie,

Morgan caught her staring at him. "Beautiful," he said slowly. "And she can cook, too." The look in his eyes was as warm as melted butter.

For a moment Kate couldn't help basking in his praise. It was nice to be appreciated—especially by Morgan Chandler. But then the practical side of her nature took over. *Don't get carried away over a simple compliment,* she warned herself, pushing back her chair. "I'd better get the dishes cleared away," she said aloud.

As she stood at the sink rinsing off the plates, she heard Morgan's chair slide back. Without even turning around, she knew by the way the hairs on the back of her neck prickled that he was heading in her direction. But she wasn't prepared for the way he molded his body against the back of hers, trapping her between himself and the counter. At the same time, his arms came up to circle her waist.

"You sure feel good." As he spoke, Morgan took a playful nibble at her ear. "Maybe I'll have you for dessert."

"You can't do that," Kate pointed out, trying to maintain some sense of control. "You've already had your dessert for breakfast."

Morgan ignored her attempts at discouragement and began to rotate his hips provocatively against her buttocks. And Kate was left without any doubt about his arousal.

"Morgan," she tried again. "You're the one who said we shouldn't set a double standard for the kids."

"I know," he groaned. "But a month is an awfully long time. Let's start tomorrow."

With that he turned her toward him, and Kate found herself clasping her arms around his shoulders, soap-suds and all. The sensual movements of his body against hers felt so good that she had no will to stop him when his lips sought and found hers. He tasted deliciously of warm apples and cinnamon. At first it was the kind of kiss that was so comfortable that it could have gone on forever. But then the tempo changed.

"Kate," Morgan whispered, his lips against hers. "Go upstairs and see if Tony is asleep."

"But . . ."

"Do it," he urged, sliding his hands down to pull her hips more firmly against his. The knit material of his jogging suit and the thin fabric of her robe were scant barriers to their intimate contact. Kate could feel every taut muscle in his lower body pleading his case.

"All right," she agreed. But when he released her, she had to grab the counter to keep her knees from buckling. "You haven't exactly made it easy for me to climb the stairs," she accused.

He only chuckled. "It's going to be worth the effort."

Tony was sleeping soundly, Kate discovered a few minutes later. And when she returned to the stairs, she could see Morgan waiting for her at the bottom. The expectant look on his face sent tingles of anticipation through her body. "You don't have to tell me we have the all clear," Morgan mouthed as she approached, the tension in her body growing stronger the closer she came.

At the second-to-the-bottom step, he reached for her, pulling her against him so that her shoulders were level with his face. With a sigh of pleasure, he nestled his head against the softness of her breast. The contact, although light, did funny things to her equilibrium. And when Morgan turned his head and found one straining nipple with his mouth through the fabric of her robe, she felt as though an arrow of erotic heat were traveling downward through her body. As it found its mark, she gasped.

Morgan lifted his head. "I think it's time to withdraw behind locked doors."

The suggestion made Kate look around in perplexity. Her first-floor living area was notable for its open floor plan. The only door that locked was to the tiny powder room off the foyer. She didn't think two people could fit inside, much less do what Morgan had in mind. Despite her arousal, the thought brought a smile to her face.

"I can see you doubt that I'm prepared to follow through with that suggestion," Morgan observed dryly.

Kate nodded imperceptibly.

"Don't you remember that first time I took you to my townhouse that I told you I was a boy scout? I wouldn't have made the suggestion if I wasn't prepared."

Taking Kate's hand, Morgan began to lead her toward the kitchen. But the look of doubt in her hazel eyes testified that she really wasn't convinced. However, when he put his hand on the basement door, she was forced to reevaluate her assessment.

"Didn't know your basement door locked from the inside, did you?" he questioned smugly. "Frankly, I think the fools who built this place put the lock on backward. But right now, I won't argue with the arrangement."

Ushering Kate inside, Morgan secured the door. And then, unexpectedly, he pulled her backward against the length of his hard body, holding her captive against himself with one arm pressing firmly against her breasts and another splayed across her hips. "Now that I have you in my power, my lady, I'm going to have my wicked way with you," he rasped, his hot breath feathering her ear.

Although deep down, Kate knew his sudden show of aggression was an act, it nevertheless sent a shiver of excitement down her spine. The slight mustiness of the basement helped her imagine she was being led down into the dungeons of a medieval castle. And the thought of being Morgan's captive under those circumstances was somehow intoxicating. As he began to maneuver her slowly down the stairs, her body jostled against his, increasing the height of her arousal. But it was more than the contact; it was this little game he had initiated as well.

Throwing her head back, she swiveled slightly so that her gaze could meet his. At once his progress down the stairs stopped.

"Please, my lord, I beg of you; do not do this thing against my will," she began, letting go of her twentieth-century persona as she got into the role of captured damsel. "My father is a great lord in the west, and he will pay a handsome price if I am returned to him unharmed."

"I care not for your father's wealth," Morgan returned, forcing her to the bottom of the stairs. The counterfeit hauteur in his voice matched the tone of her performance perfectly. "And what is more, I have no intention of taking you against your will." As if to illustrate his point, he began to move his hands over the curves of her body.

"My lord!" Kate exclaimed. If her words had started playfully, they quickly ended on a note of passion as Morgan's teasing touch became more and more intimate. Kate found herself leaning back against him for support as one roving hand slid higher and higher up her leg to find the womanly juncture where her thighs met.

"Oh God, Morgan," she moaned, forgetting everything except the rising urgency of the need he was creating.

Although Morgan had planned on ending their tryst at the couch, the two of them never made it any farther than the thick shag rug that covered the recreation room floor. She had originally installed the rug to try to warm the room, where the temperature always seemed to hover around sixty degrees. But this morning, neither she nor Morgan felt the least bit chilled. The heat of their passion was too great.

Somehow their clothes landed in a tangled heap on the carpet, while they ended up similarly entwined only a few feet away. There was no teasing banter now. The desire that had built between them all morning mandated its inevitable release. They sought and found, gave and partook in a heated exchange that swept away every thought except of each other and this unique moment together. Last night had been tender. This morning was frenzied, as though having tasted each other once, they were caught up in an insatiable addiction for more.

Somewhere in the back of her mind, Kate marveled at the speed of her response. It was as though Morgan were reaching out to her on the most elemental level— his masculinity demanding an answer from her femininity that it was impossible to deny. The intensity built and built to a dizzying summit. And at the shattering climax of their ecstasy, Kate felt as though only the hard reality of Morgan's body kept her spirit from being flung off to the far reaches of the universe.

It was a moment before Kate realized how tightly she was holding his shoulders, but as the aftershocks of pleasure subsided, she gradually loosened her grip.

One look at the dreamy expression in Morgan's golden eyes told her that he was experiencing the same delightful disorientation as she.

Neither of them spoke. But words were not necessary for each to understand just how much this joining had meant to the other. Kate looked around, beginning to recognize where they were. All at once she was aware of the cold, hard floor beneath the carpet on which they lay. And now that the fires of their passion had been banked, she shivered in the chilly air. Morgan shifted his weight so that he could wrap his arms around her. The contact was warmly comforting and Kate felt reluctant to move.

Morgan, too, seemed to want to prolong this time together. "How about if I keep you locked in my dungeon and visit you morning, noon and night?" he questioned playfully, stroking the smooth skin of her shoulders.

It was tempting to keep up the fantasy they had begun on the stairs. Yet she knew that they both had to return to reality. "I'd like that. But we both know it's impossible." To soften the words, she nuzzled her face against the wiry hairs of his chest. "Besides," she teased, "you told me this was going to have to last us for the next month."

Morgan sighed. "Are you trying to bring me back to the real world?"

"I wish I didn't have to," Kate admitted.

"Listen," he began hopefully. "I have a proposition that will let us have our cake and eat it too. Why don't we get married tomorrow? That way we don't have to try and be saints."

Kate couldn't help giving his suggestion serious consideration. Up until she'd met Morgan, doing without a man hadn't really been a sacrifice. But his lovemaking had awakened the long-dormant needs of her body. And there was more to it than that. They seemed to communicate on so many different levels. If there was any man with whom she wanted to share the rest of her life, it was Morgan Chandler.

And yet, there were still so many unanswered questions—questions that might well be resolved over the next month. Giving in to Morgan's proposition *was* tempting. But somehow she knew she had to be the one to be strong on this point. Marriage and the commitment it represented should not be taken lightly. If eleven long years of marriage to Bart had taught her anything, it was that. She owed it to herself and Tony to be sure before she said yes. And Morgan deserved that kind of consideration as well.

Kate opened her mouth to speak, but the man who held her in his arms shook his head. "You don't have to say anything. I can read the resolution in your eyes. You're going to put us both through a month of agony, aren't you?"

"What's a month, when you consider the rest of our lives together?" she philosophized, trying to sound as positive as possible. "And, if we keep busy, we probably won't notice," Kate added, knowing as she spoke that a full schedule during the day wasn't going to make the nights alone in her bed any easier.

"I'll just have to keep thinking about feasting on you for Thanksgiving," Morgan promised, getting up and helping Kate to her feet.

"That's an appetizing thought," she agreed, slipping on the robe that Morgan held for her. "But then, Thanksgiving was always one of my favorite holidays."

# Chapter Nine

$\mathcal{M}$organ suggested that they put the new plan into operation that very evening—with a cooperative dinner at his house. But though she outwardly shared his enthusiasm, Kate couldn't help wondering how she'd be received by Julie. The last time she had been at Morgan's, Julie had caught them together on the couch. And although Kate tried to tell herself she had nothing to be ashamed of, she couldn't help feeling almost as though she were returning to the scene of a crime.

But the open confrontation she secretly feared never materialized. When she and Tony arrived with the au gratin potato casserole and chocolate cake, which were to be their contribution to the meal, Julie was politely cordial—if a bit guarded.

Kate wasn't sure, when Morgan's daughter volunteered to let Tony have his pick of her discarded collection of comic books, whether she was trying to be friendly or get him out of her hair. But she was nevertheless grateful that Julie didn't simply disappear into her room.

"What did you tell her about our experiment?" Kate asked Morgan as she prepared a salad in the kitchen while he spread tangy barbecue sauce on the spare ribs he was readying for the grill.

He shrugged. "I didn't make a big deal out of it. However, I think she can read between the lines."

Kate nodded. Julie undoubtedly had a good idea what was in the wind.

"But so far—" Morgan stopped and rapped his knuckles against the wooden cabinet above his head— "things seem to be going okay."

Kate reached for a tomato and began to cut it into sections. She certainly hoped Morgan's optimism was warranted and not simply a product of his own wishful thinking. He wanted very much for things to work out, and so he had to believe that Julie would not be a problem.

"What did you say to Tony?" Morgan questioned.

"I tried not to make a big deal out of this with him either," Kate related. "But he was so excited about coming over to your house that he spewed out a dozen suggestions for group activities."

"I'll bet all twelve of them involved sporting events," Morgan chuckled.

"You're wrong. Only eleven. He also wants to go to the Air and Space Museum down in Washington."

"Well, I don't mind a bit. It's you and Julie who are going to have to come up with some alternatives if you don't want to spend the whole month down at the Civic Center rooting for the Baltimore home team."

At dinner, Morgan brought up the topic. "Well, ladies, I have two votes for the game next Saturday night at the Civic Center. But I'm open for other suggestions for that or the next weekend."

Julie looked surprised. "I thought you told me we had to get the kitchen walls painted before the men hung the cabinets and laid the floor at the townhouse."

Morgan snapped his fingers. "You're right! I'd forgotten all about that." And then he looked at Kate and Tony. "We could always use some help. Want to have a painting party?"

"That sounds neat," Tony agreed. "Can I wear coveralls and one of those white caps?"

"I can get you a white cap at the paint store," Morgan told him. "But I don't think your mother wants to buy a special outfit just for painting."

Tony looked thoughtful.

"But we can go out for dinner after we're done," Morgan added, sweetening the pot.

"Yeah," Tony agreed. "But I was going to say yes anyway."

Kate smiled at her son and then looked at Julie. "Are you sure you don't mind our horning in on your afternoon with your dad?"

The girl hesitated. "I don't care one way or the other," she finally mumbled.

"Okay. Then why don't we meet here and all go in one car?" Morgan suggested.

Kate nodded. Although she wasn't really sure that Julie wanted her and Tony along, it seemed as though the decision had already been made.

After dinner, Morgan asked the youngsters to help. "If you clear the table, we'll do everything else," he offered. "And then we can play a game of cards if you like."

"I have homework to do," Julie demurred. "But I'll help Tony with the table first."

When they were alone in the kitchen, Kate began rinsing dishes and handing them to Morgan, who stuck them haphazardly into the dishwasher. The disorganization of his technique made her shake her head. "You'll never get everything to fit in there unless you have a system," she informed him. "Let me switch jobs with you."

As she wiped her wet hands on a terry towel, Morgan came up to stand behind her as he had that morning in her kitchen. Before she could slip out of the way, he had wrapped his arms around her waist so that they pushed upward against the undersides of her breasts.

"What's wrong with my technique?" he whispered huskily in her ear.

For a moment, Kate leaned back against him, remembering the passion they had shared earlier in the day and enjoying again the feel of his taut muscles against her hips. "I'm beginning to think that housework turns you on," she teased.

In response, he playfully nuzzled the back of her neck. "Actually, I hadn't thought about it before. But I've noticed recently that, under the right conditions, doing the laundry and dishes can be very erotic."

Kate silently agreed. Right now she wanted nothing more than to give in to the delicious sensations Morgan was arousing. But she knew the dangers all too well. "If this is your secret plan for getting through the month, I don't think it's going to work," she observed dryly.

"You never let me have any fun," Morgan complained. But instead of pressing the issue, he drew back.

Kate turned and looked up into his face. "We both knew this wasn't going to be easy."

"You can say that again."

"We both knew this wasn't going to be easy," she repeated.

Morgan gave her a pained look. "There you go again, taking everything literally."

"Somebody has to," Kate reminded him, turning

away and forcing herself to think about the randomly loaded dishwasher rather than the disturbingly attractive man at her back.

To her surprise, she was rewarded by a playful pat on the rump. "You're right, of course," he conceded. "We'd better finish up in here and move on to something safer—like a quiet game of crazy eights."

Kate had to admit that the evening had gone surprisingly well. The next afternoon when Morgan called to get her reaction, she allowed herself to be guardedly optimistic.

"Good, then let's try it again at your house Wednesday," he suggested. "That way you don't have to drive all the way over here after a day at the office."

"Are you inviting yourself to dinner?" Kate asked.

"What does it sound like? And on second thought, let's make it Wednesday *and* Friday."

Kate found herself agreeing. After all, it was she who had wanted to put their "family relationship" to the test.

Again, everything seemed to go well. In fact, Kate hadn't realized how comfortable Tony was getting with the arrangement until the second dinner when he surprised her by blurting in the middle of dessert, "Hey, are you guys planning to get married or something?"

Kate almost choked on a forkful of carrot cake. But Morgan seemed unperturbed. "If I do a good enough job with the laundry and the dishes, your mother is considering it."

The boy's eyes lit up. But before Julie looked quickly down at her plate, Kate spotted a look of dismay on the teenager's face.

"There's more to it than that," Kate hastened to add. "If we decide anything definite, you two will be the first to know. How would you feel about it if we did get married?" she asked, turning to Julie.

"I'm surprised you asked me. I thought that's what you were going to do anyway," Morgan's daughter returned, managing to avoid a direct answer.

Kate's brows knitted. The girl hadn't been openly hostile, but Julie's evasive reply hadn't given Kate any insight into what she was feeling.

"But we do care about what you think," Morgan told his daughter. "That's why we're getting together, so we can all try out the idea of being a family."

"Well, I think it's a great idea," Tony enthused, shifting attention to himself before Kate could pursue the topic with Julie.

Kate was still wondering how to find out what Morgan's daughter was really thinking that Saturday when, dressed in worn denims and sweat shirts, they all piled into Morgan's car for the trip down to his Federal Hill townhouse.

"Gee, if you all make this arrangement permanent, you're going to have to give up your sports car, Dad," the girl observed from the back seat where she and Tony were scrunched together.

"Maybe we can get a sedan, and I'll keep this one as a reminder of my bachelor days," he quipped.

"Or you can turn it over to me when I get my license," Julie suggested hopefully.

Morgan groaned. "That prospect is enough to make my hair turn gray."

"Well then, just what would I get out of your marrying Kate?" Julie blurted.

"The mother who would understand your point of view," Morgan shot back.

Kate thought she heard a snort from the back seat. But she wasn't sure.

By the time the foursome reached the townhouse, the conversation had turned to less controversial subjects—like who was going to get to paint the ceiling. Tony had his heart set on using a roller attached to a stick, but Morgan was doubtful.

"The ceilings in these old houses are higher than you think," he pointed out. "But I'm sure you'll have just as much fun taping the trim so your mom and I don't get paint on it. That's one of the most important jobs."

"Yeah," Tony agreed. "In fact, Mom never even let me in the room when she was painting before. You must trust me, huh?" There was a note of pride in his voice that Kate hadn't heard in a long time.

As the car pulled up to the curb, Kate looked around. There were pickup trucks and vans all up and down the street. Men, women and children were busy unloading everything from ladders and walnut paneling to the proverbial kitchen sink. And there was quite a spirit of camaraderie about the whole enterprise, Kate noted. Before Morgan's feet had hit the curb, he had already acknowledged several friendly greetings.

"Where'd you get your new helpers?" inquired a tall blond-haired man who was just emerging from the townhouse next door carrying a bundle of scrap insulation.

"I found a crew that would work cheap, Chris. All I have to do is feed them dinner this evening."

"Send them over when you're finished. Their price is right."

"Only for me," Morgan cautioned with a wink. "I get special consideration."

"You'll get your special consideration later," Kate threatened sweetly without thinking about the implications of the words. The speculative look Chris shot in her direction made her want to hurry inside, but by the time Morgan had unlocked the door, his neighbor had already gone back to his own project.

In the living room, Kate looked around with interest. Although the floor was still cluttered, she could tell that a lot of progress had been made. Dry wall had been installed, and the antique oak staircase had been restored to its former beauty—complete with carved banister and newel post.

"When did you get the time to do all this?" she asked.

"As you've noticed, I've been devoting a lot of my evenings to continuing education—and assistant deans thereof," Morgan observed. "Luckily, most of what you see is the handiwork of my subcontractors."

Before Kate could think of a suitable reply, Tony staggered through the front door wearing the white cap Morgan had promised him and lugging two gallons of paint.

"Easy," Morgan cautioned. "Those are heavy."

"I can do it," the boy grunted, setting them down with a loud thunk that made Kate glad the subfloor in the entrance was not yet covered with anything important.

"I'll help you with the rest of the paint," Morgan offered. "Where's Julie?" he added.

"She stopped to talk to some guy outside. I didn't know she could be that friendly."

Morgan shook his head knowingly. "Julie can be very charming—when the mood suits her. I think I'd better round her up—if we want to get any work out of her this afternoon."

He was about to head out the door when he turned back to Kate. "Why don't you show Tony around? You can explore the top floor now that the stairs have been finished."

Kate took the opportunity to admire Morgan's architectural abilities. Even in this roughed-in state, the master bedroom suite was fabulous. The oversized room not only had broad window seats and a spacious dressing alcove, but two walk-in closets and a fireplace. And then there was the marble master bath, the side of which opened onto a redwood deck which was the upper story of the greenhouse.

"Hey, neat," Tony said with enthusiasm.

But it was the sunken marble tub that caught Kate's eye. Obviously meant to accommodate two, it was enough to set her thoughts along lines that she had trouble controlling as she fought to banish a mental image of Morgan and herself scrubbing each other's backs. Hastily she stepped out of the room and almost bumped into Tony, who was on his way to discover what other wonders Morgan had designed.

As it turned out, there was plenty of time to look around. Julie was reluctant to leave her new acquaintance, until Morgan invited the boy to share their dinner—with the understanding that his daughter would put in several hours' work first.

Kate watched with interest as Morgan organized the work party. His take-charge attitude reminded her of the way he'd behaved in the seminar where they'd first met. Since then she'd learned that he was willing to let others lead in some areas. But when something was really important, he just couldn't stand idly by and let someone else mess things up.

Of course, this townhouse was his baby, and he wasn't going to settle for a half-baked job. He soon had Julie and Tony putting masking tape on the trim and along the edge of the natural brick wall, while Kate went to work on the plasterboard walls with a roller. As promised, he tackled the high ceiling himself.

Kate found that working this way in a group was more fun than she had imagined. Morgan offered constant encouragement, praising both the kids and herself. And when the work flagged, he was always there with a joke or a teasing remark.

After Kate had painted for a while, Morgan let Tony take over briefly, and the boy's pride in "doing just as good a job as your mother" was obvious.

It took only a few hours to finish with the kitchen, and Kate was impressed that the novice crew had really done a first-class job.

Morgan glanced at his watch. "We have some time before dinner. You kids go out in the back yard and use the hose to get the paint off your hands and arms." Then he turned to Tony. "After you get cleaned up, do you want Julie to show you around the neighborhood while your mom and I get things put away in here?"

The boy nodded eagerly, and Julie was already heading toward the door. Maybe she wanted a chance to round up her new friend, Kate speculated.

When they were alone, Morgan turned to her and grinned. "You're a pretty neat painter. But you seem to have added some white freckles to the collection on your nose." Reaching up, he ran his thumb along the bridge of her nose and down one side.

At his touch, Kate closed her eyes. She hadn't realized how much she would miss such simple pleasures.

"You've got paint here, and here and here," Morgan whispered huskily, continuing his exploration of her face and neck. Kate found herself leaning forward slightly against the hand.

"And then there's your sweat shirt," he continued, his fingers walking down from her shoulder to lightly touch a splotch of paint that happened to cover one swelling breast. It was impossible for Kate to hide her reaction. She knew that Morgan could feel her nipple harden even through the cotton fleece of the heavy fabric.

"Are you sure you don't want to elope this evening?" he groaned, pulling her into his arms, paint-splotched clothing and all.

For a long moment, they simply stood together, thigh against thigh, chest against chest. It was impossible for Kate not to press her breasts more closely against Morgan's hard frame or lean more intimately into the cradle of his hips. Morgan's hands had begun to move restlessly on her back, pulling her even closer as he began a sensual caress. She heard a sigh of pleasure escape his lips. And then, all too quickly, he was forcing himself to pull back. "I think this way lies madness," he muttered. "Although I am willing to risk it."

"Are you willing to risk embarrassment, too?" Kate questioned. "What if the kids come bursting back in?"

"They'll just see us exchanging some healthy affection," Morgan assured. "Or maybe we could take a chance and go upstairs. The walls are in place, you know."

"But there aren't any doors yet, are there?"

Morgan snapped his fingers. "Darn. I thought I might be able to get you so caught up in the heat of passion that you'd say to hell with the doors."

"Listen, wasn't it your idea that we abstain from sex for a month?" Kate inquired, unable to keep the note of irony out of her voice.

"I never claimed that all my ideas were good. Let's drop the kids off at a movie and go to a motel."

Kate started laughing. "You're incorrigible. But we'd better show some progress on cleaning up, or the younger generation may ask us what we've been doing."

"Right as always," Morgan sighed, looking around at the brushes, rollers and paint trays that needed washing. "Let's take these out in the back yard and get started. Lucky the patio has been laid, or we'd be awash in a sea of mud before we finished getting these rinsed."

Half an hour later, everything was as clean as it could be under the circumstances. Kate was just about to ask Morgan where to look for the kids when they came bursting through the back gate with Julie's new friend in tow.

As the trio came forward, Kate noticed Tony's and Julie's speckled clothing, and suddenly she realized how she must look as well. "Morgan, what restaurant is going to let us in like this?" she challenged.

"Not to worry. The local hangout will be perfect. And it's just two blocks away, so we can walk."

Kate looked doubtful. But Julie giggled. Apparently they had been in this predicament before.

Happy to be in on the gag, Julie and her friend led the way down the block of partially restored townhouses. Morgan, Kate and Tony brought up the rear.

Around the corner, Kate stopped for a moment to look with interest at the progress that had been made. These houses were beautifully painted and restored on the outside. Many sported flower boxes that still held golden and purple chrysanthemums. Behind the windows Kate could see curtains and furniture.

"These houses went up for sale last year," Morgan told her. "Next year, our street should look the same way."

Kate smiled, noting his use of the word "our."

"The neighborhood may be new, but it already has a

number of traditions," he added. "That building used to house a tavern. But by popular demand, it's been turned into the local eatery and hangout called Spanky's."

As they stepped inside the door, Kate understood why Morgan and Julie had been unconcerned about appearances. The place was so dark that the waitress had to lead newcomers, whose eyes had not yet adjusted, to their tables with a flashlight.

"This must be a pizza place," she told Morgan, as they took their seats.

"How can you tell without looking at the menu?"

"Well, your fondness for pizza might be a clue. But actually, it's the telltale aroma of oregano and melted cheese."

"Can you smell the green peppers, anchovies, onions, and pepperoni, too?" Morgan challenged. Although she couldn't see it, she could hear the grin in his voice. "Oh boy, can we get all of that on our pizza?" Tony chimed in.

"Well . . ." Kate hedged.

The question led to a lively discussion on the merits of the various toppings. Although Kate put up a strong resistance, she was outvoted by the younger set—and Morgan. The group finally ordered two supersized pizzas with "the works."

After the waitress took their order, she handed out tokens for the video games in the other room. There was a clatter of chairs, and Kate and Morgan found themselves suddenly abandoned.

"Well, here we are alone at last," Morgan quipped from across the table. "And it's almost dark enough in here to take advantage of the situation." As he spoke, he pushed back his own chair and came around the table to sit next to Kate.

"Do you remember the first time we had pizza together?" he whispered.

"Umhum. In fact, I was just thinking about it."

"Were you wishing we were squeezed into a booth like that again?" Morgan asked.

Kate gave him a sideways look. "At the time, that was pure torture, you know."

"And now?" he persisted, his hand dropping to her thigh as it had that first time. Only now he made no move to take it away.

Kate leaned over and put her head on his shoulder. "You know how I feel," she whispered.

While they waited for the pizza to arrive, they sat close together, enjoying the chance to be alone—even in the middle of a noisy crowd.

Even though she was hungry, the reappearance of the waitress with their food and a pitcher of soda was a disappointment. "I'll go get the kids," Morgan volunteered, forcing himself to break the warm, comfortable contact.

When Morgan came back and took a good look at the monstrosity they had ordered, he lifted his eyes upward. "I hope I'm not going to regret this in the morning—if not before," he leaned over and confided to Kate.

She gave him an affectionate look. "You always say that," she reminded him. "But you always go right ahead and eat hearty."

"So you're getting to know my weaknesses and you still haven't broken things off," he observed. "Well, that's a good sign."

"Only if you agree to take my anchovies," Kate shot back.

Morgan passed his plate in her direction.

Despite her reservations, Kate enjoyed both the

meal and the company. Julie's friend, whose name was Keith, seemed nice enough. And he seemed to have a good effect on Morgan's daughter. The girl was relaxed and happy—and, as her father had said, charming. Kate began to get a sense of how she'd be without the usual chip on her shoulder.

Morgan must have been on the same wavelength. The next day, when he called Kate to lament the fact that they weren't sharing breakfast, he made a similar observation.

"Nothing like a new boyfriend to make her less possessive of Dad," he commented.

"Sounds like a good strategy to me," Kate agreed.

"Speaking of strategies, have you made any arrangements for Tony's Thanksgiving vacation?"

"As a matter of fact, I have the feeling he's going to get a plane ticket in the mail from my folks next week."

"Do you have ESP or something?"

"No. But my parents have MCI. When they called last night, I dropped a broad hint. They're delighted at the prospect of getting Tony all to themselves for a week. In fact, they had me wondering why I haven't sent Tony out for a visit sooner."

Kate heard Morgan's deep chuckle. "Funny thing about last night. After yesterday's clean-up session, I was inspired to call my mother, too."

"As I remember, it wasn't the type of thing you'd be talking to your mom about," Kate teased.

"Oh, you'd be surprised. Actually, I didn't give her any of the details, but I whetted her curiosity enough so that she insisted I bring you along to Harrisburg when I drop Julie off on the twentieth."

"Good grief! What did you tell her?" Kate exclaimed.

"You'll just have to ask her when you get there.

Actually, things are going to work out perfectly," he continued. "One of my partners has a luxury cabin near Kettle Creek that he's willing to lend us for the week. It's only a couple of hours from Harrisburg.

"And what exactly did you tell *him*?" Kate asked.

"Enough, but not too much."

"Did you ask him what activities they have at Kettle Creek?"

Morgan chuckled.

"All right, that's enough. I was trying to find out what clothes to bring."

"If it were up to me, you wouldn't need anything but that famous nightgown we both like so much. But if you insist on getting out of bed, they do have hiking trails, fishing, and winter sports."

Kate couldn't repress a grin. This conversation was making their vacation plans real at last, and she couldn't hold back the wave of excited anticipation that suddenly swept over her.

However, as the end of the month grew closer, she found her anticipation tempered with anxiety. Things did seem to be working out well with their families—almost too well. So one hurdle had been overcome. And now she was closer than ever to giving Morgan the answer he wanted to hear.

And yet there was such a riot of emotions inside her that she sometimes wished that he weren't forcing the issue. It was hard to think clearly when they were together. The month of abstinence had built her physical need for him to a fevered pitch. And it didn't help that he was so obviously feeling the same needs. It was harder and harder for Kate to remember all the reasons why she had insisted that they not rush into marriage.

She had told Morgan that this vacation together would be another test of their relationship. And yet, deep down she knew that if she lived with him for a week, she would never be able to let him go. She had fallen in love with him, she acknowledged. But he had said that love was just an illusion and what they had was stronger. How could she marry him knowing that she could never admit her real reasons? Or might her love for him be enough to change him? When he really grew to trust her, might he also love her too? That was the thought on which she had to place her hope.

And then there were all her own doubts about casting her lot with another man. The voice of experience still told her to be wary. But now her heart was urging her to take the risk and reach for the happiness she hadn't found before.

All these thoughts were still simmering below the surface of her mind as she forced herself to concentrate on packing Tony's clothes for his week's vacation with his grandparents in New Mexico.

She'd already given her parents the phone number of the cabin where she could be reached if there was an emergency. But she hadn't actually told them that she would be vacationing alone with Morgan.

The only person she'd confided her real plans to was Mary Ellen. And she'd sworn her to secrecy.

"You're crazy if you let a guy like Morgan get away," her friend had admonished. "Why don't you elope while you're there?"

Kate had given Mary Ellen a shocked look. She couldn't imagine taking such a reckless step. "You know, with my hangups, it's not that simple," she'd insisted. "And besides, Morgan hasn't said he loves me. All he talks about is *trust*."

"Well, he may not have said it, but from the things you've told me he's sure acting like it. I think he does love you and he's afraid to admit it."

Mary Ellen's words were reassuring. That was exactly what Kate was hoping. It would be hard to imagine another man as considerate and as ardent as Morgan. And that put an optimistic spring in her step as she headed for the downstairs storage closet to get out her own suitcases.

# Chapter Ten

When she tried to think about it later, Kate could hardly remember the trip up to Harrisburg to leave Julie at her grandmother's. The anxiety of meeting Morgan's mother, coupled with the anticipation of what was to follow after that, kept her mind swirling. However, she must have made the right responses to Morgan's light conversation—or he was too understanding to call attention to her tenseness—since the trip was outwardly uneventful.

Kate seemed to snap out of her trance when they pulled up in front of the stately colonial-style stone house where Morgan had grown up. She could see immediately where he had gotten his love of old homes. This one, with its twin chimneys, large dormers and proud portico, was a charmer. Set back from the road, it was surrounded by well-tended shrubbery and magnificent spruces and balsam firs.

As Morgan opened the door, Kate caught the crisp sharpness of the air, mingled with the scent of the evergreens. It was amazing, she thought, how much more like winter it seemed only a few hours farther north. Suddenly she was glad she'd worn wool slacks and a heavy Shetland sweater.

"Gee, Julie, this looks like a terrific place to spend the week," she enthused, taking a deep breath of the clean country air.

"Then why don't you stay here and I'll go off with Dad," the girl retorted.

Kate gave the girl a shocked look. But before she could think of something to say, Morgan stepped in.

"That's enough," he threatened. "Your grandmother's been looking forward to your visit for weeks, and I'm sure she's got some exciting plans."

Morgan didn't see the mask that dropped over the girl's face. He was already walking toward the back of the car. Opening the trunk, he began setting his daughter's luggage on the sidewalk. Before he had finished, the forest green front door was flung open by a surprisingly tall, white-haired woman. As she made her way quickly down the walk, Kate noticed her springy step and trim figure under her burgundy wool dress.

"Morgan! Julie!" she called. "I'm so glad to see you. And this must be Kate," she added, turning to include the younger woman in the greeting. Although Kate had been dreading this meeting, she felt instantly at ease. It seemed so natural when Mrs. Chandler gave her a quick hug after doing the same with her son and granddaughter.

Even Julie's mood improved almost immediately. It was impossible to keep up the pretense of being a victim when her grandmother seemed prepared to grant her every wish.

"I've got a wonderful dinner planned for Thanksgiving. But I knew you wouldn't want to spend the whole week cooped up with an old lady like me," she bubbled, "so I've arranged a special treat. How would you like to go to the big Penn State Thanksgiving weekend football game?"

Julie's eyes lit up. "You mean a real college game?"

"Yes. My friend Gloria Conners has the cutest grandson—who's been dying to meet you. He also happens to be a freshman at Penn State, and he's got two tickets for Saturday." The older woman looked back at Morgan. "Of course, that's if your father approves."

Kate could see the hesitation on his face. He was probably remembering his own wild college weekends. Taking his arm, she gave it a squeeze. "It's only a football game," she whispered.

He nodded imperceptibly and then smiled at his mother. "I guess I'm outnumbered. Three against one. But Julie has to promise to be back at a reasonable hour."

The easy interchange set the tone for the rest of the short visit. While Julie unpacked upstairs, Mrs. Chandler—who urged Kate to call her Margaret— served tea and cake in the drawing room.

Kate had felt herself growing tense again as she sat down next to Morgan on the Victorian-style red velvet sofa. But Margaret was as diplomatic with Kate as she had been with Julie. Skillfully she turned the conversation to a number of topics, but she was careful to skirt the issue of Kate and Morgan's little vacation.

However, once the two women had retired to the kitchen to wash up the dishes, the older one turned to Kate with a small confession. "You don't know how nervous I was about meeting you," she confided.

Kate's eyes widened. "*You* were nervous about meeting *me*?"

Margaret chuckled. "It's been years since my son brought someone special up here. And he's told me that the two of you will be getting married soon."

"He did?" Kate questioned. "But I warned him that I wasn't sure yet."

"Well, apparently *he* is. And I must say, I think my son has made a wonderful choice." She smiled as if to herself and then continued. "You know, he hasn't talked about it much, but a mother knows her child. I think you're very special to him, Kate."

The younger woman didn't know quite how to respond. Although she'd admitted to herself that she was in love with Morgan, she felt she couldn't yet share her deepest emotions with his mother—especially when she was afraid to even tell the man himself how much she cared for him. "Did—did he mention my son, Tony?" she finally asked, unaware that the catch in her voice betrayed the strong feelings she had not expressed in words.

"Of course. You don't know how excited he is about having a ready-made ten-year-old son. It sounds like he's gearing up to coach the local soccer team next year."

Kate smiled. "They've gotten along famously right from the start. Tony practically worships Morgan. I can't tell you what a difference it's made for my son." She paused, wondering if Margaret Chandler understood just how hard it was going to be for her to establish the same sort of rapport with Julie. "You know, sometimes I'm afraid I'm not going to be able to reach Julie on that kind of level."

Morgan's mother nodded sympathetically. "It's harder with a teenage girl," she commiserated, "especially one who never really knew her mother. She doesn't know how to behave with you, or just how much she can get out of the relationship."

Kate hadn't really thought of the problem in those terms before. But Margaret Chandler's words made sense.

"I think that if you get to know my granddaughter," the older woman continued, "you'll find it's worth the effort."

Her words were still echoing in Kate's mind as she watched the heartfelt hug Julie gave her father at the door when they finally left, and the way he returned it. Despite the father-daughter differences, they obviously loved each other very much, and they'd had only each other to depend on for a long time. Despite herself, Kate couldn't help feeling a small twinge of envy. She wanted Morgan's love, too.

However, once they were alone in the car together, it was obvious that all his attention was focused on her—as hers was on him. Suddenly she realized she was alone with this man, and would be for the next week. She had expended so much effort recently trying *not* to think about that week alone in a secluded cabin in the woods, that the freedom to let her mind go off on a delicious tangent was exhilarating.

Apparently, Morgan was enjoying that same exhilaration. To Kate's astonishment, instead of heading straight for the highway, he turned the car off onto the first side road, stopped the engine, and pulled her into his arms. Her surprise quickly gave way to eager cooperation.

Before she could speak, his lips were on hers in a heated kiss that expressed perfectly all the pent-up frustrations she had been feeling during the month.

"God, Kate," Morgan finally whispered, his breath warm against her face. "I've been aching to do that for so long."

"Me too," she acknowledged.

"It's been a long four weeks, hasn't it?" he chuckled.

"Umm," Kate sighed, leaning over to snuggle her cheek against the soft wale of his corduroy jacket. The musky tang of his after-shave lotion was decidedly intoxicating. But Morgan wasn't content just to snuggle. His lips and then his teeth sought her earlobes where he began to nibble gently but erotically. At the same time, his hand began to massage purposefully up and down her ribs through her sweater.

"You always feel so damn good," he murmured. "And I'll bet you'll discover I feel just as good. See?" As he spoke, he took her hand and placed it strategically on the soft wool flannel covering his thigh.

Kate hadn't known exactly what to expect. But now that she found her hand so propitiously positioned, she couldn't stop herself from flattening her palm to increase the contact and then beginning to stroke the taut muscles of his inner leg. He was right. It did feel so good to touch him that she wanted to go on and on. And his thigh wasn't all she had in mind. However, in the next second, his groan of pleasure made her realize the consequences of this dangerous little game he had started and she had been so eager to continue.

"Morgan, we've got to stop this," she implored.

"Why? I like it. Don't you?"

"Too much," she sighed. "But that's just the problem. Were you planning to make love to me in the car half a mile from your mother's house?"

"No, but now that you mention it . . ." The look of mixed exasperation and frustration in her hazel eyes made it impossible for him to continue.

His own sigh was a lot more regretful than hers. "I would have to pick a practical woman," he lamented. "But my practical Kate is right as always. It's going to be a lot better if we wait till we get to Kettle Creek. I just have to convince my body to go along with your resolve." As he spoke, he lifted her hand, which was now resting only lightly on his thigh, and pressed her fingertips against his lips.

For a moment, Kate leaned her head against his shoulder. Then she heard the engine spring to life.

Back on the road, Morgan turned to her with an impish grin. "All right, this is going to be a two-hour drive. How do you propose to take my mind off making love to you?"

Kate racked her brain. It was hard to think of anything except the man so tantalizingly close to her. And then an idea struck her. "When you were a kid, did your family play games in the car to make the time pass faster?"

"You mean like making words out of license plate letters or finding the alphabet on road signs?"

"Yes, that sort of thing. But I have one that's really fun. It's called 'I Spy.'"

Morgan quirked an eyebrow. "I'm, ur, game. But why don't you go first, and I'll pick it up as we go."

Kate studied the passing Pennsylvania scenery. They were just drawing near a large barn with a colorful hex sign painted just under the wide gable. Should she tell him she had seen something that began with *h*? she wondered. No, that would be too hard for his first try. But they were seeing barns every mile or so. That should be an easy one to start off with.

"All right, I spy something that begins with a *b*," she announced.

"Is that all the help I'm going to get?" he retorted.

"Yes."

"Okay. Does it have to be outside the car?"

Kate thought for a minute. "I guess not," she answered.

"How about *body*, then?"

"No."

"Breast?"

"No!"

"Bed?"

"Morgan, I don't think you're quite in the spirit of the game. And where would you have seen a bed, anyway?"

"But it's what I'm thinking about," he protested with a cherubic grin.

"Well, try concentrating on things outside the car. I'll give you three more chances."

Morgan was silent for a minute, scanning the wooded roadside along the country highway. "Bush?" he finally guessed.

Kate gave him a sideways glance.

"Why is it you're always so willing to think the worst of me?" he asked. "See, there's a bush right over there." He pointed to a hedgerow in front of a white clapboard house.

Kate shook her head and sighed. Morgan certainly wasn't doing a very good job of trying to take their minds off each other. And his next words confirmed her skepticism.

Pointing toward a distant pair of suggestively rounded hills with a natural cleft down the middle, Morgan grinned. "I won't even tell you what *they* remind me of."

"That's right, you wouldn't dare," Kate agreed. "But somehow, I don't remember this game being quite so erotic when I was a kid."

"You're in the big leagues now, honey," he shot back, giving her a pat on the knee. He might have intended to remove his hand at once, but she noticed that his fingers couldn't stop themselves from investigating the contour of her calf.

Resolutely, Kate placed the wayward hand back on the steering wheel.

"Maybe we should try the radio," she suggested,

flipping on the FM. However, the first station she tuned in was playing a rock and roll song about "spending the night together."

"I hope that's not your idea of music to soothe the savage beast?" Morgan retorted.

Kate quickly turned the knob. Luckily there was a station that had already started cranking out its Christmas music.

Kate began to sing along with Bing Crosby, and Morgan joined in—off-key as usual. Could he tell how bad he sounded? Kate wondered, sneaking him a loving look from under her lashes. Probably not, judging from his obvious enthusiasm.

Somehow his lack of musical ability was endearing, and Kate felt a sudden rush of warmth toward this man. Here in this cozy car, in the middle of the Pennsylvania countryside with the nip of winter in the outside air, everything seemed so right. Morgan must have sensed it too. Reaching over, he gave her hand a quick squeeze before launching into another chorus of "Winter Wonderland."

It seemed only a short time before the rocky pastureland gave way to pine forest. Reaching in the glove compartment, Morgan pulled out a sheet of directions. "Look for Route 120," he instructed. "It should be around here somewhere."

"Are we staying in the state park?" Kate questioned.

"No. Roger's cabin is in a privately developed area. Although I've never seen it, he's assured me it has a few luxuries you won't find in the park. And there's a lodge nearby which is known statewide for its country-style Thanksgiving feast. I've made reservations."

"That sounds wonderful. I see you've thought of everything," Kate acknowledged appreciatively.

After they found Route 120, the private road to the cabin was only a few miles up the road. Morgan turned off onto a winding gravel road that led upward into the thick pine forest and passed widely spaced vacation homes that were barely visible from their individual driveways.

"How do you know which one it is?" Kate asked.

"We're supposed to look for a sign that says "Roger's Stronghold.""

"You're kidding."

"Nope. Roger's a real individualist—even if he does design condominiums."

Kate could tell what Morgan meant when they pulled up in front of the "cabin." Instead of the usual rustic wood, it was a stone chalet with a wide front porch and a balcony overlooking the picturesque mountainside.

"Let's leave the luggage in the car and have a quick look around," Morgan suggested when they had parked near the entrance.

The sun was low in the west and the temperature had dropped as they had ascended into the mountains. Kate found herself shivering while she waited for Morgan to unlock the dead bolt that protected the front door. Suddenly, she realized that it wasn't just the temperature. Now that they were finally there, it was impossible to deny all the excitement, anticipation and nervousness that she had repressed during the drive.

Morgan saw the slight tremor and pulled her close. "It should be warmer inside," he promised. But the spacious living room with its thick shag rug and freestanding fireplace was almost as chilly.

"I should have realized that the furnace would be off," Morgan mused. "Let me switch it on and start a fire. Want to have a look around while I make things a bit cozier in here?"

Kate nodded before wandering off to find the bathroom. She was grateful that Morgan had given her a little time to be alone before making any demands. A few minutes later, she felt more ready to explore. The cabin only had one bedroom on this floor, and its furnishings were opulent to say the least. Besides a king-size platform bed that seemed to float several inches off the thick brown carpet, there was a wet bar with a small refrigerator in addition to a tiled corner with a huge wooden hot tub.

Kate was still marveling at the plush accommodations when she sensed rather than heard Morgan's steps on the carpet behind her.

"Your friend Roger must have been holding out on you. This place has more than 'a few luxuries.' In fact, it's hard to think of it as a mere cabin at all."

"Oh, he told me all about it, hot tub and all," Morgan confessed. "I just didn't want to scare you off by enumerating all the goodies."

"So you think I scare easily?" she quipped, knowing deep down that she did.

The challenge inspired Morgan to close the distance between them quickly. "Let's see," he suggested, turning her to face him and pulling her into his arms.

Despite having looked forward to this moment with keen intensity all month, Kate found that she was trembling now—and not only from sexual anticipation. In a way she was scared—on a lot of different levels. Had she built this up in her imagination to such gigantic proportions that the reality couldn't possibly live up to her expectations? And what about Morgan? If her mind had been playing endless phantom home movies of the two of them making love, then he had certainly been doing the same thing. Only, his had probably been in 3-D.

"God, I've been dreaming of this for an eternity," he whispered huskily, confirming her suspicions.

As he spoke, he slipped his hand inside the back of her pants, familiarly cupping the swell of her bottom and giving it a little squeeze. The intimacy of the gesture might have increased her anxiety over what was to follow, but in fact, because it felt so good, so right, it had just the opposite effect. All at once, she felt able to meet him on the sensual level they had shared before and had both craved for so long to have again.

"Morgan," she breathed, snuggling closer to his solid length. And then, on impulse, she slipped her hand between their bodies to boldly stroke the evidence of his arousal. "And I've been wanting to do that for just as long."

Morgan's light brown eyes took on a tiger's gleam. "If you knew just how good that felt, you'd be afraid to continue."

"Does that mean you want me to stop?" she challenged, recklessly ignoring his warning.

"Let me put it another way. If you keep that up much longer, I'll be able to guarantee you exactly sixty seconds of fevered lovemaking." Without waiting for a reply, Morgan continued. "I think I've got a way to divert your attention." With that, he grasped the bottom edge of her sweater with both his hands and pulled it upward over her head.

"Are you going to leave me trapped like this?" she questioned, her voice muffled by the bulky wool.

"Not if you cooperate and lift your arms."

"You leave me no choice, then," she conceded, obeying his dictate.

The maneuver allowed Morgan to make short work of the sweater. When her head emerged from underneath the knit material, the naked look of desire blazing in his eyes almost took her breath away.

"You don't know how bewitching you are with your hair all mussed up like that," he murmured. He reached up to comb his shaky fingers through the thick chestnut waves. And then, molding his hands around the back of her head, he slowly brought his lips down to merge with hers.

It was a kiss that spoke of pent-up longing as well as passion and promise. And for Kate it swept away any remnants of doubt about being alone with Morgan. She swayed in his arms, hungry for even closer contact. But the motion made her suddenly conscious of her sensitive skin rubbing against the rough texture of his sweater. Grasping the bottom edges of the offending garment, she began to treat Morgan to the same remedy he'd just prescribed for her. But even standing on tiptoes, she was too short to complete the maneuver. It was impossible for her to pull the sweater up past his eyes.

"I'm going to need some help with this," she admitted.

"What do I get if I cooperate?"

"The same thing you get if you don't cooperate— only not in the dark," she retorted.

Morgan chuckled. "In that case, I suppose I'd better help." Leaning over, he stretched his arms out and let her tug the sweater off. As soon as it had fallen to the floor beside them, he pulled her into his arms again.

The warmth of his heated torso seemed to radiate through her. And the roughness of the hair on his chest against her delicate skin was much nicer than the feel of the sweater. Morgan, too, sighed luxuriously at the contact. And yet he was not quite satisfied. Reaching around her, he felt for the catch of her bra and unhooked it. And then, holding her slightly away from himself, he slid the straps off her arms.

Kate shivered in delicious anticipation as he peeled away the lacy garment. Somehow the gesture, more than any other that afternoon, made her feel an intoxicating sense of liberation. It was as though she were finally realizing that she and Morgan were really alone with each other and could do anything they wanted.

It seemed to Kate at first that Morgan's look of delight as he tossed her bra to the floor was as much an aphrodisiac as anything else she could imagine. But a moment later she was forced to revise her conclusion.

With the merest of touches, Morgan began to graze the tips of her nipples with his thumbs. Although the touch was butterfly light, Kate's reaction was so intense that she gasped. The sensations rippled downward through her body, coalescing in a sweet ache in her abdomen, which made it hard for her to keep her balance. To prevent herself from falling into the swirling vortex that Morgan was creating, she reached up quickly and grasped his shoulders.

"If you keep that up, I'm not even going to make it to bed," she protested, her voice thick with the longing he had conjured up so easily.

"In that case . . ." Instead of finishing the sentence, he swept her up in his arms and laid her gently on the quilted velvet coverlet before quickly stretching out beside her.

Kate's body was alive with sensations—the feel of his body against hers, the now-familiar intoxication of his after-shave lotion, the warmth of his breath against her hair, and the exquisite softness of velvet beneath her naked back. Suddenly a pang of conscience swept over her.

"Morgan, we can't," she whispered.

His eyes widened. "What do you mean, we can't," he demanded.

"I mean, we can't make love on your friend's coverlet," she qualified. "We've got to get up and turn back the covers."

"Thank God," Morgan growled. "I thought you had

something more serious in mind." Sighing, he clambered up off the bed and pulled Kate after him. "All right, let's turn back the covers."

The task was accomplished quickly, but not without some further grumbling from Morgan. "I did have to get involved with a practical woman," he mumbled under his breath as he helped her fold the coverlet to the foot of the bed.

"Satisfied?" he asked.

"Not yet," she replied impishly. "But I do expect to be shortly."

Taking her words as a challenge, Morgan reached for the buckle of his belt. It took him only a moment to shed his slacks and briefs. But Kate had only a quick impression of his well-muscled body, for in the next second, he had begun to remove the rest of her clothing as well. And all she could think about again was the feel of his sorcerer's hands on her heated flesh.

Dimly Kate marveled at how attuned her body was to this man. With few preliminaries they were both so aroused that the passion was almost unbearable. Morgan's mouth sought hers now in a demanding kiss that she was eager to match. And then he was pulling her back down to the bed and covering her body urgently with his.

It seemed to Kate that if she had to wait another moment for the completion of their union, she would die. And without conscious thought, her fingernails raked across the smooth skin of his back, conveying her own elemental need.

"I can't wait any longer, either," she heard him growl as she felt him enter her with a magnificently satisfying thrust. The erotic pleasure of it was so incredible that his name was on her lips like a cry of joy. But there were even greater heights to scale.

Slowly he began to move inside her, and then more quickly so that the elation of their joining increased with every glorious stroke. It was as though the two of them were building up a charge of kinetic energy that could light the very universe. And when the release of that energy exploded within them and all around them, it was so powerful that they clung together in a oneness as old as time and as endless as the cosmos itself.

Even the descent from the stratosphere was heavenly, Kate mused, secure in the tight embrace of Morgan's arms. And for a long moment, she snuggled against him, silently contemplating the beauty of making love with Morgan Chandler.

Looking up at him from under lowered lashes, she was surprised to see him wearing a grin of satisfaction. "And just what exactly are you thinking?" she demanded.

His grin spread ear to ear. "I'm thinking that if we keep practicing like this, we'll be a shoo-in for the Olympic You-Know-What Team."

Kate found it impossible to suppress a giggle. She knew exactly what he meant. And although she realized he needed no encouragement to stay in this silly yet endearing mood, she couldn't resist adding her own frivolous touch. "Were you thinking of the two-minute dash?" she questioned, playfully tickling his ribs.

"That's okay for starters. But with a week of intensive training, I'm sure we'll be up to tackling the marathon."

Kate snuggled closer against him, already very glad that she had agreed to this vacation with Morgan.

"Sleepy?" he asked her.

"Umm."

"I guess you've earned a rest."

* * *

It had been dark for hours when the two of them finally woke up.

"And just who needed a rest?" Kate couldn't help teasing as she sat up and stretched.

"Both of us," Morgan pointed out, looking at his watch. "What a luxury, to be able to sleep at odd hours—and to wake up next to you," he added, reaching over tenderly to brush a lock of chestnut hair away from her face.

Kate captured his hand with her own. "Did I remember to tell you how glad I am to be here?" she asked.

"Not in so many words. But I think I got the message."

Kate smiled and gave his hand a gentle squeeze before letting it go. "Do you want me to help you bring in the luggage?" she offered.

"Nope. It's my fault that it's still out there." As he spoke, he began looking for the clothing he had discarded earlier on the floor.

"Don't get up until I get back," he told Kate after he'd put on his pants and sweater. "Because I brought along a surprise for you."

Before he reappeared in the bedroom, Kate heard Morgan putting more logs on the fire and rearranging furniture in the living room. What was he up to? she wondered.

She was almost about to disobey his orders and get out of bed to investigate when he brought their suitcases into the bedroom, along with a large department store box.

"Open it," he prompted as he handed it to Kate.

Inside was a long peach-colored robe of delicate silk.

"Oh," Kate exclaimed as she unfolded the very feminine garment and held it up. "It's beautiful. But, Morgan, you shouldn't have."

"But I wanted to. Put it on so I can see how it fits."

Slipping out from under the covers, Kate reached for her bra.

But Morgan shook his head. "Listen, Kate, indulge me in the fantasy I've been having since I bought this for you three weeks ago."

"And just what do I have to do?"

"Wear it with nothing underneath. The silk is opaque, so you can feel entirely modest. But I'll know."

Kate couldn't help smiling as she pulled on the robe and belted it demurely. It fit perfectly. And despite what Morgan had said about modesty, the soft silk against her naked flesh made her feel quite wanton. Turning, she modeled it for Morgan. "Is this satisfactory?"

"Perfectly. And now for the next part of the fantasy," Morgan advised, leading the way into the living room.

Kate saw that he had turned the lights down very low, moved the couches aside and spread a soft velour blanket in front of the flickering fire. On it was a bottle of wine cooling in a silver bucket, and a large wicker hamper next to a veritable mountain of comfortable-looking pillows and cushions.

"What?" Kate began.

"A very elegant indoor picnic for two," Morgan explained, taking her hand ceremoniously and leading her to the cushions. "Make yourself comfortable."

Kate did as she was told, arranging the pillows so that she was propped comfortably facing the fire.

For a moment Morgan stood looking down at her warmly, a self-satisfied smile on his face. And Kate was struck once again by what a ruggedly handsome man he really was. Even in such casual knockabout clothes as the bulky sweater and brown cords, he still looked fantastic. As she watched he settled himself next to her. Reaching over, he took two delicately etched, long-stemmed crystal glasses from the hamper.

"First I'm going to ply you with drink," he warned, taking a bottle of white Rhine wine from the cooler.

"Aren't you afraid I'll get sleepy?" Kate questioned.

"No. Giddy maybe. But definitely not sleepy." Confidently, he handed her a glass of the pale liquid.

Kate took a sip. It was smooth and delicate, with the kiss of the grapes from which it had been fermented. "Umm, good," she acknowledged appreciatively.

Morgan leaned over and kissed her lightly on the lips. "Umm, better," he decreed before filling his own glass.

"And what do you have in that basket that's a little more sustaining?" Kate wanted to know.

Morgan opened the other side of the lid. "Let's see. Brie, Vermont Cheddar, crackers, olives stuffed with almonds, sliced smoked turkey, German potato salad, pâté, French bread, double chocolate brownies, fresh strawberries . . ."

"Fresh strawberries? Where did you get fresh strawberries this time of the year?"

"The world-famous Lexington Market; where else?" he explained, naming the large red brick building full of individual food vendors which had been a Baltimore institution for over two-hundred years. "But you should have something more sustaining first. Do you prefer Brie or Vermont Cheddar?"

"The Cheddar." Kate watched as Morgan cut a slice and placed it on a cracker.

"How did you decide on this amazing assortment of foods?" she asked.

"Well, they're some of my favorites. I walked around the market yesterday afternoon collecting them—and thinking about you."

Kate smiled as she watched him cut a slice of the pale, tangy Cheddar for himself.

He dispatched it quickly and then turned back to the hamper. Taking out a creamy damask cloth, he spread it in front them and then added two white bone china plates, two beautifully worked silver forks and two damask napkins.

Kate was overwhelmed at the attention to elegant detail. "Morgan, this is lovely," she breathed.

"Do you really like it?"

She could tell by his expression that her opinion was of the utmost importance. "Oh, yes. You really have been busy, haven't you."

"Well, I had to have something to do this month. And as I said, permit me my indulgences. I want this first meal up here to be special, Kate."

She nodded, understanding what he had done. This was the kind of luxury few people had the imagination to create or the time to enjoy. Reaching for his hand, she turned the fingers upward and pressed them to her lips. "This is lovely. You're lovely," she whispered.

"Thank you."

For a moment they simply sat there together before the flickering fire, enjoying the warm, close feelings flowing between them. And then Morgan turned back to the hamper and began to take out the rest of the food.

"How did you know this was one of my favorites?" Kate questioned some time later as she polished off her third small open-faced sandwich of rich pâté and crusty French bread.

Morgan smiled. "I was just hoping your taste matched mine. But if it didn't—more for me!" As he spoke, he turned and poked up the fire, making the glowing logs spring up in flames again.

"Oh, am I eating *your* pâté?" Kate teased.

"No. I'm not going to be greedy—at least for pâté."

As he spoke, he reached across her for the crystal bowl that held the strawberries, lightly brushing his arm against her breasts.

It was only the merest suggestion of a touch, and yet Kate felt her instant, deep response.

Morgan's smile was warm as he selected a perfect strawberry, dipped it in sugar and raised it to her lips.

"Wonderful."

"Want another?"

"Umm."

He reached across her again, his arm tantalizing her once more. This time Kate couldn't stop herself from placing her hand on his sleeve and pressing his arm even more firmly against the front of her body.

"Do you want your strawberry or not?" he questioned.

"I think so."

Placing another in her mouth, he watched her enjoy the sweet red fruit. And then his hand came up to brush against her hardened nipples through the soft silk of the peach robe.

"Tempting," he murmured.

"Want some more?"

"I think so."

The words were a caress, as he settled her more comfortably among the cushions.

"You're not wearing anything under that robe, are you?" he asked innocently.

"You know I'm not."

"Oh, yes, indeed I do," he agreed, circling her nipples with his thumbs so that they stood out in sharp relief under the filmy fabric. "You couldn't be, could you?"

Kate closed her eyes, letting the delicious sensations he was creating so easily wash over her. She hadn't realized just how erotic a thin layer of material between her skin and Morgan's hand could be.

"Wait right there," he advised. "I'm going to stow the food back in the hamper."

In just a few moments he was again at her side among the pillows, and she felt the light touch of his lips against hers.

"Sugar and strawberries," he whispered.

Her lips parted, eager for the invasion of his tongue. But he began with only a light skirmish followed by a quick retreat, teasing Kate into making her own foray into his mouth.

"Better than strawberries for dessert," he breathed.

"Yes."

Tenderly his finger traced the line of her cheek as he smiled down at her. "I knew what was going to happen as soon as we got here, Kate," he admitted. "But this time is going to be quite different. This is going to be silky and slow and tantalizingly sensual until you're on fire with wanting me inside you."

The provocative words were like a tide of wanton pleasure washing over Kate's body. "And if I want that already?" she inquired weakly.

"Then I'll just have to slow down a bit."

Delicately he began to comb his fingers through her thick hair, spreading it out in a halo around her head on the pillow. When she reached up and tried to pull him closer, he shook his head. "Let me play out the fantasy to the end, Kate. Let me make love to you the way I've dreamed of making love to you."

Kate nodded and wordlessly lowered her arms. For a moment she closed her eyes, until she felt his fingers on the sash of the peach robe. Deftly, he undid it, and then she felt him part the two sides of the wrapper very slowly and push them back to expose her to his view. She felt his gaze on her like a burning caress.

"So lovely," he exclaimed. "You're so lovely, Kate."

She watched as he shed his own clothing. And then, with passion and tenderness, he began to work his special sorcery on her body, touching, kissing, caressing—rousing her to the very peaks of sensual pleasure.

Again and again she reached for him. But he always eluded her pleading hands.

"Not yet," he whispered. "Not yet." Until she found that, as he had promised, she was indeed on fire with wanting him inside her.

"Morgan," she gasped, twisting now under his hands. "Please."

His own passion was at the same fevered pitch. Swiftly he entered her, beginning to move with an almost unbearable urgency. And Kate had no difficulty following the rhythm he set, her questing hips eager to meet his every stroke.

Their climax was quick and explosive—a supernova that flared with the white heat of mutual need.

And afterward, as she drifted gently down to earth, she knew Morgan had given her something very special.

The week went on and on being special. It was as though they were savoring each moment together. And yet at the same time, the joyous hours sped by so, that she found herself packing up to go home all too quickly.

As Kate was folding a pair of jeans to tuck into her suitcase, Morgan slipped up behind her and wrapped his arms securely around her waist. "A little sad to be leaving?" he questioned, nuzzling the soft skin behind her ear.

"It's been wonderful," Kate sighed softly, her eyes suddenly moist at the thought of having to share

Morgan with anyone else. His strategy had been effective. This week had convinced her that what they had together deserved a chance.

"What did you like best?" Morgan wanted to know.

The question took Kate by surprise. There had been so many wonderful things. How could she pick just one? Take their lovemaking, for example. She wouldn't have believed it possible, but over the week it had gotten better and better. That alone would have made this time out of time a magical interlude. And with a sudden insight, she realized he had taught her more about making love in one week than a man like Bart could have taught her in a lifetime. It was a matter of caring, she knew. He cared about the joy he gave her as much as the pleasure she gave him.

But there had been so much more than just their lovemaking: Thanksgiving dinner at the Kettle Creek Lodge, when she and Morgan had played the part of newlyweds for their tablemates—a judge and his wife who had been coming there every fall since their own honeymoon.

"Our children are all grown now," the still-handsome silver-haired man confided. "But I'll let you in on a secret. Having a family is one of the best things about being married."

"Although it may not seem like it when your teenage daughter is pushing her curfew to the limit," his apple-cheeked wife qualified.

Morgan and Kate had exchanged knowing smiles. Little did this friendly couple know that they had already experienced both the joys and tribulations of parenthood.

And then there was the afternoon they had spent at a local Christmas bazaar. While she'd been admiring the handmade quilts, Morgan had gone off and bought a set of red felt Christmas stockings—customized with each of their names in silver glitter across the white cuff.

"We'll put them up over the mantel in the townhouse," Morgan had explained. "And the kids will be surprised to find that Santa Claus has visited us even though we haven't moved in yet."

"Actually, they'll be surprised to discover that *you* still believe in Santa," Kate quipped. But under the humor, she was touched by the casual way Morgan was already referring to their future married state. He was already looking past their wedding to their life together. And, in truth, she was finding it hard not to do the same thing. With every passing moment she was finding herself bound more tightly to this man.

"Well?" Morgan prompted, bringing her out of her reverie.

"I can't just pick one thing," Kate finally admitted. "It was all so special. What did you like best?" She turned to throw the question back at him, although she suspected she already knew the answer.

"I know what you're thinking I'll say." He grinned. "Actually, you *are* fantastic in bed."

Kate had gotten past the blushing stage. "You're not bad yourself."

"But I can't honestly say that was the only best thing. It was the whole week. Waking up with you in my bed. Having breakfast with you. The tramps through the woods. That fantastic afternoon we spent in the hot tub."

Kate didn't even have the decency to blush at that particular reference.

"But I can sum it all up in one word," Morgan added quickly. "You."

"That's how I feel," Kate replied softly. Standing on

tiptoes, she gave him a kiss expressing all the love she felt for him that she still couldn't admit out loud.

"Does that mean that after this wanton week of living together outside the bonds of matrimony, you've decided to make an honest man of me?"

The question didn't really take Kate by surprise. She had accepted Morgan's terms of a month to make up her mind, and now that month was over. Her answer wasn't really as hard to voice as she'd thought it would be. In truth, she'd already made up her mind. There were still a lot of unknowns, yet when was the future ever certain? What Kate did know was that she loved Morgan with every fiber of her being.

The only dent in her happiness was that she was still afraid to voice her love to Morgan, because—despite what they had shared—he still thought love was an illusion. But she knew his love for her existed. He had let her know how much he cared in a thousand different ways. If he still wanted to see his feelings for her in terms of "trust" and "honesty," that was all right. Some day soon, he'd be able to put another label on his emotions.

Looking up, she met his warm gaze. "Yes," she breathed. "Oh, yes." And then her face clouded slightly. There was one more thing she hadn't been able to bring herself to tell Morgan, but it was something that might make a difference about his wanting to marry her.

"What is it?" he asked, instantly aware of the distress in her hazel eyes. "Have you changed your mind already about having me?"

Kate shook her head. "No, I haven't changed my mind. But I do have to be honest with you about something before you decide you really want me for your wife."

"There's nothing that could possibly make any difference," Morgan assured her. "But what is it you feel you need to tell me?"

"Do you remember that first night we spent together?" Kate began.

"How could I forget—starting with the dramatic newspaper article and ending up in your bed." His eyes began to twinkle as his agile mind began to embellish a wayward thought. "Say, don't tell me that while I was asleep you wrote up an account of our Thanksgiving vacation for the *Baltimore Sun?* Should I be prepared to read about our unwed bliss in the travel section next month?"

Kate couldn't hold back the ghost of a smile, but then her features sobered again. "This is serious, Morgan. Can't you ever be serious?"

"Not when I can help it," he acknowledged.

"That first night," Kate continued resolutely, "when you asked me if I was protected and I told you not to worry?"

"Yes, I remember every detail of that evening."

"Well, what I didn't say—what I didn't want to explain then—was that I'm pretty sure I can't have any more children."

At Kate's words, Morgan reached out a reassuring hand to clasp hers. "And you're worried that might make a difference to me?" he asked.

She nodded silently.

"Listen, Kate, I think we've got the perfect family already. Besides, fifteen years of bachelorhood more or less made me give up the idea of becoming a father again."

"You're not just saying all this to make me feel better?" Kate persisted.

He squeezed her hand and pulled her close. "It's you

I want, Kate," he rumbled. "And I won't have my future wife thinking any less of herself because she can only provide me with one terrific kid like Tony Davenport."

Looking up into the warmth of his gaze, she couldn't doubt his words.

## Chapter Eleven

$\mathcal{K}$ate couldn't believe how much activity one little word set into motion. And yet, once she said yes to Morgan, there was suddenly so much to do that she was convinced it was impossible to accomplish it all in the three weeks he had given her.

"Isn't it enough that I've agreed?" she asked him. "Why do we have to rush to get married before Christmas?"

"Because I want to spend the holidays with you," he answered.

"But we could do that anyway," she pointed out.

Morgan shook his head. "It wouldn't be the same. Don't make me wait any longer than I already have, Kate."

She gave him a warm look. In truth, now that she had made up her mind to marry him, she didn't want to wait any longer either. The memories of that wonderful week they had spent together at Kettle Creek were all she had to keep her warm at night. And she had to admit she was as anxious as Morgan for the real thing. But she did understand better than he just what it would take to get everything organized in so short a time.

Since she had already taken a week off at Thanksgiving and wanted at least a few days to spend alone with her new husband, Kate knew there was no question of asking for leave now. So, even though it was going to be a small wedding, all the arrangements had to be made during her lunch hour or in the evenings.

Briefly she considered trusting some of the details to Morgan, but then she shook her head as she thought about just what havoc he might wreak. She could just see him impulsively ordering pâté for the reception—or more flowers than they really needed. He'd be completely at the mercy of salesmen who knew an easy mark when they saw one. Of course, she could sit down and go over all her specifications—with their reasons. He'd insist on the reason for every decision; she knew him well enough to be sure of that. So by the time she finished with all the explanations, she might as well go ahead and do the work herself. Actually there had been a few things she'd turned over to Morgan in the end—like finding a suit and new shoes for Tony to wear. But with each delegated task, Kate had supplied a checklist to make sure her requirements would be well met.

To her relief, one thing she didn't have to contend with was her parents' surprise. Tony had evidently informed them that a fantastic guy named Morgan Chandler was going to be his new dad. And so, when she called to give them the news, they were eager to come east for the wedding and even volunteered to stay with both Tony and Julie while she and Morgan got away for a few days.

Another problem quickly solved was where to hold the ceremony. Morgan, with what Kate considered boundless optimism at the time, suggested the university chapel, and by some minor miracle, the date he had selected was free.

But still she was kept busy locating a photographer who didn't charge an arm and a leg, a florist who didn't try to talk her into a display that would rival the botanical gardens, and a place where they could have a reception for thirty.

Even finding the right dresses for herself and Julie was no easy task. Kate knew the simple but elegant look she wanted. It was just a matter of locating it for less than a month's salary. But Julie was a different proposition. Even though she tried on dozens of dresses that would have been fine, the girl found fault with all of them and refused to wear any to the wedding.

After several evenings spent with Julie in the dressing rooms of every major department store in the Baltimore area, Kate found her nerves beginning to fray.

Is she trying to make me angry? Kate wondered, as she got ready for bed one evening after a particularly exasperating session in which Julie had steadfastly rejected a beautiful red velvet gown in which she looked really lovely. Or is this a way of letting me know that she's still worried about how marriage will affect her relationship with her father?

Whatever was bothering Morgan's daughter, the best course would be to get it out in the open, Kate reasoned. And yet, once she'd made the decision to initiate a pre-mother-daughter talk, she found herself hesitating. Julie was still the unknown in this whole proposition. If she couldn't establish a good relationship with the girl, what kind of tensions might that create in her marriage to Morgan?

Finally, after she had pulled to a stop one evening in the Chandlers' driveway, she turned quickly to her passenger before the girl could get out of the car.

"Julie, is there anything bothering you?" she began.

The girl looked up in surprise and then quickly shook her head with a jerky motion. "No."

However, now that Kate had made up her mind to open the lines of communication between them, she wasn't willing to let the conversational door be slammed in her face so abruptly. "In a few weeks we're going to be living in the same house, and it's going to be awfully uncomfortable if you can't come to grips with the fact that your father and I are getting married."

The girl sat for a moment with her head bowed and then turned to Kate with a defiant look. "Why do you think I'm worried about you and my father?"

Kate suddenly felt out of her depth. This was never the kind of reaction she got from Tony. If he didn't want to talk about something, he simply clammed up instead of answering a question with a question. Could it be she was jumping to the wrong conclusions, after all? Kate wondered. "Julie, I can't know what's bothering you unless you tell me. But I want you to know that if you need to talk to me or if you need me for *anything,* I'll be here."

Morgan's daughter looked thoughtfully down at her hands. "Okay," she finally said, and then, after a long pause, added, "Listen, I've decided I like that red velvet dress that we saw a couple nights ago after all. Can we go back and get it tomorrow?"

Was this some sort of peace offering? Kate wondered. There was no way of knowing. Suddenly she found herself wishing that Morgan were home so that the three of them could sit down together and talk things over. But this evening, as on the previous two, he was working late at the office finishing up a shopping center design that was due the week after the wedding.

In the end, Kate had to simply be thankful that Julie had found a dress. There was just so much to do that she couldn't devote as much time as she wished to the girl's problems.

*After Morgan and I get married,* she told herself, *I'll break through her barrier.*

Although the weeks before the wedding were hectic, they weren't without their bright spots. One afternoon, she returned from a lunch hour spent at the florist to find her office decorated with crepe paper streamers.

"Surprise," Mary Ellen and the female half of the continuing-education department shouted in unison.

For a minute, Kate could only stand wide-eyed in the doorway. And then, as her knees started to turn to Jell-O, somebody pushed a chair forward. Gratefully, she sank into it. This was so unexpected.

"You don't know how hard it's been all week, trying to keep this little party a secret. In fact, it could be the first secret I've kept in my life, and it almost killed me," Mary Ellen confessed.

The group giggled appreciatively. And suddenly a warm gush of sentiment overwhelmed Kate, making her vision blur with a film of tears. Feeling foolish, she groped in her purse for a tissue. As she dabbed her eyes, she looked around at the ring of smiling faces.

"You really shouldn't have—" she began.

"Oh yes we should. You deserve it," one of the staffers interrupted.

"Besides," another voice piped up, "even if you've only been here a few months, you should know that office policy dictates never to pass up a party."

There was another ripple of laughter.

"All right, I surrender," Kate acknowledged.

"Then let's get down to business," Mary Ellen suggested, handing Kate a department store box wrapped in silver-and-pink foil paper and adorned with a large wedding bell.

It was almost too pretty to open, Kate thought, and definitely too pretty to tear. Carefully she began to loosen the tape at the ends.

The group waited expectantly, as if they shared a secret. And suddenly Kate felt self-conscious at being the center of attention. As she pulled the top off the box, she understood their banked excitement. Inside the tissue paper nestled an almost transparent gown of the palest aqua.

"Oh, how beautiful," Kate exclaimed, lifting the fabric and touching it to her cheek as she looked around again at the gathering. The circle of friends that had enclosed her so tightly had opened up a bit as chairs were pulled up and people made themselves comfortable. Now into the spirit of the occasion, Kate held up the sexy gown against her bodice in order to show it off. At that moment, her eyes collided with a pair of amused tawny ones that had been hidden by the press of female bodies around her.

Simultaneously, Kate's mouth dropped open and her fingers released the silky material, letting the gown fall into a shimmering pool in her lap.

Morgan grinned. "Oh, don't stop," he encouraged. "I was enjoying being an undetected voyeur back here in the corner."

Everybody else laughed appreciatively.

"I hope you don't mind my accepting Mary Ellen's invitation," Morgan added. "Being offered a chance to find out just exactly what goes on at a wedding shower was just too tempting. But more than that, I really wanted to share it with you."

The last admission was uttered so wistfully that Kate found herself swallowing hard in order to dislodge the lump that had suddenly materialized in her throat. "Of course I want you here," she whispered, hoping her voice would carry across the room. She knew exactly what he was trying to tell her in those few words. He wanted to share the joys of life with her. But more than that, he was simply seizing the opportunity to spend some time with her—if even in a crowd of giggling women. These last weeks had been so hectic that they had hardly gotten the chance for that. Although she had missed the intimacy, at least every second of her days and evenings had been filled. But what about Morgan? Maybe all this was actually harder on him than it was on her.

Meeting his eyes, she nodded her head almost imperceptibly, trying to tell him with the gesture that she understood. And then, on impulse, she raised her fingers to her lips and blew him a kiss.

Morgan nodded back. But his warm smile was her real indication that he had received the unspoken message.

"I hope you two haven't forgotten about the rest of us here," someone in the room joked.

"How could we?" Kate questioned, conscious all at once that it wouldn't be fair to spoil everybody else's fun. "You made this wonderful surprise possible."

"Well, Morgan had a lot to do with it," Mary Ellen explained. "He's the one who suggested a lingerie shower."

"He did?" Kate couldn't keep the surprise out of her voice.

"Yes, I did," her husband-to-be clarified from the back of the room. "I told Mary Ellen that the two of us had enough pots and pans, small appliances and linens to outfit two households, and what practical Kate needed was the kind of thing she wouldn't ordinarily indulge herself in."

Kate looked from her fiancé to her administrative assistant. "So the two of you cooked this up together?" she prompted.

"No," he clarified quickly. "She did all the work. I was just the technical advisor."

Mary Ellen didn't dispute his words. Instead, she handed the guest of honor another beautifully wrapped box—this one with green-and-silver paper. Inside was an incredibly feminine, delicately sexy peach-colored teddy, trimmed in narrow lace at the deeply veed neckline. "What is it? Hold it up," someone urged.

"Uh, um . . . a teddy," Kate exclaimed.

"Let's see. Pass it around," several voices in the crowd suggested.

As Kate started to obey, Mary Ellen leaned over and whispered in her ear. "It's from Morgan."

Kate looked up quickly enough to catch the satisfied smirk on his face. "It'll look great with your robe," Morgan mouthed silently above the heads of the other women.

"So you were just the technical advisor, were you?" she teased. She might have thought herself incapable of engaging in this type of banter in front of a group of her co-workers, but much to her surprise, she was actually starting to get into the spirit of the thing and really enjoy herself. *Have three and a half months with Morgan changed me so much?* she wondered. But it was true. She *had* changed. It had been a subtle process. But Morgan had helped her become more open to new experiences, more able to let her hair down, and less self-conscious about how her behavior might look to other people.

"Well—you've got to let me have some fun. And believe me, picking this out was *fun*," he was saying.

Kate couldn't suppress a knowing grin. She could indeed picture him in the lingerie department of some local department store asking to see an assortment of the sexiest teddies available. "And when do you expect me to wear something like this?" she challenged, blissfully unaware of the implication of her words.

Morgan's response was a wolfish grin. And, despite herself, Kate flushed prettily. Maybe she hadn't come quite as far as she imagined, after all. But before she had more time for reflection, another box was thrust into her hands and she was automatically beginning to loosen the pastel wrapping paper.

As it turned out, the week of the shower was probably the most hectic for Kate. After that, the plans she'd made finally seemed to be coming together. And, as she told Morgan over the phone a week before the wedding, it actually looked as though they were going to be able to pull things off.

"That's good," he told her, "because whether there's a wedding ceremony or not, I have some rather specific plans for you that evening, and the next day, and the day after that."

"Oh?" Kate pretended to sound mystified, although she knew exactly what Morgan had in mind. Her hunger for him was as intense as it had been during the weeks before their Thanksgiving vacation together—only more so, if that were possible, because now she knew exactly what she had to look forward to.

Morgan didn't even bother answering her implied question. "I miss you, you know. It's hard to believe two people can be so close and yet so far away at the same time," he murmured huskily instead.

"Yes," she agreed.

"Listen, I have an idea," he began. "Tomorrow's Saturday. Why don't you and Tony come over? You can put some of your clothes in my closet, and he and I can do some fixing up in the room where he'll be sleeping until we move down to the townhouse."

"Okay," Kate agreed.

"Gee, I thought you were going to give me some sort of argument about how busy you are."

"No, your plan makes perfect sense. Is ten-thirty too early?"

"Of course not. In fact, if Tony and Julie weren't around, I'd ask you to come tonight."

"Yes, well, uh . . ."

"Yes, well, uh, I know. I have to take what I can get. See you at ten-thirty."

What Morgan was able to get the next morning was a long, lingering kiss in his front hallway, after he had sent Tony upstairs to have a look at his new room.

"Let me pull you into the coat closet where we can be alone," he murmured after they had finally broken apart slightly.

"You must be kidding."

"Only partly." As he spoke, he drew her around the corner into the kitchen. And then, before she could protest, he slipped his hand inside her coat and cupped her breast lovingly. "God, you feel so good," he whispered, "even through all these bulky winter clothes."

Kate sighed, letting herself melt against the length of his strong body. She knew what he meant. He felt so good, too, that she could hardly stand it.

His fingers had just drifted downward to the edge of her sweater and slipped underneath to caress the eager flesh of her torso when a loud "ahem," made them jump apart guiltily.

Kate looked over Morgan's shoulders to meet the look of disapproval in Julie's eyes. But, by the time he turned around, it had vanished. "Hope I wasn't interrupting anything important," the girl apologized. Although the words were appropriate, Kate could detect no note of sincerity in her future stepdaughter's voice.

"Are you looking for some breakfast?" Morgan questioned.

"Yes. But Tony wants you upstairs," she told her father.

As Kate turned to follow Morgan up the stairs, Julie surprised her with a light tug on the sleeve. "Want to have a cup of coffee with me?" she asked.

Kate was speechless for a moment. This was the first time the girl had actually made some sort of overture toward her. "Why, why yes, thank you," she finally managed.

Morgan turned around and winked before going off to find Tony. *See*, he seemed to be saying, *you are making progress.*

Kate slowly hung up her coat before joining Julie in the kitchen. This was such an unexpected development, that she didn't know quite how to respond. As she pulled out a chair at the round oak table, she watched the girl get down cups and saucers with such unsteadiness that they vibrated together. And when she handed Kate a steaming cup, some of the black liquid slopped over the sides and puddled into the saucer.

"Is something bothering you?" Kate asked, remembering the offer she'd made in the car after they'd gone shopping.

Julie stood unmoving at the counter. And then she turned quickly to face Kate, a look of deep distress in her golden brown eyes that were so much like Morgan's. After darting a quick glance at the doorway to assure herself that they were alone, she began to speak in a halting voice. "I . . . I think . . . I mean . . . Oh, sh—" She stopped, mumbled an expletive and hesitated for a long moment. Then Julie seemed to gather the courage to plunge ahead. "I missed my period last month and I'm really worried."

Of all the things that could have come out of Julie's mouth, this was the last one that Kate had expected. But with an effort, she struggled to keep her shock from showing on her face. "Have you told your father?" she finally managed.

The words made the blood drain from Julie's face. "No!" she exclaimed in horror. "And you have to promise you won't tell him either."

"Why?"

"Have you ever seen him when he's really angry?" Julie shot back.

Kate nodded slowly, remembering the awful night when Morgan had thought she had been responsible for that revealing newspaper article about the seminar. She did know what it was like to be the focus of his anger. In fact, she hoped she was never on the receiving end of anything like that again.

"Don't you think if we went to him together . . . ?" she proposed, knowing that in this case he had the right to know what was happening with his daughter.

But Julie only shuddered. "I'm sorry I told you," she said, "if that's all you can suggest."

The admission made Kate feel trapped. On the one hand, this was the first time Julie had opened up with her, and the girl obviously needed help. But on the other hand, how could she go behind Morgan's back? However, his daughter's very real distress seemed to make the decision for her. And then, too, there was the possibility that Julie really had nothing to worry about. In that case, Morgan need never know. Maybe if she agreed to Julie's terms for accepting her help, they *could* solve this problem together.

Kate cleared her throat. "Okay, I promise not to tell your father anything unless you decide it's all right," she agreed.

Relief—and something else that Kate couldn't identify—washed across the girl's face. "Thank you," she whispered.

One hurdle had been crossed. At least they both knew where they stood. But that didn't make things any easier for Kate. "Do you have some reason to think you might be . . ." She hesitated, trying to find some delicate way to say "pregnant." But there was none. And so she finally had to ask the direct question.

Julie looked down at her fingernails. "I don't know," she confessed.

"Well, have you and one of your boyfriends ever been . . . intimate?"

"I don't want to talk about it. I just want to find out what's wrong," the girl returned quickly.

For a moment Kate sat and thought about the unfortunate situation. Somehow it didn't seem fair that the first mother-to-daughter talk she and Julie had had was about *this*. But berating her luck wasn't going to do any good. Instead, she'd simply have to try to deal with the crisis.

Kate sighed. This would all be easier if Julie were willing to lay all her cards on the table. But since she wasn't, Kate would simply have to do the best she could under the circumstances. "Have you been to a doctor?" she asked.

At first, the question was met with silence. Finally Julie shook her head. "I can't talk to my family doctor about this and I don't know where else to go. Actually, I was hoping you could take me somewhere."

The note of pleading in the girl's voice hung in the air between them for several seconds while Kate thought frantically if there were any other course she could suggest. But though she racked her brain, nothing else came to mind. "Okay," she finally agreed. "And the sooner the better, I guess."

Silently she had to admit that she wasn't only thinking of the girl's welfare. There was also the wedding just a week away, and this crisis would certainly put a damper on the proceedings if it weren't resolved before then. Why did Julie have to bring this up *now* of all times? she wondered, and then stopped short. *What a selfish thought,* she castigated herself. *Here this poor girl may be in real trouble and all you can think about is yourself.*

Kate looked down at the cup of coffee she had virtually forgotten. Taking a sip, she noted that it was no longer hot.

"I could pour it back and warm it up," offered Julie, who had also taken a swallow from her own cup.

Kate gave her a wan smile. "No, that's all right. The thought of going upstairs and keeping my face neutral while I tell your father that the two of us are going out together has taken my appetite away."

Relief flooded Julie's features. "Does that mean you're going to help me?" she asked.

Kate nodded.

"And you won't tell Dad what's going on?" the girl pressed.

"No, I won't tell him." The assurance was against Kate's better judgment, but under the circumstances, how else could she help Julie? she rationalized.

While she thought about exactly what to do, Kate went upstairs with the clothes she had brought over, and hung them in Morgan's closet. Then she phoned a walk-in family planning clinic near the university that catered to students. Before she knew it, she and Julie were in the car and heading downtown.

When Kate had finally screwed up her courage enough to tell Morgan they were going out, he and Tony were so absorbed in a discussion of how to decorate his new room that both of them had hardly glanced at her carefully expressionless face.

"I'm glad you and Julie are finally enjoying each other's company," Morgan had told her a bit absently before turning back to Tony. And, on this particular morning, Kate could only be grateful that he didn't press her for details.

*Enjoying each other's company,* Kate thought as she fought the Saturday morning traffic near the campus. Julie seemed to have retreated behind some sort of silent, protective wall, steadfastly resisting all efforts to draw her into conversation now that her future step-mother's help was assured. Finally Kate had given up and turned on the radio. Under the circumstances, she herself might not be too talkative, she mused, as she began to search for a parking space near the clinic.

Inside, Kate waited while Julie nervously filled out a medical history form. She couldn't help noticing sympathetically that the girl's hand was trembling as she handed the green sheet and ball-point pen back to the receptionist. Reaching over, Kate put her arm around Julie's shoulder. "It's going to be all right," she murmured.

Julie seemed to shrink away from the contact, and Kate quickly removed her arm. *She probably doesn't know me well enough to accept the comfort,* she told herself, as she watched Julie return to her seat in the crowded room.

The girl picked up a fashion magazine and began thumbing through the pages too rapidly to really see the glossy models in their winter finery. But Kate was too tense even to pretend interest in a magazine. Instead she found herself looking at the other anxious faces in the crowded room. Most seemed to belong to college girls—a few accompanied by boyfriends. But all of them looked as alone as shipwreck survivors on their own individual desert islands.

It seemed to take forever before Julie's name was finally called. But when Kate checked her watch, it had only been twenty-five minutes.

"She'll be back in a jiffy," the cheery receptionist assured Kate, who nodded her thanks. Yet once Julie had left the room, Kate was so fidgety that she couldn't sit still. Getting out of her seat, she went to the window and looked out at the traffic crawling along Charles Street. But it couldn't hold her attention for long. Sitting back down, she sighed and picked up a magazine, but instead of reading, she began to absentmindedly roll it into a tube.

With Julie gone, time seemed to crawl by even more slowly than it had before. Kate couldn't stop from looking at her watch every few minutes, nor from glancing up every time someone came down the hall. However, it was a good forty minutes before Julie finally reappeared at the entrance of the waiting room. Kate scanned her face anxiously for a hint of the verdict. But there was none.

"Well?" Kate blurted, letting out the breath she had unconsciously been holding.

"I'm not . . ." Julie didn't finish the sentence.

"Thank God."

"I guess I just panicked," the girl stated with more coolness than Kate would have believed possible. "But I really want to thank you for bringing me here."

Kate nodded. "I'm so glad things worked out."

"Me too," Julie agreed, her expression suddenly lightening.

Kate went to retrieve their coats from the nearby closet. Julie waited by the reception desk, where she took one of the clinic's business cards and stuck it quickly in her pocket.

Once out on the street, Kate turned to Julie. "Listen, I have an idea. Let's go to lunch so we can tell your father that's what we did without fibbing."

Julie couldn't repress a giggle. "Good idea," she agreed.

After they had ordered chicken salad sandwiches at a nearby luncheonette, Kate wondered if she should try to get Julie to talk about the events of the morning and what had led up to them. Now that everything was all right, the girl seemed to want to pretend that the whole crisis had never happened.

But Julie seemed so relieved that Kate hated to spoil her new sense of well-being. *There will be plenty of time to talk about this later,* Kate told herself. *Maybe I should just consider this a beginning we can build on.*

She was probably making the right decision, Kate decided as Julie became even more animated and began to chat about her school and friends.

Kate, too, found her spirits lifting. She'd offered Julie her friendship. But more than that, she had actually been able to help her future stepdaughter with a real problem—and she had probably saved Morgan a few more gray hairs as well. It *was* a good first step toward establishing the kind of relationship she'd been hoping for since she and Julie had first met. And now that the first step was taken, there was no reason why they couldn't keep making progress.

# Chapter Twelve

$\mathcal{K}$ate had planned some time for herself on Sunday morning. As Morgan had pointed out at the shower, the two of them wouldn't need all the kitchen utensils and equipment they had accumulated. And so she wanted to go through her own drawers and cupboards and decide what should be kept and what should go to the Salvation Army or some other worthy cause. It was a task that most people wouldn't enjoy. But for Kate there was a lot of satisfaction in finally being able to discard some of the battered pots and pans, threadbare dish towels, and now-dull knives she'd been using ever since she'd first set up housekeeping.

Since Tony would only be in the way, she had suggested that he spend the night with one of his friends. And so she was working alone in the kitchen, humming along with the radio, when the doorbell rang several times in quick succession at nine-thirty. Sleepovers usually meant late awakenings for her son. Could he be coming home early for some reason? she wondered, tying the belt of her green robe more securely around her waist and heading for the front door.

"Hold on, I'm coming," she called, as the bell jangled yet again. Somebody was certainly impatient, Kate mused as she peeped outside through the curtained window. On the doorstep stood Morgan and Julie. He had turned away toward his daughter and so Kate couldn't see his face.

Well, this was certainly an unexpected pleasure, Kate thought, a warm smile turning up the corners of her mouth. Had she mentioned the kitchen sorting chore to Morgan? And had he and Julie given up their Sunday morning to come to help? It was the kind of thoughtful gesture she had come to expect from the man who would be her husband in less than a week.

But the smile of welcome froze on her lips as she threw open the door and Morgan whirled around. She had expected to see his face filled with the warmth that had become so important to her over the past few months. Instead, his features were set in a rigid mask as cold as the freezing air that rushed in through the open doorway. The anger that flashed in the depths of his tiger eyes was like static electricity.

Involuntarily, Kate jumped back, as though she'd just shuffled across a nylon rug and inadvertently touched a metal lamp base. Ignoring her reaction, Morgan stepped inside the small hallway, pulling Julie after him. With a quick backward push of his free hand, he slammed the door shut.

Without realizing that she had even moved, Kate found her shoulders suddenly pressed defensively against the far wall of the little entryway, the rational part of her mind trying to comprehend what was happening.

For several moments they stood facing each other, the pounding of Kate's own blood in her ears seeming to fill the hallway. Julie had receded so far into the background that Kate momentarily forgot her existence. When Morgan finally spoke, his voice seemed to be coming to her through layers of ice. "All right, I told you I'd never condemn you again without giving you a chance to explain first. Suppose you explain."

At first Kate stared at him uncomprehendingly. And then, from somewhere deep in her paralyzed mind, an awful thought began to form. Somehow Morgan must have found out about yesterday.

As if to confirm the growing realization, the angry man confronting her pulled out a white business card and held it up for her inspection. In neat black letters across the front was the name, address and phone number of the clinic she and Julie had visited less than twenty-four hours ago.

"Well?" Morgan prompted.

Out of the corner of her eye, Kate caught a flash of movement behind Morgan. It was Julie. In her own distress, Kate had forgotten all about the girl. But now, over Morgan's shoulder, their eyes met and held for an instant. And then Kate took in her pallor and drawn features. As she watched, silent syllables formed on Julie's lips and Kate made out the words *"you promised."*

"I'm waiting," Morgan grated impatiently. "Aren't you going to tell me why you took it upon yourself to whisk Julie down to a family planning clinic without consulting me? I can only imagine what you think of my daughter's morals, but if you'd decided she was in need of contraceptive advice, you might have brought up the topic for discussion."

"I didn't . . . I mean I . . ." Kate began and then trailed off before she could make any real explanation. She was acutely conscious of Julie's eyes on her face.

"I know I told you I wanted you to be a mother to

Julie," Morgan shot back, apparently unwilling to wait for whatever she was trying to get out. "But don't you think this is a little more responsibility than you should assume without consulting the girl's father?"

"All this isn't what you think," Kate began to defend herself.

Morgan's dark brows lifted expectantly. "Yes? Then what is it? When I asked Julie what the card from this clinic was doing on her dressing table, she told me that you had taken her."

The sardonic expression in Morgan's eyes told her that he didn't really expect she was going to come up with a satisfactory response. And suddenly Kate was seized with a sense of *déjà vu*. Hadn't all this happened before? And in this very hallway?

The realization made Kate feel like a small animal who had blundered into a hunter's snare and could now sense it tightening painfully. Only this time, somehow, she felt as though she had sprung the trap on herself. What could she say to defend herself without breaking her word to Julie?

"I trusted you with my daughter," Morgan was saying, the unsteady timbre of his voice signaling that his emotions were less under control than when he had first slammed the door. "And this is what I get in return."

Kate looked at him bleakly, seeing the wounded look in his eyes behind the blazing anger. So that was it. She should have suspected. Just as when she'd roused his ire before, everything came down to *trust* and *honesty* again. And why not? It was the concept on which Morgan had painfully rebuilt the foundation of his life after Julie's mother had run out on him. And now once again, when he thought that trust had been broken, he was reacting with fury to cover his feelings of hurt and betrayal. How ironic, she thought grimly. There was no way to explain without breaking Julie's trust. However, the insight was of little use to Kate. She simply didn't know how to get through to him when he was in this kind of state.

It had become hard for Kate to catch her breath, as though a vise were constricting her chest. Taking several deep breaths, she tried to calm herself and fill her lungs. But the effect was not what she had intended. Unconsciously she was taking too much oxygen into her system and all at once she began to feel lightheaded. "I—I've got to sit down," she whispered.

"I'm afraid I haven't got time to stay for a social chat," Morgan informed her curtly. Glancing back at Julie, he added, "Wait for me in the car. I'll be out in a moment."

Just before his daughter turned to leave, she shot Kate a look that was part pity and part something that Kate's muddled brain was not capable of assimilating.

When the door had closed behind Julie, Morgan shifted his full attention to Kate once again, who could now only stare at him wide-eyed. His hands were balled into fists. And though he kept them rigidly at his sides, she wondered fleetingly if he were actually going to hit her. He certainly looked angry enough.

However, as he caught the direction of her gaze, he only snorted derisively. "I don't assault women," he informed her curtly, "even when they deserve a good thrashing."

Kate fought for control. Simply standing here facing Morgan like this was almost more than she could manage. But she had to try to get through to him—to break through that defensive barrier of anger that masked the feelings of vulnerability he couldn't admit. However, he was too caught up in his own pain to give her a chance.

And apparently the only way he could deal with that

pain was to strike back at the person he held responsible. His next words seemed to hit her with such force that she literally doubled over.

"You realize, of course, that the wedding is off. I certainly couldn't marry you now under the circumstances."

"But what do you expect me to do about . . . about all the arrangements?" Kate found herself blurting, realizing in some corner of her mind that he had turned the conversation away from the real issue.

"Cancel them." Without uttering another word, he turned and strode out of the house, closing the door firmly behind himself.

The full impact of what his leavetaking meant had not yet hit. And so there were no tears. Kate could only stare blindly at the closed door, feeling numb and confused. He had called the wedding off? Was that really what he had said? It couldn't be. Not just like that, without any real discussion. But she had heard the edict. And though it was almost unthinkable, she knew that in his present distraught state, Morgan had meant it. Unable to focus on the pain to come, her mind clutched at practical details. There were calls she was going to have to make—to the florist, the photographer, chapel, the wedding guests. But the sheer magnitude of it all made her suddenly weary.

The next few hours would always be a blur in Kate's memory. She could never recall going upstairs, taking off her robe and getting back into bed. But that was where she found herself when Tony banged noisily into the house just before lunchtime.

"Hey, Mom, where are you?" he called. And then, "What's the matter?" after he had pounded up the stairs and found her in the darkened bedroom.

"I'm not feeling very well," Kate explained, suddenly realizing that it was no lie. The emotional turmoil of the morning had left her feeling sick and shaky. "Let me rest for a little while, and then I've got to talk to you about something," she forced herself to add. Although she couldn't yet face telling Tony what had happened, she knew it would have to be soon.

And yet, part of her couldn't help hoping that when Morgan had a chance to calm down and see things more rationally, he might change his mind. That had happened before, after all. Or just maybe, Julie would realize her role in all this and make a confession. However, as the day wore on and the phone failed to ring, Kate's hopes for a reconciliation grew dimmer. By Monday morning she was forced to admit that the future she'd imagined with Morgan Chandler had vanished like a morning mist in the hot sun.

It was then that the tears came—tears for what had happened, but most of all, tears for what might have been. Despite everything, Kate knew that she still loved Morgan—even flawed as he was. His anger wasn't his fault, she told herself. He just couldn't stop reacting the way he had for so long—not on his own. He had been translating feelings of betrayal into anger for so long that it was an ingrained pattern. Kate had been confident that building a trusting marriage relationship with him would heal the wounds that Julie's mother had inflicted. But now she wasn't going to get the chance, and the realization made her tears flow even more heavily.

Morgan Chandler might not believe in love, but Kate did. It was love, and nothing else, that had made *her* vulnerable to *him*. She had worked hard to make herself independent and sure of her ability to cope with life on her own before she'd met Morgan. But her love for the man had made her open herself up to him in a way that she thought she never would again. And now that love was causing her so much pain that she wanted to pull the covers up over her head and hide from the world while she wrapped her misery around herself as tightly as the protective bedcovers. But that was impossible, of course. There was just too much to do. With bitter irony, Kate allowed herself to picture wedding guests assembled in a flower-decked chapel looking mystified at each other as the time for the arrival of the bride and groom came and went. Well, if that wasn't going to happen, she was going to have to get busy.

What was the hardest part of the whole miserable episode? Kate wondered afterward. Canceling the florist, the reception hall, the photographer and the minister had been relatively easy. Kate had simply pretended in her own mind that she was a secretary delivering an impersonal message. The wedding guests had been a lot harder. Since there hadn't been time to write each of them a note, she'd had to phone. But, with all but a few like Mary Ellen, she'd made it clear from the tone of her voice that she didn't want to discuss the reasons for the sudden change of plans.

Telling her parents had been even more painful, but it would have been far more difficult if they had lived in the same city. At least, Kate told herself, she only had to contend with the sympathy that came over the phone lines; she hadn't had to see their shocked faces—and they couldn't see hers.

Worst of all had been Tony. If anything, the news seemed harder for him to bear than it was for even Kate herself.

"You mean Morgan's not going to be my dad after all?" he had blurted in response to her carefully prepared speech about how "some things don't work out the way we expect."

Struggling to hold back her own tears, Kate had nodded. She wanted to reach out and pull Tony into her arms and comfort him. But he wouldn't let her. Instead he stamped up to his room and wouldn't come out for the rest of the day, even for the dinner Kate forced herself to prepare.

Kate dragged herself through the next week like an automaton. After the one evening when she had let her tears flow freely, the only way she could deal with her own feelings and with the sympathetic looks everyone at work shot her when they thought she wasn't looking was to operate in a sort of numb haze. Saturday, the day that was to have been her wedding, was the worst, of course. Mary Ellen had tried to get her to agree to bring Tony over and spend the day. But Kate had begged off, explaining that she would hardly be very good company. And as it turned out, it was a lucky thing. Saturday morning she was feeling so ill that she could hardly get out of bed. And it was all she could do to keep down some dry crackers and tea.

It must be a reaction to everything that's happened, Kate told herself as she huddled under the covers. But the next morning she was feeling very little better. And the persistent nausea continued through the rest of the week, making her feel light-headed and shaky. It didn't help that Tony was becoming just as uncommunicative and unmanageable as he had been before she'd taken the parenting seminar. Suddenly, not only was Kate worried about her ability to take care of herself, she was fearful about what the loss of Morgan Chandler was doing to her son.

Her distress over Tony's anguish finally made Kate take a step that she almost wouldn't have believed possible. About a week after their canceled wedding date, she reached for the phone and quickly dialed Morgan's still-familiar number before she could lose her nerve.

As the phone rang she could feel her heart begin to pound, and she almost slammed the receiver back in the cradle. What if Julie answered? What would she say? And what if Morgan himself answered? Would he simply hang up on her?

The questions chasing one another through her mind were cut off by his brisk hello. The sound of his familiar voice sent a tremor through Kate's body and she couldn't immediately respond.

"Hello?" he repeated. "Is anyone there?"

"It's me," Kate finally acknowledged. "Please don't hang up," she added quickly. "I have to talk to you about Tony."

"What about Tony?" Morgan challenged, his manner suddenly guarded.

"He's very upset about what's happened," Kate began, surprised that she could actually talk so rationally to Morgan. Encouraged that he hadn't broken the phone connection, she pressed on. "Morgan, your quarrel is with me, not Tony. But *he* doesn't understand that. Even though I've tried to reassure him, I think he secretly suspects that we're not . . ." Kate paused, and then forced herself to go on, ". . . getting married because of something he's done."

"Yes, I think I can understand that," Morgan acknowledged with real concern in his voice. "How can I help?"

"Well, I was hoping that you might call him—even make a date to go somewhere with him, if that's not too much of an imposition. I know you really don't have any responsibility to him, but—"

"No, that's okay," he interrupted. "You're right; I don't have any quarrel with Tony. I like him and I do feel a sense of responsibility toward him. What if I come over some time this week and bring him his Christmas present, and then we could arrange something for the next Saturday, maybe a soccer game or something?"

"That would be wonderful." Kate was suddenly both relieved and very sad. Tony would be going out with Morgan, but she wouldn't.

She heard Morgan clear his throat. "I'll call him tonight, then. Around eight?"

"That would be wonderful. Thanks." There seemed nothing more to say. And so they both said their stiff goodbyes and hung up. Kate sat for a long moment staring at the phone, fighting back the tears she had promised herself she wouldn't shed. Morgan was so near and yet so far away. But, at least for her, there seemed no way to bring him any closer.

It was even harder for Kate to control her emotions in the face of Tony's glowing account of the afternoon he'd spent with Morgan.

"We had a real good time," the boy bubbled, as he told about the soccer game they'd watched and the hot dogs and Cokes they'd shared. And then his features sobered. "But I think Morgan misses you. Sometimes I'd look at him sort of sideways and he'd seem so sad—just like you. And when I tried to get him to talk about—you know—about what happened, he just shook his head and changed the subject."

Kate bit her lip and looked down at the hands clasped in her lap. When Morgan had come to pick up Tony, she'd stayed upstairs so that they wouldn't meet, but when she'd heard the front door close, she hadn't been able to keep herself from rushing to the window to watch the man and boy get into the blue Datsun parked across from her townhouse.

She'd had only a brief glimpse of the man. And yet, that was time enough to take in the many small details that made up Morgan Chandler. His jeans were the old comfortable ones he liked so much, although she wished they didn't cling to his legs quite so caressingly. She didn't need any reminders of the muscle and sinew of the man. He should have gotten a haircut last week, she noticed, as he turned to get in the car. And suddenly she found herself longing to reach out and brush back the thick dark locks that had fallen across his forehead. But that was impossible now, she reminded herself. He wasn't hers to touch any longer.

When she'd finally come back downstairs, the smell of Morgan's after-shave lotion lingered tantalizingly in the hall—another piercingly sharp reminder of what they had shared and what they would never share again.

Kate's only consolation was that at least Morgan was still a viable factor in Tony's life while the boy needed him. For example, he had obviously chosen his Christmas presents carefully. Besides a regulation soccer ball, he'd given the boy the fancy clock radio he'd been wanting for months and a keyboard that turned his game computer into a more sophisticated, programmable machine. The latter was accompanied by several instruction and programming books.

"Which do you like best?" Kate had asked, not quite sure Morgan should have spent that much on her son but pleased that he seemed to like the gifts so much. Most of her own presents had been much more practical. Since they were back on the old familiar tight budget, she had concentrated on shirts and jeans for school.

"The programming stuff," Tony had answered her question. "At least, if Morgan wants to help me learn to use it."

Kate's face had clouded, and she looked away so that Tony wouldn't see. She wasn't sure how much time Morgan would be spending with her son in the future. But she couldn't explain that to Tony yet.

"I wish Morgan were here now," the boy had added. "It would seem more like Christmas."

"Yes," Kate agreed simply, remembering how Morgan had pressed to get married before the holidays. Suddenly, an image of the bright red-and-white stockings he had bought when they were at Kettle Creek leaped into her mind. What had he done with them? she wondered. Had he still hung his and Julie's on the mantel at the townhouse? Somehow she didn't think so.

The sudden cancellation of their plans had made it very hard for Kate to work up any enthusiasm for Christmas, and she suspected the same might be true for Morgan. Nevertheless, although her heart really wasn't in it, she had tried to make the holiday season as festive as possible for Tony's sake. But somehow, she just didn't seem to have the energy to get much done. They'd skipped the lights on the evergreens near the front door. And she'd only been able to force herself to bake two kinds of holiday cookies—neither one of which she wanted to eat.

In fact, she was still queasy every morning and was hardly able to eat anything during the day. And much as she tried to tell herself that this was just a reaction to everything that had happened, she finally had to admit that she was worried about her health—if not for her own sake, then for Tony's, since she was entirely responsible for his welfare.

One morning, after the holidays were finally over, Kate faced her hollow-eyed reflection in the mirror and made a decision. She had better go see the doctor, if only to reassure herself that her physical symptoms were just the result of emotional distress.

Picking up the phone, she dialed Dr. Fitzpatrick's office, expecting that she might have to wait another week for an appointment. But to her surprise, after she described her symptoms, the nurse fit her into the schedule before lunch that day.

Kate got dressed hastily and then phoned the office to say she'd be in late. Luckily Mary Ellen was not yet in, so that she didn't have to explain where she'd be. Lately her administrative assistant had been so solicitous that Kate had been afraid to mention feeling sick for fear that she'd be bundled instantly off to the infirmary.

*Maybe I should have let her do that,* Kate mused on her way downtown to the doctor's office. *Dr. Fitzpatrick's nurse wouldn't have had me come in right away if she hadn't thought there was something to all this.*

As it turned out, there definitely was something to Kate's persistent symptoms. But the news she received as she sat across from Dr. Fitzpatrick's desk after her exam made her eyes widen in disbelief.

"You're about two months pregnant," he told Kate.

"But I can't be. I mean, I thought I couldn't have any more children," she blurted.

Dr. Fitzpatrick raised a shaggy eyebrow. "And what made you think that?"

Feeling confused and disoriented, Kate began to explain how, when Tony was two, she had finally persuaded Bart that they should stop using contraceptives. Although he hadn't really wanted any more children, he had finally given in to her plans. But it hadn't made any difference after all, because she had failed to conceive again during the next six years of their marriage.

"Maybe there's something your physician in Santa Fe knows about your previous medical history that can shed some light on this," Dr. Fitzpatrick suggested. "Suppose you have a seat in the waiting room again while I give him a call and find out."

Still dazed from the unexpected news, Kate plopped down into a vinyl chair and sat staring across the room at nothing in particular. How could she possibly be pregnant? she wondered. Could Dr. Fitzpatrick have made some mistake? And yet he'd seemed so positive.

Ten minutes later, the mystery had been unraveled and Kate was feeling so faint that the doctor made her lie down again in an unoccupied exam room.

"You mean you really didn't know that your husband had had a vasectomy?" he asked sympathetically.

Kate could only shake her head dumbly.

"Are you absolutely sure? You know, your signature was on the consent form."

"Bart must have forged it," Kate mumbled weakly, comprehension dawning. Suddenly she was remembering some of the angry words they'd had when she'd brought up the subject of another baby. "He told me he really didn't want to share me with anyone else besides Tony, but when he finally agreed to let me try and get pregnant, I thought I'd changed his mind," she explained now.

Dr. Fitzpatrick shook his head, as if trying to figure out what kind of man would pull this particular kind of stunt on his wife. "I suppose he was counting on the fact that you'd assume Tony's difficult birth was responsible. But why didn't you have a fertility workup if you really wanted another baby?"

Kate looked up at Dr. Fitzpatrick, wondering what he must think about all this. "Don't you remember the timid little mouse who used to be Kate Davenport?" she questioned. "Don't you remember the woman whose husband had her convinced that she was a failure? Not being able to get pregnant again was just another one of the failures I accepted."

"I guess in a crazy way that does make sense," Dr. Fitzpatrick acknowledged, patting her arm. "It's just so hard to reconcile the woman you are now with that other Kate Davenport."

Kate nodded, only half listening. She was still almost unable to come to grips with the trick Bart had played on her—and how it had affected her life now.

"You know, if you don't want to continue this pregnancy . . ." Dr. Fitzpatrick began gently.

But Kate's look of horror stopped him from finishing the sentence. "No, I *do* want this baby," she protested, realizing as the words came out of her mouth that they were true.

"I had to ask," he said simply. "But now I know where you stand. Let's go back in my office, and I'll give you some information on how to take care of yourself."

As she left the doctor's office clutching a prescription for prenatal vitamins and a sheet of instructions, Kate felt a surge of something close to happiness, now that the reality of her condition had had a chance to sink in. *How ironic,* she thought. *It wasn't Julie who was pregnant, it was me. And even if I don't have Morgan, I have something he can't take away.*

Protectively she crossed her arms in front of her abdomen for a moment, still unable to detect the swelling of the new life inside her body but confident now of its existence.

*A baby,* she thought again as the corners of her mouth turned up. *The baby I was so sure I was never going to have.* And then, as a new thought took hold, the smile faded from her lips. This was also the baby Kate was going to have to raise all by herself.

Had she been hasty in refusing the way out of her predicament Dr. Fitzpatrick had offered? No, Kate told herself firmly. She wanted this child. And more than that, she wanted *Morgan's child*—even under these particular circumstances.

Glancing at her watch, Kate grimaced. The doctor's appointment had taken almost the entire morning. And

Kate certainly didn't want to take any more leave now that she really might be needing it later.

She had decided not to tell anyone about the baby right away. But she had forgotten about Mary Ellen. Her administrative assistant had been watching over her with such protective intensity since she'd learned the details of the canceled wedding plans that it would have been impossible for her not to know that *something* was up.

"Okay. Out with it," Mary Ellen demanded, coming into Kate's office and closing the door.

"What are you talking about?" Kate tried to play for time.

But her perceptive friend was not to be put off. "Something's different about you today. If it didn't sound so corny, I might say that you're fairly glowing with some sort of inner light."

Kate smiled at the aptness of the observation.

"Don't tell me," Mary Ellen continued. "Has that blankety blank Morgan Chandler had a change of heart or something?"

The suddenly bereft expression on Kate's face told Mary Ellen she had made a mistake. "Sorry," she apologized, real pain in her voice. "The question just represented wishful thinking, I guess. But what is it? What's happened to make you look like a madonna in a Renaissance painting?"

"I just found out I'm going to have a baby," Kate announced before she could change her mind about the revelation.

Her assistant's mouth fell open, and it was several seconds before she could say, "But I thought you couldn't."

"So did I," Kate agreed, the wonder of her new discovery evident in her voice. Quickly she proceeded to explain the whole unbelievable story.

"So, of course, you and Morgan weren't using anything," Mary Ellen finished for her.

"Right."

"Are you going to tell him?"

The question brought Kate up short. A week ago she might have answered with an instant no. But now she hesitated. "I don't know," she said slowly. And then she added an admission that she had voiced aloud to no one, not even her son. "I still love him," she acknowledged in a low voice. "But I don't want him to come back to me just because he feels responsible for my pregnancy."

"After what he did to you, I'll just have to take your word that he's worth taking back," Mary Ellen returned, "even if you still want to argue that he's got a perfectly reasonable excuse for his miserable behavior."

Kate opened her mouth to protest, but her friend shook her head. "I don't want to debate the merits of Morgan Chandler. But I do have one more point to bring up. If you want to make sure his motives for coming back are pure, you're going to have to patch things up before the pregnancy starts to show."

Kate nodded. "I just found out about the baby this morning, and I haven't had any time to think things through. But you're right, of course. I'm going to have to get the reflective stages over with as soon as possible. I don't even know what I'm going to tell Dean Porter yet, much less Morgan Chandler."

That evening after Tony was in bed, Kate reached for the jug of white wine she kept in the refrigerator. A relaxing glass might help her deliberations along. But a sudden realization made her stop in the act of pouring the pale golden liquid into a goblet. Dr. Fitzpatrick had emphasized that alcohol—even in moderation—wasn't good for unborn babies. After emptying the glass into the sink, she turned back to the refrigerator and pulled out a carton of milk. *Much more appropriate,* she congratulated herself with a grin.

It was odd, she reflected, sitting down in the rocking chair in the corner of her bedroom, what a good mood the baby had put her in. By rights the prospect of raising another child alone should have made her quake in her boots. But she just couldn't work up any enthusiasm for such negative emotions. And besides, was she really going to try to do it by herself, or was she counting on Morgan's help? Was that the real reason for her equanimity?

That question brought her up short. *All right, here it is, time to analyze your real feelings,* Kate told herself firmly. Did she want Morgan back? The answer to that was a resounding yes. But what if she tried to set things right between them and only earned another scathing rejection? The thought sent a tremor through her body. Even if she understood the reasons for Morgan's pain and anger, she honestly didn't know if she were strong enough to confront it again. And it was a definite possibility. After all, if she decided to make the first move, there was absolutely no guarantee that he would take the overture kindly.

Struggling to get control of these troubled reflections, Kate set the rocker in motion, letting the gentle, rhythmic movement calm her spirit. There was one key element that she had been steadfastly avoiding, but now she had no other choice. She had to think about the role Julie had played in all of this.

*Well, what about Julie?* Kate asked herself, taking a contemplative sip of milk. As if in response, the girl's face as she had last seen it came into her mind. Stamped on the features was the expression Julie had worn just before turning to leave that terrible Sunday morning. At the time, Kate had not been able to analyze what Julie's look had meant. But now, with the leisure to consider the expression, she suddenly understood. She had seen pity in the girl's eyes. But she had also seen triumph.

The realization was so startling that the almost-finished glass of milk slipped from Kate's fingers and landed with a soft thump in her lap. Luckily she was able to pull it upright before much of the white liquid had trickled out onto her bathrobe. But the rescue action was automatic as Kate's mind struggled to come to grips with the truth of what had happened.

Julie had deliberately set her up. The girl hadn't really thought that she was pregnant. That had simply been a convenient excuse to get Kate to "help her" without telling Morgan. After all, she had been living with Morgan for fifteen years. She knew his strengths and weaknesses. All Julie had to do was make sure her father then found out and she could be confident of his reaction.

Despite the logic of her reasoning, Kate's mind reeled away from her conclusion. Would Julie actually do something that drastic? But the evidence was just too great. Slowly Kate went back over the Saturday she had taken Julie to the clinic. There had been her evasive behavior, her unwillingness to answer questions, her oddly quiet reaction to the "good news," followed by her bubbly demeanor at lunch. Now she could see that it all fit. Julie had been reluctant to talk about her "problem" because it didn't exist. She had been nervous not because she was worried about her condition but because she was wondering if she could pull off the deception. She hadn't been relieved after her exam because she had known all along that she wasn't pregnant. And she had been elated at lunch because she knew her plan was going to work.

Julie hadn't wanted Morgan to get married. She had broken up other relationships before, he had said. But doubtless she had never before gone to such extremes.

Unbidden, a great feeling of sadness descended over Kate. Had Julie really seen her as that much of a threat? And was it still possible even to contemplate marriage with Morgan when his daughter was willing and able to throw up such drastic impediments? Kate shook her head. She just didn't know. And now she wasn't sure exactly how to proceed.

## Chapter Thirteen

$\mathcal{K}$ ate was still wondering what to do when, as if on cue, the phone rang a half hour later. Who would be calling now? she wondered, glancing at the clock and noting that it was close to eleven.

However, not in her wildest imagination would she have guessed who was on the other end of the line.

"Kate, I'm sorry to be calling you so late," Margaret Chandler apologized, "but I've been thinking about you all evening and I finally decided I had to speak to you."

"You've been thinking about *me?*" Kate questioned incredulously.

"Well, about you and Morgan, actually," the older woman was saying. "Kate, I should have called you weeks ago to tell you how upset I am about the way things have worked out."

"Yes, well . . ." Kate began uncertainly, not knowing quite where this unexpected conversation was leading.

"Morgan wouldn't tell me exactly what happened

231

between you two," Margaret continued. "He's too upset."

"Oh?"

"Kate, Morgan misses you terribly. I know he does."

"I miss him, too," Kate whispered before she could bite back the words.

For a moment there was silence on the other end of the line, as though Margaret Chandler were as uncertain about this conversation as Kate.

"I don't know exactly what this call is going to accomplish," she finally admitted. "I was just hoping that there might be some way I could help you work things out." She hesitated again and then seemed to reach a decision. "Kate, I'd like to ask you a very personal question. Did you break things off, or was it Morgan?"

"Morgan."

"I thought so. Kate, you don't have to tell me what happened. Morgan has been so afraid of letting himself be vulnerable, of committing himself to anyone since Charlotte left him, that I thought he'd never marry again. But when I met you, I knew you were the woman who could make him whole again."

Kate drew in her breath. "I guess you were wrong."

"No, I was right. Give him another chance, Kate, for your sake as well as his."

"I'm not sure he'll let me."

"But you won't know unless you take a chance, will you?" Mrs. Chandler persisted.

The younger woman's brow furrowed. There were factors that Morgan's mother just didn't know about, and Kate was not really free to bring them up in detail. But she did have to say something to indicate the breadth of the problem. "And what about Julie?" she finally asked. "How does she feel about all this?"

"Julie misses you too."

It was lucky, Kate mused, that Mrs. Chandler couldn't see her look of disbelief. "But surely that can't be true," she challenged. "Couldn't you tell when we were up there Thanksgiving how jealous she was of me?"

"Yes, I could tell. And I think that when you and Morgan broke off, Julie was elated. But she's been up here several times recently, and I know she's beginning to realize what her negative attitude has done to her father, and what she's lost, too."

Could it be true? Kate wondered. Or was this just another part of a well-calculated act? It was hardly a question she could ask Mrs. Chandler without giving away more than she should. However, the older woman's next words made Kate's heart leap. "It was Julie who suggested that I call you, actually."

Kate felt suddenly light-headed. "She did? Are you sure?"

"Absolutely. We're both on your side, Kate. So why don't you see if you can shake some sense into that pigheaded son of mine."

Mrs. Chandler's words were just the spur Kate had needed. She wasn't going to give up Morgan without a struggle, she told herself. And now that she knew about Julie's change of heart, she had more reason to believe that things could actually work out.

The next morning at breakfast, she made Tony part of her plans. "Do you think you could get Morgan over here this Saturday and then spend the day at a friend's house instead of meeting him?" she asked.

Her son looked puzzled. "Why should I do that, Mom?"

"Because I want to try and work things out between the two of us, and I'm afraid Morgan won't come over if he thinks I want to talk to him."

"You mean you want to talk to him about getting back together?"

"Yes."

"And the two of you might really get married?" Tony dared to elaborate.

Kate reached over and ruffled his hair. "That's what I have in mind," she confirmed, hoping that she could keep the same note of confidence in her voice when she actually confronted Morgan.

"All right!" Tony grinned and waved his fist in the air. Pushing back his chair, he started across the kitchen toward the phone. "I'm gonna call Jimmy and set things up right away. And then I'll call Morgan."

Her son played his part superbly. By ten that Saturday morning he was out of the house and Kate was waiting nervously in the family room for Morgan—who thought he was in for a session at the roller rink with the boy.

Had she made a mistake? Kate wondered. Should she have simply called Morgan up and explained that she wanted to talk to him? No, she assured herself. That would have given him time to anguish over the meeting. And she had done enough anguishing for both of them.

How should she dress? How much makeup should she wear? What should she say? Should she offer Morgan something to drink or eat? Where should they sit? Every detail of this important confrontation had been considered and reconsidered.

Just picking an outfit had taken more than an hour. Her first impulse had been to wear something long and flowing that would completely disguise the shape of her new curves. But then she decided that Morgan might wonder what she was trying to hide, since she had never appeared in anything similar before. In the end, she selected a softly tailored russet wool dress that emphasized the still-narrow line of her waist. The barely detectable fullness of her abdomen was covered nicely by the gathered skirt. Her bust was another matter, she noted, as she inspected her silhouette critically in the mirror. She was definitely a bit more voluptuous in that department. But there was nothing she could do about it except think small.

Kate permitted herself only a touch of makeup. She didn't want to look as if she were trying to get Morgan back with her beauty—that would be a lost cause anyway, she told herself wryly. And there was no point in trying to hide her freckles; he had seen them already. But she did brush her thick mane of chestnut hair until it shone.

Stepping back to observe the effect, she had to admit that she didn't look too bad. Since she'd learned about the pregnancy she'd started to feel better and had begun eating properly again. So there must have been an emotional component to her morning sickness, after all, she mused. It must have had something to do with worrying about what was wrong.

However, as she waited for Morgan to arrive, new and quite different feelings of uncertainty assailed her. And it was all she could do to keep from chewing on her fingernails, a habit she thought she'd given up back in junior high. Trying to take her mind off the coming interview, she stood and began to look at the titles of the books in the shelves beside the fireplace—pretending that the collection belonged to someone else.

When the doorbell rang she jumped. She had unlocked the door so that Morgan could let himself in. Somehow she didn't want to meet him in the foyer this time.

"Come in," she called in response as the bell sounded again. She heard the door open and then footsteps in the hall.

"Tony?" Morgan said. Not getting any response, he started down the hall.

When he finally strode into the family room, Kate was standing with her back to the bookcases, one hand unconsciously gripping the back of the lounge chair beside her. She felt her heart catch in her throat as Morgan's tall form filled the doorway. It had been so long since she had been even this close to the man she loved. For a moment all she wanted to do was drink in every detail of his presence. He had finally gotten his haircut, she noted. But were there a few more strands of gray in among his dark waves? And what about his face? It seemed different, somehow, as though the laugh lines around his eyes had deepened into more permanent furrows.

Had she really forgotten how tall and imposing he was, she wondered, and how he seemed to fill a room with his presence? The scent of his after-shave drifted across the space between them, almost like a caress, and an unconscious smile lit up Kate's eyes and then gently lifted the corners of her lips.

At the first sight of Kate, Morgan had stopped in his tracks. She watched as strong, unreadable emotions flickered across his features. For several heartbeats, it seemed as if both of them were caught and held by some witchery designed to immobilize the body but not the mind. And then Morgan, with what looked like obvious effort, broke the spell.

"I came to pick up Tony," he announced, his voice thicker and deeper than Kate remembered.

"Morgan, he's not here," Kate admitted, her own voice foggy with all the emotions she felt.

For a moment he stared at her uncomprehendingly.

"I wanted to talk to you," Kate added.

As she spoke, she could see that familiar defensive anger begin to cloud his features. Apparently he was still terribly hurt by what he thought she had done behind his back. "We don't have anything to say to each other," he pointed out very quietly, obviously trying to keep his own emotions under control. Without another word, he turned away.

*He can't just walk out,* Kate's mind protested silently. Before she had time to think about what she was doing, she was already across the room, her hand gripping the sleeve of his heavy car coat.

The contact made him whirl back around. "I said, we don't have anything to say to each other," he repeated, emphasizing each word as though he were talking to a two-year-old.

Kate shook her head forcefully. She wasn't going to let this end before it had even begun. "Yes we do," she insisted. "The last time we—we talked, I was so unprepared that I didn't know what to say in my own defense. Now I do."

Morgan eyed her warily. "Yes, you've had more than a month to think up an explanation for your behavior."

"That's not fair," Kate shot back. "You said you'd let me give my side of the story. And you really haven't."

Morgan shrugged. "All right, what's your side of the story?"

"Well I'm certainly not going to give it to you standing in the hall like this. Why don't you take off your coat and come into the kitchen. I'll fix you a cup of coffee."

"I don't want your hospitality," Morgan reminded her. "I came here to see Tony, remember?"

Without waiting to continue that particular argument, Kate turned toward the kitchen. If Morgan wasn't willing to even listen, then she had lost before she had even started. Nervously she began to get down cups. But to her relief she heard footsteps behind her and then the scrape of a chair at the table.

Trying to keep her hands from trembling, Kate turned on the hot water. "Is instant okay?" she asked. "I haven't been drinking coffee lately and . . ."

"Fine," Morgan agreed.

Kate opened the cabinet and brought out the jar of instant crystals, along with one of the herb teas she had begun using since her visit to the doctor. She didn't really like the stuff, but she knew caffeine wasn't good for the baby.

"I didn't know you drank that," Morgan commented from behind her back.

"I . . . I'm trying something new," Kate returned, hoping he wouldn't ask why. She was glad for an excuse to keep her back to him as she got out milk and sugar and waited for the water to boil. But finally she had to turn around and bring their cups to the table.

Now that he had agreed to this talk, Morgan, too, seemed to want to put off the inevitable as long as possible. Carefully he poured milk into his coffee before stirring the dark liquid slowly. But finally, when he placed his spoon in the saucer with a soft clink, Kate knew she had to say her piece.

"Morgan, I've gone over and over this in my mind," she began, trying to control the tremor in her voice, "and if there were any other way to . . ." She had been about to say "get you back," but had stopped just in time.

He waited patiently for her to continue, the quizzical, expectant expression on his face not making things any easier.

"I'm going to have to betray Julie's confidence," Kate went on resolutely.

It had been the wrong way to start, Kate realized instantly. Morgan's light brown eyes fixed her with such a piercing look that Kate unconsciously pushed her chair back several inches. But there was no way she could take the statement back. After only a small hesitation, she continued talking. "But I think that's what she'd want me to do now."

"And just how are you able to read my daughter's mind," Morgan challenged.

Kate shook her head. This wasn't going the way she had expected at all. "That's not the point," she finally offered.

"And what *is* the point?"

"I took Julie to that clinic because she came to me and told me she thought she might be pregnant," Kate revealed. "She made it clear that she was afraid you'd be angry, and she begged me not to let you know we were going down to the clinic. That's why I couldn't say anything when you dragged her over here the Sunday before—" Kate stopped short. She had almost said "before the wedding."

"That Sunday," she amended.

"I see," Morgan said carefully. But the tone of his voice told her that he didn't really see at all.

Kate looked down into her teacup, waiting for him to say something more. But he didn't, and the silence between them only stretched tauter, like a rubber band about to snap back in her face with a wicked sting.

Finally he cleared his throat. "Don't you think this would sound more credible if you'd explained it right away?" he questioned. Somehow, here in her sunny kitchen, his calm delivery was more ominous than his anger would have been.

"Yes," Kate was forced to agree. "But I told you I had to think things through."

"So you say," he shot back.

Kate pressed her lips together to keep them from trembling. Deliberately she laced her fingers tightly in her lap, knowing that the pressure must be turning her knuckles white.

When she didn't say anything, Morgan was forced to continue. "You're asking me to believe that my daughter thought she was pregnant?"

"No. That she *said* she thought she was pregnant and that she *asked* me to act without informing you."

Morgan's face darkened. "Just what is it that you're trying to imply? That my daughter was lying?"

"Yes," Kate whispered miserably, wondering how she had lost control of the conversation, "if you insist on putting it in those terms. She didn't want us to get married, and so she . . ."

Morgan pushed back his chair and stood up. "I believe I've had enough of this," he announced.

Kate followed suit, stumbling sideways in her haste to get up. "Wait," she pleaded. "Why do you think I asked you here? Why do you think I started this discussion in the first place?"

"I wouldn't know," he ground out.

What could she say, Kate wondered desperately, that would make him see what was at stake here?

"Morgan," she began, "I had given Julie my word that I wouldn't tell you anything about this. I couldn't betray her confidence lightly. It was a matter of trust, as you're so fond of saying. But finally I decided that whatever I'd promised her wasn't worth losing you."

"So you broke your word to her?" Morgan clarified helpfully.

Kate shook her head. None of this was coming out right. It was all tangled up in her mind. Or was Morgan the one who was deliberately obscuring the real issue? What did she have left to offer that would make any kind of sense to him? she wondered. Was there any way she could make him see what was trivial and what was important?

"Morgan," she began. And then before she could lose her nerve, she plunged ahead. "Morgan, none of this would make any difference except that I love you. I don't want our—our relationship to just end like this."

"Our relationship, as you put it, already has ended," he informed her curtly.

Kate looked away, unable now to take the coldness of his gaze. She felt the pressure of tears behind her eyes. But she wouldn't shed them here in the kitchen, not in front of Morgan. There was one more thing she longed to tell him, the thing that might just make a difference. But she knew she must hold back. She wasn't going to bind Morgan Chandler to her with their child. She was too proud for that.

But somehow she wasn't able to prevent herself from reaching out and brushing her fingers across his hand where it rested on the kitchen table. It was something she would never be able to do again; she knew that now. And she couldn't deny herself that one last goodbye. Even if it didn't mean anything to Morgan, it did to her.

Quickly then, before she made even more of a fool of herself, Kate turned and hurried out of the kitchen, her vision blurred with the tears she couldn't hold back. Not even thinking about where her feet were taking her, she climbed the stairs with leaden steps, intent on putting as much distance between herself and the man in the kitchen as possible. Why had she thought she could change his mind? she wondered. Why had she been so stupid as to think that anything she could say to Morgan would make a difference now? He couldn't open himself up to her because he was afraid of getting hurt. Why hadn't she been smart enough to realize that and spare herself this final bitter scene?

She was crossing her room when she heard the front door pulled shut with a resounding slam. Feeling her knees buckle, she caught herself on the edge of the bed and sat down heavily.

Well, she thought dismally. If she'd had any doubt that her relationship with Morgan Chandler was over, the slamming of the door had set them to rest.

It was several moments before Kate could move. Not even bothering to brush away the tears streaming down her cheeks, she unbuttoned her dress, pulled it over her head and tossed it on the chair. Still wearing her ecru slip, she crawled under the bedcovers. After pulling them up over her shoulders, she rolled on her side, drew up her knees and clasped her arms around the pillow. *What a pitiful comfort,* she thought. *Am I really reduced to hugging pillows?* But at the moment, she knew she was. *Go ahead and cry,* she added. *No one's going to know. You don't have to square your shoulders and hold your head up until Monday at the office.*

After the flood of tears subsided to a tiny trickle, she finally pulled herself together enough to reach for a tissue and blow her nose. Despite the new life inside her, she felt strangely empty—and numb. Rolling over onto her back, she looked upward, suddenly remembering that as a little girl lying in bed, she'd often wondered what it would be like to walk on the ceiling upside down. Life had been so much simpler then, she mused. No husbands who tricked you into thinking you couldn't have any more children. No shattered love affairs. No children to support by yourself. Just quiet speculations about walking upside down like a fly.

Suppose the ceiling were iron, she wondered idly. Could you walk on it with magnetic boots? It would have to be thin sheets of iron, or the whole thing would be too heavy. Or what about Velcro? Could they put strips of Velcro on the ceiling and on people's shoes? That wouldn't be as heavy. But they'd have to use a special glue.

The line of thought was so absorbing that she didn't hear the front door open or the quiet footsteps in the hall outside her bedroom.

"Kate?"

Turning her head, she wondered if wishful thinking were making her imagine Morgan framed in the doorway, his face full of anxiety. But no, his image was too solid, too detailed not to be real.

"What are you doing here?" she whispered in amazement, pushing herself to a sitting position but still clutching the bedcovers tightly around her shoulders.

"Loving you," he said simply.

Kate stared at him uncomprehendingly. What had he said?

His face clouded as he searched her features anxiously. "Kate, is it too late to tell you that I love you? Can you ever forgive me for what I've put you through?"

Although these were the words she had been longing to hear for so long, they seemed to make no sense. There was no way they could penetrate the protective insulation she had drawn around herself like the bedcovers she still hugged to her chest. She could only look at him numbly, the tears still glistening in her eyes.

"Oh, Kate." He was almost sobbing. "Have I destroyed any chance we might have had for happiness?"

As if in a dream, she saw him close the distance between them. And then he was on the side of the bed, reaching out to her with a naked longing that was impossible to hide now. Tenderly, he pulled her into his arms so that she was enfolded by the soft wool of his pullover. She felt his cold hand stroke the damp skin of her face, tracing the tear tracks on her cheeks with the side of his finger. The icy contact was like a shock, bringing her at last to the reality of what was happening.

"Kate, I love you so much," he repeated. "Please, for God's sake, say something. Tell me it's not too late."

This time she realized just what he had revealed. The sudden knowledge made her heart skip a beat. Morgan had said he loved her. *He loved her.*

It was as though the world had turned upside down—not only because she had never heard words of love from Morgan before, but because of what they must mean now.

"No. I mean, no it's—it's not too late," she stammered, feeling a sudden surge of wonder that this was really happening.

It was then Kate reacted to the physical cold of the hand against her cheek. "You're half-frozen! Where have you been for the last hour?"

"Sitting in the car thinking about us and realizing what a damn fool I've been," he admitted. "I was just too wounded to see the obvious when it was staring me in the face. Can you forgive me for not believing you?" he asked again.

Kate reached up to press her warm fingers tenderly against his cold cheek. "I think I already have, Morgan."

The love and gratitude shining along with the unshed tears in his eyes were her reward. "Oh, God, Kate," he murmured. "What if I'd lost you?"

Before she could speak again, his lips descended to claim hers in a kiss that said as much as his words of love and contrition. It was a kiss that Kate returned with all the yearning that had been pent up inside her for so long.

Her happiness was so overflowing now that more

tears spilled over onto her cheeks. And she knew as Morgan pressed her close that they were mingled with moisture from his eyes, too. They clung together, then, each drawing strength and love from the other. Finally Morgan drew back slightly, his lips a caress against her damp cheek. "Even your tears taste good," he breathed, "and you feel so good, too."

Kate snuggled closer, reveling in the ecstasy of his mouth against her face and the touch of his hands as they stroked her bare shoulders. All the pain between them was gone. And now she was free to express the emotions she had held in for so long.

It must have been the same for Morgan. Suddenly he was tugging the covers aside and kicking off his shoes.

"Kate, Kate," he murmured, lying down beside her on the bed and pulling the length of her body tightly against his. For a long moment, he simply held her close, letting the heat of her body seep into his own. Just as he had that first time they made love, he seemed to need to assure himself that they were really in each other's arms like this again. And then his hand moved between them, seeking and finding the fullness of her breast.

"Oh," she gasped, astonished at the intensity of her response.

His answer was a muffled groan as he bent to nuzzle his face against the soft curves at the lacy top of her slip. And then his hands were on her hips, sliding around to cup her bottom and pull her against him so that she could feel the hard, throbbing ache of his need for her.

She had thought, when conscious thought had been possible, that they wouldn't make love until after she'd told him about the baby. But now, caught by the tide of feelings he had created, she could only respond to his closeness and his touch. The joy of being in his arms again was just too much to deny. And now that he was here with her again, she was free to admit just how tremendously she had missed him.

Instinctively seeking to increase the pleasure of the contact with this man she loved so much, she began to move her hips against him, the intimate rhythm a symptom of her own building need to have him inside her.

Morgan had lowered the straps of her slip and bra to her shoulders. And as his thumbs dipped underneath the lacy fabric to find the hardened peaks of her nipples, she trembled at the sensations of heat rippling through her body.

Her name was on his lips again, repeated over and over like an endearment, before his mouth sought hers in a long, thirsty kiss that told Kate yet again of the depth of his need for her. As if by mutual agreement, they drew apart so that they could shed their clothes.

She felt his eager hands on her unencumbered breasts then, lifting and cupping them from underneath before he bent to press his face appreciatively against their softness. And when his thumbs found her taut nipples again, she moaned at the keenness of the pleasure.

"Kate?" Morgan whispered, his breath warm and moist and exquisitely exciting against her ear.

"Oh, yes, Morgan, please."

"I love you," he affirmed, covering her body with his.

"I love you, too," she echoed, overwhelmed at the joy of being able to say those words as he entered her.

She felt him plunge deep within her, unable to contain the urgency of his passion. But there was no need to hold back. She was right there with him at that sharp, aching peak of desire which could lead to only one conclusion.

It was as though all the colors of the universe were kaleidoscoping around her, merging and melding and shimmering in their brilliance. And as Morgan began to move more quickly within her, she knew the focus of that intensity.

Eagerly she matched his rhythm, meeting him thrust for thrust, feeling the beauty and the power of the bright, pulsing colors build until there was no way to hold them in check. They seemed to explode in glorious chromatic bursts that went on and on, carrying her with them on luminous shock waves of rapture.

She heard mingled words of love, then, knowing that some had tumbled from her lips and some from Morgan's. And she knew for a certainty that it had been the same for him as it had been for her.

Kate felt Morgan shift his weight, bringing her along with him to nestle at his side. His lips moved in her hair and on her face, and she snuggled against him, glowing with the aftereffects of their shared ecstasy. Gently he pulled the covers up around them, making the bed into a warm, comfortable nest.

It was sometime later that she felt him stir beside her and clear his throat. "I hate to make you move," he whispered, "but the arm you're lying on is asleep."

"Oh, Morgan, why didn't you tell me?" As she spoke she rolled away and watched as he began to flex the limb in question.

"Because you seemed so comfortable," he answered. "And because I couldn't bear to let you go."

"I really didn't want to move away either, but actually, I've been thinking about a trip to the bathroom," she admitted, sitting up. "However, I do promise to come right back."

Morgan grinned. "See what happens when two people don't communicate their needs?"

Kate wrinkled her nose and then swung her legs over

the side of the bed, feeling suddenly a bit self-conscious. But since her robe was hanging near the shower, she had no choice except to walk across the bedroom naked.

When she emerged from the bathroom a few minutes later, she had put on the green velour wrapper and was belting it around her waist.

"Gee, I knew something terrible would happen if you went away," Morgan sighed. "Take that damn robe off. I want to see your gorgeous body, not fuzzy green stuff."

Kate couldn't keep a hot flush from spreading across her cheeks.

"If you don't take it off, I will," Morgan pledged, holding up the covers so she could slip under. "I promise to keep you warm," he added, "if that's what you're worried about."

"That's not what I'm worried about," she retorted, obeying his instructions before slipping back into bed. Suddenly she knew she had given away more than she had intended by the intensity of her voice.

"Then what?" Morgan asked gently, smoothing back the hair from her face and looking questioningly into her troubled eyes.

Kate felt her heart begin to pound and her gaze skittered away from his.

"What is it?" he persisted. "Whatever it is, you can tell me about it."

"Morgan, I . . ." She stopped. She had told him she couldn't have children. What if he didn't want their baby? What if it really wasn't all right? And yet, if that were true, wouldn't it be better to know right now?

"Kate," he began, and then hesitated, wetting his lips as though engaged in some inner debate. Slowly he reached out to stroke her cheek with the side of his hand. "Trust me, this time," he whispered.

"I . . . we . . . I'm pregnant," she finally managed.

Morgan pulled her into his arms. "Oh, Kate. I thought that might be what you were going to say. But I couldn't do it for you, in case I was wrong—not when I knew how sad you felt about not being able to have any more children." He hugged her tightly.

Her eyes widened. "How—how did you know?"

"I didn't know for sure. But when you came back to bed in that damn robe, a lot of little things that I hadn't thought about sort of clicked into place."

"What does my robe have to do with anything?" Kate demanded, pulling slightly away so that she could meet Morgan's amused gaze.

"Only that you've never been self-conscious with me about your body before."

"And what else gave me away?" she persisted.

"Well, there was the herb tea," Morgan continued. "I couldn't imagine why you were drinking that stuff instead of coffee, until I had some other clues."

The grin on Morgan's face made Kate cock her head to the side and raise her eyebrows. "I can't wait to hear about these 'other clues,'" she challenged.

"There are two of them, actually," Morgan clarified. "Your breasts. They're a lot bigger, you know. I mean, they were nice before, but now—*ho boy.*"

Kate looked at him helplessly. "You mean you don't mind?" she asked softly.

"About your breasts? Hell no. They're wonderful."

"No, I mean about the baby."

Morgan pulled her close again, nuzzling his cheek against hers. "I knew you meant the baby," he admitted contritely. "I just couldn't resist kidding you a little bit more. Actually, what I told you was true up at Kettle Creek. I guess I had given up the idea of ever being a father again. But now that it's going to happen, I'm delighted."

Kate closed her eyes and clung to him. "Don't you want me to explain what happened?" she finally asked.

"Not if you don't want to tell me."

"But I do." Haltingly at first and then with more sureness, she told him the story of how Bart had tricked her.

As she spoke, she could feel Morgan's body tense. "That rotten s——" he started to curse, but Kate put her fingers to his lips.

"That's all in the past now," she soothed. "And we have the present together."

"We wouldn't have the present if you hadn't had the guts to give me another demonstration of just what a jackass I've been," Morgan reminded her.

"But that's in the past now, too," Kate echoed.

Morgan's arms tightened around her. "Yes, that's in the past, too. I love you, Kate," he whispered. "And I trust you."

Kate turned and pressed her lips to his cheek. She knew just how much those words meant to Morgan.

"Me, too," she agreed.

"Kate."

"What?"

"When I get home I'm going to talk to Julie. You know, several times over the past few weeks she asked if I was going to start seeing you again. And I think she wanted to tell me what she had done. But she was afraid." He stopped and chuckled ruefully. "I can imagine why. It takes real backbone to face an angry Morgan Chandler."

"Oh, Morgan, you won't be too hard on her, will you?" Kate questioned. "She only wanted . . ."

"I know what she thought she wanted, Kate. But not now. You showed her the kind of person you are, and if she has any sense at all, she'll be glad to welcome you to our family."

"Oh, I certainly hope so." Kate crossed her fingers for luck, wishing wholeheartedly that the prophecy would come true.

"Downstairs in the kitchen, you mentioned Julie wanting us to get back together. Was it just motherly intuition?"

Kate smiled at his remark. "In a way it was. Your mother called me last week, Morgan. She told me that she thought Julie was really sorry for all the grief she'd caused us both. Actually, your mother's the one who gave me the courage to get you over here. She told me you wanted me back, even if you wouldn't admit it to yourself."

For several moments neither one of them spoke. And then Morgan stirred beside her. "Can I ask you one more question, Kate?"

"Anything."

"You didn't tell me about the baby this morning, even after you'd been brave enough to let me know you love me. Does that mean that if I hadn't come back you would have—" He stopped, fumbling for the right words, his eyes searching hers. "You wouldn't have told me? You would have raised our child by yourself?"

"Yes," Kate admitted. "I wasn't going to try and hold you to me with that if you didn't . . ." Emotion choked her voice and she stopped.

"Oh, Kate." Morgan's own voice had deepened and he paused again. "Do you remember," he finally asked, "a long time ago when I told you that love was just an illusion?"

She nodded.

"It always would have been a transparent illusion for me, hovering on the edge of my expectations, if you hadn't taught me how to bring it into focus and make it real."

Kate smiled warmly at the man she loved. "And am I turning you into a poet, too?" she asked.

"That's about as poetic as I'm going to get," he assured her. "At least with words. But with my hands, now that's a different story." As if by way of illustration, he began to stroke the soft skin of her naked back, before tangling his fingers gently in the rich fullness of her hair and bringing her lips up to meet his.

"And by the way," he murmured, his lips pausing millimeters from hers. "We're getting married next week."

"Next week!" Kate exclaimed, her practical mind suddenly enumerating all the things that had to be done to make even just a small "family" wedding. Reaching over to the nightstand, she located the note pad and pencil she kept there, and with a quick shift of positions, she was able to prop the pad against Morgan's shoulder. "Let's see, we'll need . . ."

Gently, he took the pad from her hands. "Oh no you don't," Morgan warned playfully. "I've got a much better idea for handling this." With that he tore her yet-unwritten list from the pad and proceeded to shred it into tiny pieces. Then with a few off-key bars of "Here Comes the Bride," he ceremoniously showered them both in the confetti.

Kate raised an eyebrow as she brushed a speck of paper from her hair. "Well, it better be good."

"We'll drop the kids off at my mother's and elope. This time we'll do it first and talk about it afterward."

The smile began in the depths of Kate's hazel eyes before spreading into a knowing grin across her face. "Just what I've always wanted—a very practical man."

"For once I thought so, too," he observed before sealing the words with a kiss that was as much a promise of his love and trust as a token of their future together.

# Silhouette Special Edition

## MORE ROMANCE FOR
## A SPECIAL WAY TO RELAX
### $1.95 each

| | | | |
|---|---|---|---|
| 2 ☐ Hastings | 21 ☐ Hastings | 41 ☐ Halston | 60 ☐ Thorne |
| 3 ☐ Dixon | 22 ☐ Howard | 42 ☐ Drummond | 61 ☐ Beckman |
| 4 ☐ Vitek | 23 ☐ Charles | 43 ☐ Shaw | 62 ☐ Bright |
| 5 ☐ Converse | 24 ☐ Dixon | 44 ☐ Eden | 63 ☐ Wallace |
| 6 ☐ Douglass | 25 ☐ Hardy | 45 ☐ Charles | 64 ☐ Converse |
| 7 ☐ Stanford | 26 ☐ Scott | 46 ☐ Howard | 65 ☐ Cates |
| 8 ☐ Halston | 27 ☐ Wisdom | 47 ☐ Stephens | 66 ☐ Mikels |
| 9 ☐ Baxter | 28 ☐ Ripy | 48 ☐ Ferrell | 67 ☐ Shaw |
| 10 ☐ Thiels | 29 ☐ Bergen | 49 ☐ Hastings | 68 ☐ Sinclair |
| 11 ☐ Thornton | 30 ☐ Stephens | 50 ☐ Browning | 69 ☐ Dalton |
| 12 ☐ Sinclair | 31 ☐ Baxter | 51 ☐ Trent | 70 ☐ Clare |
| 13 ☐ Beckman | 32 ☐ Douglass | 52 ☐ Sinclair | 71 ☐ Skillern |
| 14 ☐ Keene | 33 ☐ Palmer | 53 ☐ Thomas | 72 ☐ Belmont |
| 15 ☐ James | 35 ☐ James | 54 ☐ Hohl | 73 ☐ Taylor |
| 16 ☐ Carr | 36 ☐ Dailey | 55 ☐ Stanford | 74 ☐ Wisdom |
| 17 ☐ John | 37 ☐ Stanford | 56 ☐ Wallace | 75 ☐ John |
| 18 ☐ Hamilton | 38 ☐ John | 57 ☐ Thornton | 76 ☐ Ripy |
| 19 ☐ Shaw | 39 ☐ Milan | 58 ☐ Douglass | 77 ☐ Bergen |
| 20 ☐ Musgrave | 40 ☐ Converse | 59 ☐ Roberts | 78 ☐ Gladstone |

### $2.25 each

| | | | |
|---|---|---|---|
| 79 ☐ Hastings | 87 ☐ Dixon | 95 ☐ Doyle | 103 ☐ Taylor |
| 80 ☐ Douglass | 88 ☐ Saxon | 96 ☐ Baxter | 104 ☐ Wallace |
| 81 ☐ Thornton | 89 ☐ Meriwether | 97 ☐ Shaw | 105 ☐ Sinclair |
| 82 ☐ McKenna | 90 ☐ Justin | 98 ☐ Hurley | 106 ☐ John |
| 83 ☐ Major | 91 ☐ Stanford | 99 ☐ Dixon | 107 ☐ Ross |
| 84 ☐ Stephens | 92 ☐ Hamilton | 100 ☐ Roberts | 108 ☐ Stephens |
| 85 ☐ Beckman | 93 ☐ Lacey | 101 ☐ Bergen | 109 ☐ Beckman |
| 86 ☐ Halston | 94 ☐ Barrie | 102 ☐ Wallace | 110 ☐ Browning |

# Silhouette Special Edition

## $2.25 each

| | | | |
|---|---|---|---|
| 111 ☐ Thorne | 128 ☐ Macomber | 145 ☐ Wallace | 162 ☐ Roberts |
| 112 ☐ Belmont | 129 ☐ Rowe | 146 ☐ Thornton | 163 ☐ Halston |
| 113 ☐ Camp | 130 ☐ Carr | 147 ☐ Dalton | 164 ☐ Ripy |
| 114 ☐ Ripy | 131 ☐ Lee | 148 ☐ Gordon | 165 ☐ Lee |
| 115 ☐ Halston | 132 ☐ Dailey | 149 ☐ Claire | 166 ☐ John |
| 116 ☐ Roberts | 133 ☐ Douglass | 150 ☐ Dailey | 167 ☐ Hurley |
| 117 ☐ Converse | 134 ☐ Ripy | 151 ☐ Shaw | 168 ☐ Thornton |
| 118 ☐ Jackson | 135 ☐ Seger | 152 ☐ Adams | |
| 119 ☐ Langan | 136 ☐ Scott | 153 ☐ Sinclair | |
| 120 ☐ Dixon | 137 ☐ Parker | 154 ☐ Malek | |
| 121 ☐ Shaw | 138 ☐ Thornton | 155 ☐ Lacey | |
| 122 ☐ Walker | 139 ☐ Halston | 156 ☐ Hastings | |
| 123 ☐ Douglass | 140 ☐ Sinclair | 157 ☐ Taylor | |
| 124 ☐ Mikels | 141 ☐ Saxon | 158 ☐ Charles | |
| 125 ☐ Cates | 142 ☐ Bergen | 159 ☐ Camp | |
| 126 ☐ Wildman | 143 ☐ Bright | 160 ☐ Wisdom | |
| 127 ☐ Taylor | 144 ☐ Meriwether | 161 ☐ Stanford | |

- - - - - - - - - - - - - - - - - - - - - - - - - - - - - - - - - - - - - - -

**SILHOUETTE SPECIAL EDITION,** Department SE/2
1230 Avenue of the Americas
New York, NY 10020

Please send me the books I have checked above. I am enclosing $_____
(please add 75¢ to cover postage and handling. NYS and NYC residents please
add appropriate sales tax). Send check or money order—no cash or C.O.D.'s
please. Allow six weeks for delivery.

NAME _____

ADDRESS _____

CITY _____ STATE/ZIP _____